Thrown for a loop . . .

Clay felt himself slipping and strained to remain upright. Then the bull jerked forward, pulling Clay along with it. His arm was caught in the rope, stretching all the muscles and tendons to the point of tearing. Clay felt himself blacking out from the pain.

Suddenly his hand came free, and he fell completely underneath the raging animal. The big bull pushed off with its back feet and, as its hoofs came up, one caught Clay square in the side of the head. It was like being hit with a sledgehammer, and Clay went down in the dirt.

He lifted his head just in time to see the bull turn, lower its head, and charge straight at him. . . .

Rodeo Riders #1

COWBOY UP!

Mike Flanagan

A SIGNET BOOK

To the three women in my life—
my wife, Diane, and my daughters,
Jodie and Chancelee

SIGNET
Published by New American Library, a division of
Penguin Putnam Inc., 375 Hudson Street, New York, New York 10014, U.S.A.
Penguin Books Ltd, 27 Wrights Lane, London W8 5TZ, England
Penguin Books Australia Ltd, Ringwood, Victoria, Australia
Penguin Books Canada Ltd, 10 Alcorn Avenue, Toronto, Ontario, Canada
M4V 3B2
Penguin Books (N.Z.) Ltd, 182–190 Wairau Road, Auckland 10, New Zealand

Penguin Books Ltd, Registered Offices: Harmondsworth, Middlesex, England

First published by Signet, an imprint of New American Library,
a division of Penguin Putnam Inc.

First Printing, December 1999
10 9 8 7 6 5 4 3 2 1

Copyright © Mike Flanagan, 1999
All rights reserved

 REGISTERED TRADEMARK—MARCA REGISTRADA

Printed in the United States of America

PUBLISHER'S NOTE
This is a work of fiction. Names, characters, places, and incidents either are
the product of the author's imagination or are used fictitiously, and any
resemblance to actual persons, living or dead, business establishments,
events or locales is entirely coincidental.

BOOKS ARE AVAILABLE AT QUANTITY DISCOUNTS WHEN USED TO PROMOTE PRODUCTS
OR SERVICES. FOR INFORMATION PLEASE WRITE TO PREMIUM MARKETING DIVISION,
PENGUIN PUTNAM INC., 375 HUDSON STREET, NEW YORK, NEW YORK 10014.

Chapter 1

Jack Lomas wiped the sweat from his brow as he finished loading the last bale of hay onto the old battered Dodge pickup. He was silently thankful that he would only have to feed his cattle hay a few more times before the spring grass grew enough to sustain them without the need for supplemental feed.

Thinking of the arduous task ahead only served to remind him that he had hoped to have someone hired by now to help him. He hadn't been able to find anyone willing to put in a day's work since he'd run off that no-account Larry Simpson three months ago. Larry had been the last in a long line of no-accounts who wanted to get paid but didn't want to work, and he never had been able to find anyone who did. "Dad blame lazy bums anyway," he mumbled to himself. "Don't nobody want to put in a day's work no more."

Jack heard the sound of a car engine. He turned and looked down the winding, rutted road that led to the house. Shading his eyes against the morning sun, he could make out the white sedan with the red lights on top, immediately recognizing it as belonging to the Chavez County sheriff, Ben Aguilar.

Placing his sweat-soaked Stetson back on his head, Jack moved to the gate leading out of the hay barn and stood waiting for the car to arrive.

Ben Aguilar saw Jack Lomas standing by the gate

and was both thankful and apprehensive at the same time—thankful he had caught the old rancher before he left to feed, and apprehensive because of the news he had to deliver.

Ben brought the car to a stop several yards away from where Jack Lomas stood leaning against the iron gate. Getting out of the car, he closed the door behind him and walked toward the old rancher, trying to put on his friendliest smile and hoping he was succeeding.

Jack Lomas straightened up and walked toward him.

"Hey, Ben," he said extending his hand, "what brings you out this far this early in the morning?"

Ben Aguilar shook his hand, noticing the power that still remained in the older man's grip. He might be getting long in tooth but there was still strength left in this old rancher. He looked into Jack's weathered face and reflected on the man he had known since childhood. Growing up in Central New Mexico, he had known and worshipped Jack Lomas ever since he could remember. It surprised him how saddened he was to see the man grow old. It reminded him of his own mortality and he wondered if Jack ever got lonely as his days wore on. Ben and his wife Carmen had three fine boys and two sweet girls to see them into their old age. Jack Lomas had no children of his own anymore.

"I was hopin' to catch you before you started out to feed," Ben said.

"Well, you barely did. I just finished loading the hay and cake on the truck. Another five minutes and I'd've been gone. Since you caught me, let's go up to the house and have a cup of coffee. I've still got some left from this morning and it won't take but a minute to warm it up."

Ben complied and fell in beside the rancher as they walked to the house. "All the snow's about melted. I even saw some trees starting to bud out on the way out here."

"Yep," Jack responded, "I was just thinkin' I won't have to be feedin' much longer. I noticed the grass is startin' to turn green. I figure another couple of weeks and there'll be enough grass to carry my stock."

Ben only nodded as he turned and looked around at the Lazy L Ranch. Everything was neat and in working order. He knew Jack Lomas never let things go unattended and it was evident by the painted barns and corrals. Everything was in its place, and nothing was neglected.

As they entered the house he knew he would find it in the same immaculate shape, though no woman had lived there for the last ten years. Everything was neat as a pin. As they walked through the living room and into the kitchen of the one-story ranch house, Ben saw the clean dishes drying in the dish rack, the stove top and counters were wiped clean, and the plastic place mats on the table were spotless, evidence of the order the old rancher lived his life by.

Taking a kitchen match from the holder on the wall, Jack lit the gas burner on the stove and set the old coffeepot over the flame. Picking up two cups from the dish rack by the sink, he placed them on the counter by the stove then pulled a chair out from the table and said, "Have a seat, Ben, the coffee'll be ready in a minute." Ben pulled out a chair, placing his hat on the seat of another and sat down.

"I know you didn't come all the way out here to

talk about the weather and range conditions, so what does bring you out this way?" Jack asked.

Ben felt his nerves tighten. He had hoped to continue with their small talk and then ease into the real reason he'd come out to see Jack Lomas. He squirmed in his chair like a schoolboy who'd been called on to answer a question on homework he didn't do. Finally seeing there was no way to approach this but straight out, he cleared his throat and began, "Umm, well Jack, actually I came out to ask a favor and maybe do you one at the same time." He stopped there, looking expectantly at the rancher, hoping he'd interject a question at this point, but Jack Lomas just sat there with a poker face and waited for Ben to continue.

Ben squirmed again, feeling the perspiration begin to build under his arms "Uh, Jack, I know you haven't been able to find any help since Larry, and I got a fella who needs a job. I thought maybe we could help each other out."

Jack Lomas watched Ben's face for a moment, sensing there was something the man wasn't telling him. "Who is this fella that's needing a job and how come he didn't come out here and ask me himself?"

"His name is Clay Tory and the reason he didn't come out here is because . . . well . . . he's locked up in my jail at the moment." Ben cringed inwardly, knowing what the old rancher's reaction would be.

Jack rocked back as if slapped, then he slowly stood and lifted the coffeepot from the stove. He poured two cups of steaming liquid, and handed one across the table to Ben and set the other down in his place. Before taking his seat he moved the pot to the back burner and turned off the gas flame. Returning, he shook his head as if trying to clear his thoughts. "Now let me get this straight, you want me to hire this Clay fella and right now you got him in your jail." Then, with a thoughtful look Jack asked, "He any kin to Jason Tory?"

Ben sighed. He had hoped Clay's relations could be kept out of it, but he knew that was a foolish wish. Jack was too smart for something like that to get by him. "He's Jason's youngest boy, but that don't mean he's anything at all like Jason."

Jack almost choked on the swig of coffee he'd just taken; it took him a while before he could speak. When he did his voice bellowed, "You got him locked up in your jail and you're sittin' there tellin' me he's nothing like Jason Tory! Sounds to me like the apple doesn't fall too far from the tree."

Ben realized this conversation wasn't going well and if he didn't do something quick, Jack was going to end it. "Jack you're jumping to conclusions. Let me explain before you make up your mind."

"What have you got him locked up for?" Jack asked, his eyebrows arching as if to say he already knew the answer.

"We arrested him for possession of a stolen vehicle."

"Just as I suspected," Jack said. "Like father like son. Too lazy to work so they got to steal from honest folk. What makes you think I'd want to hire one of Jason Tory's thievin' brats to work for me? I doubt any of that bunch has ever done an honest day's work in their life."

"You're right about the Torys," Ben said, feeling as if the cause had already been lost, "but Clay's different. I'm not saying he's an angel, but he's certainly not like his daddy and his brothers, or those worthless uncles of his. This is the first time I've had him in jail, and I sure can't say the same thing about the rest of his clan."

"Hmph," Jack interrupted, "he must be smarter then. Not that he's any less honest or lazy than the rest of 'em. It's just that he ain't been caught."

Ben shook his head in exasperation. "Jack, I'm tellin' you he ain't like the rest of 'em. Oh I've had my run-ins with the boy before, mostly on account of his fighting. He's got a quick-fire temper and he won't be pushed by nobody, but he doesn't cross the line. If he had, I'd've known about it." He paused and let Jack consider the facts. Ben still had a hole card, but he wasn't going to play it until the time was right.

"If he ain't never crossed the line, then why you got him locked in jail right now?" Jack asked, the hint of a smile playing at the corner of his mouth.

Ben leaned back in his chair, savoring the moment. This conversation was finally going the way he'd wanted. Jack was coming into this just like he'd hoped, and now with a little luck he could win the old rancher over. "It's kind of a strange thing, I guess you could say. From what I can gather Clay borrowed a pickup from one of his friends, Joe Hanson, supposedly with Joe's consent, said he was going to see someone for a while and he'd bring the truck back." Ben stopped and chuckled, bringing a frown to Jack's face.

"What's so dadburn funny?" Jack asked, impatience bristling in his voice. "I ain't got all day to sit here listening to you carry on. I got cattle to feed."

Ben smiled again. "Well, it appears Clay did borrow the truck to go see somebody, but the somebody was Joe's girlfriend." He paused to let the fact sink in. "Apparently, Joe hitched a ride to his girlfriend's house unexpectedly, and when he got there he found his pickup parked outside. Now being the bright fellow he was, instead of confronting Clay and the girl with his newfound knowledge, and probably gettin' himself into a fight he knew he couldn't win, he walked to a pay phone and called the sheriff's office and reported his truck as being stolen. Even told them where it was and who the thief was. Of course, he claims he never loaned the truck to Clay and that the girl wasn't his girlfriend, even though she told a different story. But since he pressed charges and there weren't any other witnesses to back up Clay's story, and he did have the keys to the truck on him when the deputy showed up, we had no choice but to arrest and charge him."

Jack's face revealed nothing as he sat looking at Ben. "What did the boy say when he was arrested?"

"Pretty much what I told you, and the girl backed it up, but Clay's friend still claims he never lent him the truck and insisted on pressing charges. Judge Rynor feels the same as I do, but his hands are tied. He had to charge Clay with grand theft auto. He's waiting to hear from me before sentencing the boy."

Jack frowned at the news he'd just heard. He didn't like being pigeonholed and knew that was exactly what Ben was trying to do to him. "What will happen to the boy if I say no?"

"Well the boy's only seventeen, which makes him a juvenile. This is fortunate because it can't go on his permanent record, and because it is his first offense, the sentence won't be that stiff. In normal circumstances, the judge would release him to the custody of his family, but in this case that would be the worst thing we could do to the boy, so he'll probably get six months in Juvenile Hall."

Jack looked thoughtfully at his coffee cup, "Juvenile

Hall might be the best thing for the boy. Might take some of the edge off him."

Ben felt his spirits fall, but was determined to keep fighting. "Jack, you don't know what Juvenile Hall is like. It's not like it used to be. In the old days you could send a boy there for six months and when he came out you'd see a change for the better. But now with all these bleeding heart liberals giving these kids more rights on the inside than they got on the outside, and preventing anything close to punishment from taking place, it's more like a day camp for young criminals. They learn more about how to beat the system from the kids inside than they could ever learn on the streets.

"If Clay goes in there I feel pretty certain he'll come out like the rest of his family. Like I said he's got a quick temper and there's plenty of hardened criminals in Juvy. One of them will push him, and he'll fight back and keep on fighting until he's either dead or on top of the heap, and knowing Clay he'll probably come out on top of the heap." Ben paused and looked into Jack's face. The old rancher was lost in thought and Ben knew he was thinking about another boy, a long time ago. He felt sorry for the old man, but he knew in his heart he was doing the right thing.

Clearing his throat, Ben continued. "In eight months the boy turns eighteen. If he's still in juvenile at that time he becomes a legal adult and any time he has left will be served in the state penitentiary."

Jack looked up at him. "But I thought you said the judge was only going to give him six months?"

"He is, but that's if there's no problems during those six months. If Clay gets into trouble once, which is highly likely, he'll get more time added on. So you see, Jack, I need your help."

Jack Lomas leaned both elbows on the table and ran his fingers through his hair as if trying to straighten out the thoughts in his mind. "Isn't there someone else who could take the boy? Someone a little younger, who's had better experience with boys than me?"

"There's no one else we can think of," Ben answered, knowing that wasn't entirely true. If Jack turned him down he did have a couple of other ranchers who might consider taking the boy, but he had a particular reason for wanting Jack to take him. He was just about ready to play the final card.

"I need some time to think about this," Jack replied, feeling depression sinking in. He hadn't felt like this in a long time and he didn't relish it now. "How soon do you need an answer?"

"Sentencing is scheduled for Tuesday, so we would need an answer by Monday afternoon."

Jack nodded and took a sip of his coffee, making a face as he realized the last few swallows had gotten cold. He got the still-warm coffeepot from the stove and refilled his cup and offered more to Ben, who gladly accepted, much to Jack's chagrin. He needed time to think, to think of some way out without looking like a villain, but Ben leaned back and took a sip of his coffee. Jack knew he had more on his mind.

"There's something else you should know about the boy." When Jack raised his eyebrows in a questioning look, Ben continued. "He's probably the best all-around cowboy I've ever seen for someone his age." He paused to let the statement sink in, then went on. "Clay's been riding saddle broncs, barebacks, and bulls for the past four years, and has been winning consistently for the past two and a half. He's a pretty fair roper and with a little more meat on him, he's going to be a top contender in the steer wrestling. But what's amazing is he's done it all on his own, with no help from his family."

Jack's face was unreadable, but Ben could have sworn he saw a light spark in his eyes for just a moment before the old rancher caught himself.

"I don't see what that's got to do with anything," Jack Lomas growled. "I ain't had nothin' to do with rodeos for fifteen years now. It don't make me no never mind if the boy's good or if he ain't. If I do this—and I ain't sayin' I am—it ain't because the boy's good at gettin' on a bronc or crazy enough to get on a bull."

In spite of himself, Ben smiled.

"What are you grinnin' about?" Jack snapped. "I don't see nothin' funny about this situation, and I'm here to tell ya I don't appreciate bein' put in it. Almost makes me regret voting for ya." Jack hesitated momentarily and then resumed in a softer tone. "But then I reckon that's why I voted for ya in the first place, cause ya care about people."

"Look, Jack, I was just thinking that with all your knowledge about rodeo you could give the boy some pointers that would improve his riding. He's world champion material and you could help him. I'd just hate to see someone with his potential go to waste because of a trumped-up charge." Ben stopped, knowing anything else he could say would be pointless.

Jack sat staring at the floor, his legs crossed to the side of the table, his fresh coffee untouched. Finally he turned to the sheriff and asked, "What do I have to do if I take this boy?"

Ben's lips started to twitch into another smile, but he checked himself and with a straight face answered,

"Keep him here with you, be responsible for him, and help him see the errors of his ways."

"How long?" Jack asked.

"One year," Ben stated.

"A year?" the rancher bellowed. "But I thought you said the judge was giving him six months?"

"Six months in juvenile, but one year if he's released to someone's custody."

"I see," Jack said. "I wonder who'll be gettin' the sentence, me or him?"

Ben stifled another smile. "Well at least you don't have to pay him. The county pays you fifteen dollars a day for keeping him and gives him five dollars a day for essentials."

Jack shook his head. "If he works for me, he gets paid."

"Sorry, Jack, that can't happen. We've found that without a pocketful of money, these kids aren't as apt to up and leave, so we keep their spending money to a minimum."

Jack scowled. "I understand your reasoning but I don't like workin' somebody and not payin' 'em. Goes against the grain."

"I know, but believe me it's for the best. So can I tell Judge Rynor you'll do it?"

Jack scowled again. "Don't rush me. I'll let you know Monday. I want some time to think it over. I ain't had no one to take care of for almost ten years now. I've grown used to only lookin' out for me. I don't really cotton to the idea of havin' to look out for some youngster with an attitude problem."

"I understand," Ben said, getting his hat and standing. "If you decide to do it, you can talk to the judge. He'll fill you in on all the particulars."

"One other thing before you go," Jack said, still

seated in his chair. "What happens if I take this boy and it don't work out? I mean if we can't get along or he don't want to work? What happens then?"

"He goes to juvenile to serve his full time."

"I see," Jack said, "so it's in his best interest to make it work out too?"

"That's right," Ben said. "I'd better get going. I've got to stop and see Mrs. Turner on my way back. Seems she saw someone on their place the other day and thinks it might be the cattle thieves we been lookin' for. It's probably just some of those oil field boys checking wells, but I promised her I'd check it out anyway."

Jack Lomas stood and carried both cups to the kitchen sink. Taking his hat from where he'd hung it on the back of the chair, he followed the sheriff outside, squinting in the bright spring sunshine.

"See ya later," Ben said, heading to his car. He stopped as he opened the door and turned to the rancher. "And, Jack—thanks."

"What for?" the old man growled. "I ain't said I'd do it yet."

"I know," Ben said, "but thanks for not saying no."

Jack mumbled something about sheriffs and what they were good for, then with a backward wave walked to the hay barn and swung the gate open, turning to watch the sheriff's car head down the road. Then shaking his head in disbelief, he mumbled to himself again, "I'd better get busy or it's going to be dark before I get all these cows fed."

Chapter 2

Jack Lomas hunched over the steering wheel of his Ford pickup as he drove the last few miles into Roswell. The Ford was a new one-ton truck. He'd purchased it four months earlier when he'd turned the four-wheel drive Dodge into a ranch truck. The Ford came with more amenities than suited him, including air-conditioning, automatic transmission, and stereo, which was tuned to the local radio station. The salesman at the car dealership had set the radio and the dial had not been moved since, nor would it. Jack never used the air conditioner either, saying it made people soft to where all they wanted to do was sit inside and never get nothing done.

Garth Brooks was singing on the radio as he passed the Military Institute on the north end of town, but Jack wasn't listening to any of the lyrics. His mind was occupied with what lay ahead.

It was Monday morning and Jack was on his way to the courthouse to see Judge Rynor and Sheriff Aguilar. He had spent a restless weekend trying to decide what course of action to take. He had measured the pros and cons of the situation, and had finally come up with the scale measuring heavily on the con side. He was still wrestling with his decision as he pulled up to the Chavez County Courthouse, parking in one of the spaces marked CHAVEZ COUNTY SHERIFF'S PARKING ONLY.

"Let them give me a ticket," he mumbled. Stepping out of the pickup, he stood for a moment looking at the courthouse, and with a deep sigh, he finally walked up the sidewalk that lead to the sheriff's office.

Ben Aguilar sat in his office staring out the window. He'd seen Jack Lomas drive up and had watched him park in one of the reserved parking places. A smile played across his face as he watched Jack walk toward the office. He knew Jack Lomas wouldn't get a ticket for parking in that particular spot, even if he wasn't going to take Clay Tory. None of his deputies would have written Jack Lomas a ticket, even if he drove a hundred miles an hour down Main Street.

A few minutes later both Ben and Jack were standing in the judge's office waiting for Judge Rynor to appear. Neither spoke as they sat in chairs on opposite sides of the room. The judge's secretary was busy typing on her PC and paid neither of them any attention.

They had been waiting for about ten minutes when Judge Rynor came hurrying into the room, his hand extended as he greeted Jack Lomas. "Hi, Jack, how are you?"

"Fine I reckon," Jack responded as he rose slowly to his feet.

"Ya'll have a seat," he said, motioning to the two leather-covered chairs on the opposite side of his desk as he closed his office door.

Once both men were seated, the judge sat in his high-backed leather-covered chair and leaned back in a relaxed gesture. Jack noticed how the chair seemed to engulf the judge's bony frame and he wondered how much of the taxpayers' money was spent on that particular chair so this elected official could sit in comfort and act as lord and master over the peons of

Chavez County. A scowl crossed his face as he thought about it, waiting for the judge to begin.

As if reading the old rancher's thoughts, Judge Rynor leaned over his desk and crossed his arms. "Well, Jack, did you have time to think over the proposition Ben talked about?"

Jack Lomas rubbed his chin, looking first at the judge then at the sheriff, who were both waiting expectantly for his decision. "Yeah I thought about it, but I got a couple of questions first."

The judge had known and respected Jack for years. He knew all about the rancher's past and all the hardships he had gone through and his sympathy went out to him.

When Ben had come to him with his idea, he'd been in favor of it, but he had strong doubts about Jack agreeing to it. He was surprised when the rancher actually showed up. Looking at him now, Rynor answered, "Ask away. We'll help any way we can."

Jack glanced at both men again. "If I decide to do this, what say will his family have on what takes place? I don't want nothin' to do with that bunch of lazy no-accounts, and I sure don't want 'em out at my ranch."

The judge considered the question and replied, "I understand your concern." After a few moments of deliberation, he continued. "Under the terms of his release, young Tory will have twice-a-month visiting privileges, which means he'll be able to visit his kinfolk during daylight hours. But under the same terms they will not be able to have personal contact with him at any other time except by phone, and you will have control of that. You can set the number of calls he can receive, and when they can call—though I doubt they will. Does that answer your question?"

"How does the boy feel about going with me?"

"That's a good question," Ben chimed in. "I talked to him about it after I saw you the other day, and even though he wasn't as enthusiastic as I had hoped, he did agree it was the best alternative. He gave me his word he'd do his best to make things work out."

Jack Lomas sat without commenting, thinking about the situation and what it would mean to him. It had been so long since he'd had anyone around to care for or look after, and now they were asking him to take on a boy he didn't even know and hadn't wanted to know. He knew things would change for him and he didn't like the idea. He liked things the way they were, living alone, answering to no one and not having to worry about anyone but himself. "Well," he said after some deliberation, "I reckon if there's no other way, I'll take the boy. But if he don't toe the line I'll bring him right back here and he can serve his time in jail regardless of the final results."

The judge and the sheriff exchanged guarded looks, and it was the judge who spoke first. "Jack, I understand how you feel and I can't say as I blame you, but I do hope you're going into this with the right attitude. We feel young Tory is worth redeeming or we wouldn't be going to this trouble, but we want you to understand he is rebellious, and I believe Ben has already told you about his temper." He paused to see what Jack's reaction would be, but Jack just sat there staring at him as if waiting for him to continue, so he did.

"Considering Clay's upbringing and his relatives, I think it's admirable that the boy hasn't been before me long before now. The fact that he hasn't speaks well for him, but that still doesn't mean that what you're about to undertake is going to be easy. I can guarantee you that it won't, but I don't want you to get the idea that the first time you and the boy have a problem you can just bring him back here and dump him off and be rid of him. That's not what this is all about. Due to the circumstances of this case, we feel this young man got a bad deal and we're trying to ensure that, due to one unfortunate mistake, he doesn't feel like the system is turning its back on him, but rather trying to help him." Rynor stopped again and stared straight into the rancher's eyes. "Do you understand what I'm saying?"

Jack didn't answer immediately, returning the judge's stare without blinking. When he did answer, his voice was steady with even a hint of anger behind it. "I never shirked anything in my life and if I decide to tackle this job I promise you I won't shirk it either. I'll do everything within my power to see that this boy gets a fair shake. But I swear to God, if I see he ain't makin' an effort to get along, or if I find I can't make a positive impression on him, I'll bring him back to ya. I'm too old and set in my ways to start changing now."

Judge Rynor sat looking at Jack for a few moments before allowing himself to smile at the older man. "I think we both understand each other. I want you to know I appreciate you doing this, Jack. I don't think you'll regret it."

"I already regret it," Jack growled, "but I don't reckon I could sleep nights if I didn't at least give it a try."

The judge and sheriff exchanged knowing glances again, then the judge turned back to Jack. "You'll do fine. Are you ready to meet your ward?"

Jack looked surprised by the question and looked both at Ben Aguilar and Judge Rynor. Both men were

looking expectantly at him. Finally with a sigh of res-
ignation he said, "I reckon I'm as ready as I'll ever
be."

With a grin lighting up his face, Judge Rynor
reached over and pushed the intercom on his phone.
"Wendy, will you have Deputy Harkins bring Clay
Tory to my office?"

"Yes sir," she replied from the voice box on the
judge's telephone. He turned to Jack. "I've already
done all the paperwork to release him to your custody. He can leave with you today. No sense in you
having to make another trip into town to pick him
up."

"Looks as if you already figured I'd take the boy,"
Jack Lomas said to the judge.

"Let's just say I was being optimistic." Judge Rynor
smiled, but Jack Lomas didn't return the smile. Instead he sat stoically, wondering if he wasn't making
a big mistake. His mind went back in time, as it had
been doing for the last few days, to things he'd
thought were long forgotten. He thought about the
mistakes he'd made and what the consequences had
been. He couldn't go through that again, but maybe
through Clay Tory, God was giving him another
chance to make amends for what had happened.

"I reckon being optimistic is a good thing as long as
it's someone else who's takin' the load," Jack said, betraying none of the nervousness he felt as they waited
for Clay to be brought in.

The office grew uncomfortable as the three men
tried to make small talk, finally giving up all pre-
tenses and remaining silent, each thinking his own
thoughts as they waited.

After what seemed an eternity, the intercom on the
judge's desk announced the arrival of their awaited

ward. "Show them in please, Wendy," the judge spoke, standing as he completed the request.

Jack and Ben also rose to their feet as the door swung open. The judge's secretary led in a deputy, who was followed by a youth who looked questioningly at the three men in the room.

Jack Lomas looked the boy up and down. He was smaller than he'd expected, knowing the boy's father. Jason Tory was a big man, made even bigger by the large protruding stomach that hung heavily over his belt, but the youth standing in front of him now was trim and fit. He stood just over five foot nine inches and moved with an easy grace that reminded Jack of a mountain lion. He guessed the boy weighed around one sixty, and it was all lean muscle. But it was his eyes that struck Jack. They were pale blue, almost gray, and they caught and held his own as if he were prey. Jack shifted uncomfortably on his feet and finally held out his hand. "I'm Jack Lomas. I reckon you and I'll be spending some time together."

The boy looked tentatively at the judge and Ben Aguilar before looking back to Jack, taking the proffered hand and saying, "Pleased to meet you, Mr. Lomas." Looking Jack straight in the eye he continued. "I appreciate what you're doing for me."

Jack heard the words but noted the insincerity behind them, knowing the boy had been coached to say them. He resented the words as soon as they came out of the boy's mouth and almost made a sarcastic retort before catching himself. Instead he stared hard into the youth's eyes, noticing Clay Tory's surprise as he realized the old rancher knew he wasn't sincere. Clay dropped his gaze and Jack released his hand. "I'm sure we'll get along fine, Clay. Have you got all your things?" he asked, noticing the gear bag the boy had dropped just inside the door.

"Yes sir."

"Well if there's nothing else, I reckon we better be gettin' on out to the ranch and get you settled in."

Judge Rynor cleared his throat. "If you'll just sign the papers Wendy has typed up," he said, addressing Jack, "everything will be in order."

Jack Lomas gave the judge a venomous look. "What papers?" he asked gruffly, suspicious of any legal documents.

"Just some papers giving you custody of young Clay here. They're just a formality. I should have had you sign them earlier but I forgot about it. Sorry."

Jack Lomas looked questioningly at the judge. "Let me look at them papers."

The judge nodded to his secretary, who brought them in and handed them over to Jack. He returned to his chair and began reading each paper, satisfying himself there were no clauses he didn't understand. He asked for clarification on one or two paragraphs and continued reading only when he was satisfied with the answers. Meanwhile everyone stood waiting, glancing at each other occasionally, uncomfortable with the situation and not knowing what to do about it.

Finally Jack turned the last page over and asked, "Where do I sign?"

Wendy walked over and marked an X on each of the lines he was to sign. Jack wrote his name in his slow scrawl, and handed the pages back to Wendy. "Is that everything or is there anything else I need to know before we get going?"

"That pretty well covers it," Judge Rynor said, rubbing his hands together.

"Well I guess we better get along then. I got cattle to look after and the north pasture's fence needs some mending."

Ben Aguilar walked with them out to Jack's pickup. "You mind your *P*'s and *Q*'s," he said to Clay. "I'll be out to check on you from time to time. If you need anything, let me know."

"Thanks," Clay said sarcastically and turned to see Jack scowling at him. "Thanks," he repeated more earnestly.

Ben watched the two as they backed out and headed down the street. "This ought to be real interesting," he said to himself as he watched the truck turn the corner onto Main Street.

Chapter Three

Jack rolled down the window on his side of the pickup truck as they rode along the two-lane highway that led to the Lazy L Ranch.

Clay hadn't spoken a word since they'd left the courthouse and the silence hung heavy between the two. George Strait was singing about clear blue skies, but neither of them was listening to the lyrics, as they were each absorbed in their own thoughts. Finally Jack could bear the silence no longer. "Are you in school?" he asked.

The look Clay gave him was noncommittal. "I was, but I tested out. I passed everything so I shouldn't have any problem getting my diploma."

Jack nodded. "How'd ya do?"

"I reckon I did all right. Had a little problem with English, but I managed to pass."

"Good. An education is an important thing today. It wasn't so important when I was your age. I only made it through the eighth grade and didn't do well."

Clay nodded but didn't say anything. Instead, he went back to gazing out the window lost in his own thoughts again.

Jack sighed as he realized the conversation had run out of steam. He turned west onto a caliche road and they continued the rest of the way in strained silence.

Jack eased the truck up the winding drive to the

ranch house, avoiding the major potholes left behind by the winter snows and cold weather. "I've got to get the blade hooked up to the tractor and fix this road," he said as much to himself as to Clay. There was no reply as the boy surveyed the house and surrounding buildings.

"Is that an arena?" he asked as they passed the long equipment barn where Jack stored his tractors and various hay tools.

"Yep, only it ain't been used as an arena for a long spell now. Mainly I just use it to hold cattle when I'm workin' 'em." He watched the boy's face as he looked from one end to the other, noticing the change in his attitude when he saw the two bucking chutes at the arena's far end.

"Sheriff Aguilar told me you used to be a rodeo hand," Clay stated, "but I thought he was just pulling my leg."

"That was a long time ago. I hear you're a pretty good hand yourself."

"I do all right. I just wish to hell I had more time to practice."

Jack slammed on the brakes and the pickup skidded to a halt, dust boiling up and floating off on a slight breeze. Clay moved to brace himself against the cushioned dashboard, barely preventing himself from being thrown into the windshield. He looked wildly about, trying to locate the reason for the sudden stop. When he looked over at the old rancher and saw the baleful stare that was directed at him, his heart skipped a beat. "Let's get one thing straight right now," Jack said firmly between clenched teeth, "I don't put up with no foul language. I figure anyone who's got to cuss to get his point across ain't got enough sense to talk at all, and I don't want to be wastin' my time listening to him. I know things are different now than when I was young, and using foul language is more acceptable now than it was then, but not with me. I just cain't see no sense in it."

"Jeez, I didn't mean to get your pacemaker all upset. All I said was hell—"

"Don't say it again," Jack interrupted. "I know what you said and I'm tellin' ya right now I won't stand for it. Is that clear?"

Jack's cold eyes pierced into Clay's, and the boy held his gaze for ten seconds before finally dropping his eyes. "Sorry," he muttered.

"Now that we got that settled, let's get up to the house and get you settled in. Then we'll rustle us up some grub and get to work. I've already lost most of the day and there's things needin' to be done."

Clay's anger burned as he stepped out of the pickup. He wondered what he'd gotten himself into. Here he was stuck out in the boondocks with a crazy old man for a whole year. The sheriff had talked him into this, saying it would be better than the six months he'd have to serve in Juvenile Hall, but Clay wondered if that was true. But he knew he couldn't stand being locked up for six months. The two weeks he'd spent in jail already had just about made him go crazy. *I reckon I can always head to Montana and change my name,* he thought glumly as he followed Jack Lomas into the house.

Clay set his gear bag down in the bedroom Jack had shown him. Looking around, he decided he liked the feel of the room, though he hadn't shown it when Jack opened the door and led him in. Instead he'd shown total indifference, as if he were being shown to another jail cell.

The room was large with a single bed pushed up

against one wall. There was a large oak dresser, where he was told he could put his clothes, and a closet for anything that needed hanging. There were several pictures on the wall and glancing at them, he saw they were old photographs of the ranch and various activities that had taken place. He noticed one that showed a younger Jack Lomas sitting astride a bronc that was trying to unload the rider on its back. Clay stared at the picture and had to admit Jack was making a good showing when the picture was snapped.

"I'll bet he got thrown," he whispered to himself. He knew this wasn't a rodeo picture because Jack was riding a ranch saddle rather than the standard high-swelled, high-cantled bronc saddle, but even so he was keeping a good seat, and looking closely at the old black-and-white photo he could see the ghost of a smile on Jack's lips. Leaning closer, he read the faded hand writing on the bottom of the photo. "Jack on Old Stormy 1976. He made it to the finish." Clay frowned and was startled from his thoughts at the sound of Jack's voice.

"Lunch is ready," he called from the kitchen. Clay glanced once more at the pictures and noticed another of a younger Jack Lomas with his arm around an attractive woman, a small boy about ten years of age standing in front of them, his eyes looking with adoration at the man standing above him. He took one more look around the room before walking down the hallway toward the kitchen.

As Clay took a chair at the table, Jack sat a plate in front of him. "After we finish eating we'll load up several posts and some wire and head over to the north pasture. That runoff from the last snow washed out some gaps. I just hope none of the cattle have found it yet."

Clay remained silent, and as he ate his fried steak and potatoes, his thoughts were on Montana. They spent the next three days repairing fences in the north pasture. Tracks in the dirt where the fences had washed out showed several head of cattle had crossed to the adjoining ranch. All during the time they worked the mood remained somber between the two of them. Jack had tried several times to engage Clay in small talk but the young man had responded with single-syllable answers and had made no attempt to keep the conversation going. He worked hard and Jack was impressed at how quick the boy caught on to things. He rarely had to be told what to do, and never a second time.

At night the mood was even more reserved. Jack usually sat at the kitchen table working on his ranch books, reading the Bible, or making plans for the next day's work, while Clay, usually worn out from the day's work, went to his room or tried to watch the old television set in the living room. The TV set was at least twenty years old and the antenna had been whipped by the wind so much over the years that it could only bring in one channel, and even that one had poor reception. Clay complained about the programs that were being shown and asked the old rancher why he didn't get a satellite system.

"Don't like to watch television. I only bought that durned thing because my wife nagged me about it. Said she got bored being here all alone." He didn't tell him about the fight they'd had about it and how she'd threatened to pack up and move to town if he didn't get one.

Jack saw the frustration on Clay's face and felt the irritation rise in him as Clay stomped off, slamming the door to his room.

As one door slammed, another opened in Jack's mind, bringing back long-forgotten and painful memories. He remembered a time long ago when he was at odds with another young man. That had been so long ago. Thoughts of that time lay buried deep in the recesses of his memory, but now they came flooding to the surface. He didn't fight to keep them buried, but try as he could, he couldn't remember what had caused the rift between the two of them or when it had begun. All he could remember was single battles that been fought, with neither side winning or willing to concede.

Sitting alone at the kitchen table, the dim light of the sixty-watt bulb in the overhead light illuminating the ledgers on the table, he tried for an hour to update the figures in the columns, but his mind kept wandering to the past.

Jack Lomas had to admit he'd never been one for self-evaluation. He'd always done and said what he'd thought was right. And for most of his life that rule had served him well, but now as he sat alone, he wondered if it had really served him as well as he'd thought. For the first time ever he began to doubt himself and his philosophy and as he did, unbidden tears came to his eyes and he didn't fight to hold them back. His eyes were red and blurry when he finally turned off the kitchen light and walked down the hall to his bedroom. He paused at Clay's door and could hear the regular breathing of sleep coming from the room. Emotions welled up in him and he turned away before they threatened to swallow him. Making his way to his bed, he undressed and lay on the bed. Unable to fall asleep, Jack thought again of the young man of long ago. . . .

*   *   *

Clay was awakened at four in the morning. "Get up, breakfast's ready."

Wiping the sleep from his eyes he looked at the illuminated hands on the clock by his bed. "What the . . ." He stared at Jack, stunned by the early hour.

"We got to get started after them cattle today. They've already been gone for several days and it'll take a spell to get 'em back. Now get up and let's get goin'."

While Clay sleepily ate his breakfast of ham, fried eggs, and homemade biscuits with peach preserves, Jack hooked the stock trailer behind the Dodge pickup and fed the barn stock.

Though he lived by himself, he still kept chickens and he usually had a hog and a beef fattening for his own use, saying he didn't trust that stuff you bought at a store—no telling what was in it.

He returned to the house as Clay was finishing his breakfast. "I hope you ate enough. It may be a long time before we get back here to eat again."

Clay gave the solemn nod that Jack was used to seeing these past four days and picked up his dishes. Carrying them to the sink he began washing them, quickly picking up Jack's habit.

"Can you ride a horse?" Jack asked, already knowing the answer since Ben Aguilar had told him the boy could ride as well as anybody he'd ever seen. He was still surprised at the response he got as the boy's head jerked around, light sparkling in his eyes.

"Yes sir," was all he said, catching himself, but Jack had already seen the fire.

"Well hurry up, we got to get these horses loaded and over to the north pasture before the sun gets up or we'll never get all them cows before dark."

The sun was just making its entrance, the first fingers of dawn lighting the soft clouds in the eastern sky as they pulled up to the gate separating the Lazy L from the Two Springs Ranch. "We'll leave the pickup and trailer here," Jack said, pulling off to the side of the rutted trail that served as a road across the pasture. "We'll bring the cattle through this gate, then one of us can drive them to the rest of the herd while the other brings the truck and trailer."

They had taken a head count of the cattle in the north pasture the day before and had found twenty-three missing, and could only assume they had all wandered through the broken fences searching for greener pastures.

They unloaded the horses from the covered stock trailer and Jack handed Clay the reins of a tall sorrel. "His name is Whiskey," Jack said in the way of introduction. "He's a tough one. Took me four months of hard ridin' to get that rascal to quit bucking every time I got on him. He'll still show out from time to time, but only when you first get on him. Once you get him lined out he's all business, and can go all day and then take you to the dance at night."

The rancher's love for the horse didn't go unnoticed by Clay and something in his hardened reserve softened toward the old man for a fleeting moment.

"I'll hold him while you get on," Jack said, and Clay bristled.

"I can ride as good as you, old man. I don't need you to hold my horse for me," he spat at Jack, insulted by the offer.

Jack's eyes blazed at the boy's stinging words. Fighting to bring his temper under control, he held his tongue until he was sure he could speak. His eyes still smoldering, he spoke in a voice that was calmer than his emotions. "Suit yourself."

Jack tightened the cinch on his saddle and led his horse off a few steps before taking hold of the bridle in his left hand. He grasped the reins in his right hand and stepped up into the saddle, not letting go of the bridle until he was sure the big bay wasn't going to try anything. Mounted on his horse, he turned to watch the boy.

Clay finished zipping up the chaps Jack had handed him. Surprisingly, they had fit him perfectly and he wondered who they belonged to originally, certainly not the old rancher, for they were way too small for him. Clay noticed the leather had been well oiled and cared for, though he doubted they had been worn for a long while.

Taking the reins of the big sorrel, he flipped them over the horse's neck and grabbed them along with the saddle horn in his left hand. With the cantle in his right hand, he placed his left foot in the stirrup and stepped up. As his rump came in contact with the leather of the saddle, the world seemed to explode beneath him as the sorrel ducked his head between his legs and shot into the air, jerking Clay's neck back with the sudden jump.

Clay grabbed the saddle horn with his right hand and tried to pull against the reins to force the horse's head up, but found he only held the very end of the split reins, which didn't give him any leverage to pull. As his feet floundered to find the stirrups, he realized they had been let down for a person with longer legs and his wouldn't reach. With no stirrups and only the saddle horn to hang on to, he was like a pendulum with one pivot point, and it became painfully aware to him there was no way he was going to stay aboard.

Sure enough in two more jumps he was sailing through the air, his arms and legs windmilling frantically as he tried to fight thin air for some semblance of balance, only to find the ground coming at him way too fast. The side of his face hit first followed only a millisecond later by his left shoulder, and side, and finally his lower torso. The breath was knocked from him in a whoosh as he slid through the prairie grass and snow-packed earth. When things finally stilled he tried to get his befuddled mind to take stock of his condition, but the pain he felt throughout his body told him there was no place to begin, at least until he could get his lungs to fill with air and at present they weren't cooperating.

When at last he was able to suck in large quantities of air to replace that which he'd lost, he rolled over, groaning as he did. His eyes were blurry and he felt like his brain was floating in a thick fog that refused to lift. He shook his head, only to regret the sudden movement that sent waves of pain down his shoulders and into his back. Moving slowly he raised up on his hands and knees and finally forced himself to stand up, weaving as he tried to regain his balance.

As the haze cleared from his mind and his eyes began to focus, he looked around, trying to get his bearings. He found the pickup and trailer, and saw the sorrel was standing a good distance from it, his reins trailing the ground while he grazed on a mouthful of prairie grass, acting as if what had taken place was the normal course of events.

Shaking his head with caution, Clay looked to where Jack Lomas sat on his bay. He was leaning on the saddle horn acting unconcerned, as if this happened every day.

Clay walked shakily to the trailer and sat down on one of the fenders, feeling as if he might lose the breakfast he'd eaten only a short time before.

Jack rode over to the sorrel, who remained ground-hitched, as a good ranch horse is supposed to, and taking up the reins, led him to where Clay sat. He was still holding his head in his hands, the nausea just beginning to subside. Jack had a biting comment on the end of his tongue, ready to berate the boy for his foolishness, but when he saw how pale Clay was he remained silent and waited for the boy to look up.

Clay's stomach began to settle and he looked up expecting to see Jack gloating over his escapade, but what he saw startled him. He didn't know how to react to the look of concern that he saw on the old rancher's face. No one had ever been concerned about him before. Why should this old man who had brought him out here as a prisoner to be used as free help be concerned about him?

"You all right?" Jack asked, his voice not reflecting his worry.

Clay only nodded.

"Well, you want to try again?"

Clay looked into Jack's eyes, expecting to see him mocking him, but all he saw was a questioning look. "Yeah, but first I want to adjust my stirrups."

Jack grinned at him. It was the first time Clay had seen him smile. "That's why I was going to hold him for you to begin with."

"It would have been nice if you'd mentioned that beforehand." Clay groaned.

"Seems to me you were in too big a hurry to prove that you could ride as well or better than I could." Jack responded without malice.

Clay gave him a lopsided grin. "I guess I was, but you could have told me the stirrups were too long for me."

Jack looked thoughtful for a moment before replying. "I reckon I could have, but then you didn't exactly give me a chance to. I'll bet the next time I offer to do something for you, you'll stop and think about it before flying off the handle."

Clay stared at him a moment, then nodded. He knew the old rancher was right and it galled him to admit it, but he wasn't about to give him the pleasure of saying it. Nobody, outside his circle of friends, had ever offered him advice or help without expecting something in return, especially his lazy father and brothers. The only thing they'd ever given him was hard times because he wouldn't go along with their ideas of making easy money, but he'd seen where they had gotten with all their stealing and swindling. What they didn't spend on jail fines and attorneys they blew on whiskey and gambling, and he found both to be distasteful. They were the reason he'd left home at the age of thirteen and moved in with friends. It was one of those friends who had, four years before, taken him to his first rodeo, where he had experienced the excitement of the action and even talked to some of the hands who were participating. That night, alone in his bedroom, he had sworn he would do everything in his power to become a rodeo hand.

He had started the next day, talking to anyone around Roswell who had been or was involved with any of the events in rodeo. Soon he found Larry Craig, a lanky, rawboned cowboy who worked for one of the local ranches and rode saddle broncs on the amateur circuit. It was Larry who had helped the thirteen year old ride his first broncs. Vince Rogers, an intercollegiate bull rider had assisted him in learning to ride bulls. Gary Williams had helped in teaching him how to steer wrestle and had even hauled him to several rodeos, letting him use his dogging horse and hazing for him. He'd team-roped with Kyle Lester and calf-roped with Jerry Frazier, and by the time he was sixteen he was beginning to make an all-around hand. When he'd actually started winning, his father and brothers had taken his money, even when he'd hidden it, and he had had to find a part-time job to pay for his next entries. He'd stayed in school, and though his grades weren't the best he still passed. He took the high school equivalency test his last year so he could spend more time on the road traveling to rodeos, where he borrowed roping and dogging horses, entering either four or five events, depending on his finances at the time.

Jack flipped him the sorrel's reins, and rising stiffly to his feet, he hobbled up beside the horse and began taking up the stirrups.

"You're going to have to learn how to mount a horse properly if you want to prevent that from happening again," Jack said. He spoke as a teacher would to a student, and not as if he was trying to impress him with his knowledge.

Clay nodded and looked questioningly at him.

"Grabbing the cantle is for movie stars. A real cowboy never gets on that way." Clay fumed at the comment but remained silent, continuing to listen to the old rancher. He certainly didn't want a repeat of the earlier incident. "When you get on, hold the reins and the saddle horn in your right hand," Jack said, looking at Clay to make sure he was listening. When he was satisfied he was, he continued. "Hold the bridle's head strap in your left hand. If your horse is too big or your arms are too short, hold the left rein as close to the bit as possible and take a hold of the horse's mane. Hold him up tight so he can't jerk his head away from you. Then put your foot in the stirrup and swing up. Don't give him his head until you're firmly seated and your feet are in the stirrups. Then hold your reins tight and keep the bit pulled snug in his mouth until you see what he's going to do. Got it?"

"I think so," Clay answered.

With a small amount of coaching, Clay remounted Whiskey. This time went without incident, though the big horse did try to take his head once again, but Clay pulled him around with the left rein and the horse quickly settled down.

When Clay was in the saddle and Jack could see he was going to stay there, he rode to the gate. Dismounting, he swung the post and wire open to allow them to pass through, then closed the gate back, smiling to himself as the sorrel stepped in a rut causing Clay to wince.

Chapter Four

Jack set the pace at a ground-eating trot. At first Clay ached from the pounding pace but soon his body adjusted to the rhythm of Whiskey's gait and the pain eased.

They rode the entire section that joined the Lazy L, crisscrossing the land to make sure they covered all the ground. They had split up several times and though they found many cows wearing the Two Springs brand, they only found fourteen head with the Lazy L branded on their left hips.

It was late in the afternoon when they brought the fourteen head to the gate leading into the Lazy L. Jack loped around the cattle and opened the gate as Clay drove them through.

Clay's body felt thoroughly beaten as he pushed the last cow through. His legs were chafed where the chaps had rubbed them. His feet and legs were sore from standing in his stirrups and his back felt as if it were broken in several different places. His face and shoulder constantly reminded him of his wreck from earlier in the day and he was tired, as tired as he could ever remember being.

Jack watched the young man ride wearily through the gate and knew it had been a hard day on the boy. Riding all day could wear out the most able athlete if they weren't used to it, and he had pushed the boy hard today. He gave Clay credit though; he had done his share without complaint.

"You load your horse in the trailer and drive around to the east windmill, and I'll drive these old biddies there. There should be plenty of others there this time of day," Jack said, climbing back into the saddle.

Clay nodded, and though he wouldn't admit it, he was thankful for the chance to get off this horse. As he loosened Whiskey's cinch, he watched Jack start the cattle on their way, and he felt something close to admiration for the old rancher. Jack had ridden hard all day and didn't look any worse for wear, unlike himself. "That's one tough old man," he said quietly to Whiskey. The horse looked at him as though he understood and Clay smiled weakly.

Later on, Clay was putting away his dishes from supper when Jack spoke to him. "Reckon you can take the trailer and a horse up to the north pasture tomorrow and take another head count. There just might be a chance we miscounted or missed some."

Clay dried his plate, tired to the bone and wanting nothing more than to go to bed and sleep for three days, but hearing Jack's request, he perked up. "Sure," he responded, wondering what Jack was going to be doing while he counted cattle.

As if reading his thoughts Jack continued. "I think I'll drive over to the Two Springs headquarters and talk to Bud Canton. He's the foreman over there. I'll see if they've run across any of the missing cows."

Clay was up before the sun the following morning and trailered his horse to the north pasture. After mounting in the proper fashion without incident, he began a slow crossing pattern of the large pasture.

Jack had told him there were close to six hundred fenced acres in this pasture alone, and he knew it would take him most of the day to check every arroyo and cedar stand to ensure that he located each cow. He would check the windmills and water tanks first, knowing most of the cattle would remain close to these, and check all the other likely places in between.

The land he rode over was rangeland, dry and sparse with few trees, but with just the right amount of rainfall the hardy range grass provided sufficient protein and filler to fatten the crossbred cattle that had adapted to the harsh climate.

Used to the speedy trot of the horse now, Clay rode from one watering hole to the next, allowing his eyes to take in the range. For some reason he couldn't explain he felt at peace with the world for the first time in a long while. Maybe it was being alone in this vast country, or maybe it was the horse under him and the mission he was on, or maybe it was the warm, cloudless day. He couldn't put his finger on it, but he felt as if the weight of the world had been lifted from his shoulders. It was as if he had stepped from one world into another, and all his troubles had been left behind.

He had been at the Lazy L six days now and thinking about those days he wondered again why Jack Lomas had taken him in. He knew something had happened in the past that had changed the old rancher. Ben Aguilar had made subtle hints about it when he'd told him about Jack and the Lazy L, but he had warned him not to be too nosy, which was no problem since he'd learned early not to be too inquisitive. His father's backhanded slaps had broken him at an early age from asking too many questions, but that didn't keep him from wondering what had happened in Jack's past to make him so hard.

By three in the afternoon he had covered the entire pasture, satisfied he'd looked in every possible place where a cow might have hidden. He rode back to the pickup and trailer, still nine head short of the two hundred and thirty-two head that were supposed to be in the pasture.

When he drove up to the ranch house he noticed that Jack still wasn't home so he unloaded his horse. After rubbing him down and feeding him, he fed the other barn stock and then walked down to the arena.

Climbing the high board fence that bordered the enclosure, he jumped down to the hard-packed earth and looked around. Though the enclosure itself had been maintained, with evidence of recent repairs, he could see that neither the roping chutes on one end nor the bucking chutes on the other had had any recent use. He climbed atop one of the bucking chute gates and surveyed the setup. He was impressed with the layout and knew they had spared no expense in building the chutes or the holding pens.

As he sat atop the chute he could feel the old excitement welling up in him at the thought of riding, and was soon lost in his thoughts of past rides and future dreams. He was still sitting there when Jack Lomas drove up the lane toward the house. Clay was so engrossed in his thoughts that he didn't hear him approach. Jack looked out the windshield of his truck at the youth. "Jaimie . . ." the name slipped from him in a whisper of hope, and then he caught himself and shook his head as if to rid his mind of an unwelcome thought.

Clay heard the pickup as it came to a stop in front of the house and jumping easily to the ground, he walked up to meet Jack.

"Have any luck?" Jack asked as Clay came through the gate.

"Still missing nine," Clay replied as he walked up to the old rancher. "How about you?"

Jack shook his head, frowning. "Nope. I talked to Bud Canton, seems he's missing twelve head out of the same pasture we were in yesterday. He thinks he found some tracks where a truck might have gotten stuck on the north end. He's riding all of his pastures to see if any more cattle are missing. We'll have to do the same thing."

"We going to start tomorrow?" Clay asked.

"Nope, tomorrow's Sunday. We go to church on Sunday. We'll start again early Monday. I want to start with the pastures on the west side since those are closest to the county roads. Then we'll work the east pastures and finish with the south pastures."

Clay nodded. "If someone's rustling cattle I don't see why you want to wait until Monday. Why don't we get started tomorrow?"

"Because tomorrow's the Lord's Day and we will observe it," Jack stated gruffly, only to regret it as he saw the excitement snuffed out of the boy's eyes. He started to tell him that he wanted to talk to the other ranchers at church tomorrow. He wanted to find out if any of them were missing livestock too, but Clay had already turned and walked back toward the barn. Jack watched him until he disappeared, then with shoulders sagging, walked slowly into the house to cook their supper.

They awoke Sunday to an overcast sky, and it seemed to fit both their moods as they ate breakfast in silence and dressed for church. The drive into town was devoid of conversation and Jack was thankful when they finally arrived at the church. He was greeted by several men standing outside and was soon absorbed in conversation. He looked around occasionally to locate Clay. At first the boy was standing off to himself, but with the arrival of two boys his age he was soon leaning against the church talking, and Jack felt a strange comfort that he had friends here.

If asked about the sermon that day Jack couldn't have told you anything about it, as his mind absorbed the facts he'd learned in the last two days. He said a silent prayer as the services came to an end and he hurried out of the church. He was waiting by the pickup when Clay came out with his two friends. Jack impatiently climbed behind the wheel and started the pickup before Clay was in and seated.

They drove to the Blue Bonnet Café, still not a word passing between them. The place was packed with people and they had to wait fifteen minutes for a table. Jack left Clay standing in line and walked to the table where Ben Aguilar sat with his family. Ben was dressed in his Sunday suit and Clay had to look twice before he recognized him. He'd never seen the sheriff in anything but his uniform. Somehow seeing him dressed this way made the man seem more human in his eyes, and as the old rancher leaned on the table, he wondered what they were talking about. He surmised it was about the missing cattle but he would have liked to know more of the details. He wasn't about to ask Jack.

After a few moments Jack came back to stand in line beside him. He seemed a little less anxious and even smiled at the lady who came to seat them. After they had placed their order with the harried waitress, Jack asked, "So how did you like the service?"

"Fine," Clay responded, though he really didn't get much out of it. The preacher had spoken on the evils

of drinking and since he didn't drink, he didn't figure
the message was for him.

"Good," Jack said though his mind wasn't really on
Clay's response. Almost as an afterthought he asked,
"Who were your friends?"

"That was just Charles Stevens and Berry Smith. I
went to school with them," he answered.

Jack's eyes looked up with interest. "Is that Gary
Stevens' boy?" he asked.

Clay shrugged his shoulders. "I don't know. I
reckon. His dad owns a small ranch west of here."

"Yep, that's Gary Stevens' place. He didn't say anything about losin' cattle, did he?"

Clay looked at the rancher with a questioning
glance and suddenly wondered about the missing cattle and why Jack was so worried. Nine head of cattle
couldn't make that big a difference to him. Of course
they weren't sure if that was all that were missing, but
still it made him wonder. "Yeah, he said his dad was
missing several head after the last big runoff, just like
you. Their fences had washed out too and they
thought they were on their neighbor's place, but they
hadn't found them. Their neighbor was missing a
couple of head as well."

Jack looked awestruck. "Why didn't you tell me
this?" he asked, his voice rising.

Clay looked shocked, then angry. "Because you
didn't ask. You don't like talking to me anyway, so
why should I tell you?"

Jack's face registered shock then surprise, then understanding as he stared at the young man across
from him. "I'm sorry," he said quietly as several people turned to look at them. "I shouldn't have spoken
to you like that. Apparently everyone's been hit by
these cattle thieves, which means it's a pretty large-

scale operation. There's no tellin' how much damage they'll do before they move on or get caught. Many of my pastures have access to county roads, which makes them an easy target for cattle thieves. I've tried to make it harder by building barricades in the roads where the only way to drive in is through the main road leading to the house, but that won't stop them. They'll just drive the cattle to their trailers on horses, then rope and drag the cows into the trailer and be gone before anyone's the wiser."

"Isn't there anything we can do to stop them?" Clay asked, now more sympathetic to the old man's plight.

Jack shook his head. "All we can do is move the cattle closer to the house, but the grass won't hold out long enough to keep them there. Then when winter hits I won't have any grass left, and I'll have to move them to the remote pastures where it'll be harder to feed them. If the rustlers are smart and don't get caught they'll wait until then and lure them with feed."

Clay could see the dilemma the old man was faced with. "Couldn't we ride watch in those pastures?"

"Which ones do we watch? And while we're watching one, what's going to keep them from stealing cattle from the ones we're not watching?"

Clay nodded slowly as he began to see the problem the old rancher was up against. "Maybe they'll catch them soon," he said in the way of hope, yet knowing the odds were against it. There weren't enough deputies in the county to patrol the vast amount of rangeland and cover all the roads in and out of the area. A smart thief would have lookouts and radios and would be monitoring the police band radios. "Does Ben have any ideas?"

"He says they're doing everything they can. They

just learned about it a week ago. He says they don't
have any suspects but they're talking to everyone
who has a history, and they're calling all the surrounding sheriffs' offices to see if they have had any
reports of stolen cattle. Right now it doesn't look
promising."

They finished their meal in silence and drove home
in the same manner. "Get changed," Jack said as they
pulled into the yard. "We'll drive over to the west
pasture and have a look around."

Clay started to say something about it being the
Lord's Day, but thought better of it and hurried inside
to change.

Rain began to fall as they reached the west pasture.
It was coming down in a fine mist and added to the
mood of the day as they drove across the cattle guard
and continued on the winding pasture road.

"We'll check a couple of water holes on the way,"
Jack said, trying to see through the dirty windshield.
The windshield wipers were running but they only
seemed to mix the mist with the dust that had accu-
mulated on the glass, making more of a muddy
streak. They stopped at two water tanks and counted
the cattle they saw on the way. Jack had loaded two
sacks of cake into the back of the truck before leaving
the house, and now he fed small amounts to the cows
while getting a head count.

They continued on to the gate that led to the county
road. As they neared it, Clay could see where trees
and dirt had been pushed up in the road by a dozer.
There was only enough room for the pickup to
squeeze through, and it brushed against the sides as
they pulled up.

Both Jack and Clay got out of the truck and exam-
ined the road by the gate. Sure enough, they could

both see a mixture of horse, human, and cattle tracks around the gate. A little ways past the gate and before the county road, they could see where a truck and trailer had backed up and loaded the cows.

"They used the barricade as part of a pen and drove the cattle up here and loaded them," Jack said looking at the ground. "Looks like they got maybe ten or twelve head and they cut the chain I had around the gate." The severed chain had been put back in place so the casual observer would think the gate was still locked.

Looking at the sky, Jack started back toward the pickup. "It's too late to do any more looking. Let's head back to the house and I'll call Ben and report this to him, though I don't see what good it will do. Them cattle are probably already in Texas hangin' in a meat locker somewhere."

Both Jack and Clay were somber as they drove back to the house. Clay wondered what this was doing to the old rancher. He could understand him being upset over the theft of his cattle but for some reason Jack seemed to be taking it really hard, as if this were some kind of personal war and he was losing.

Jack called Ben's office when they got back to the house and was told he was out at another ranch looking into some missing cattle. Jack hung up the phone with a sigh and slumped into a kitchen chair. Clay pulled out a chair and sat down, watching him as he ran his fingers through his white hair. He seemed to age right in front of Clay.

"It's all right, Mr. Lomas, Ben'll catch 'em," he said, not knowing what else to say.

Jack Lomas looked up at the sound of his voice. "I hope so, son, I surely hope so."

Chapter Five

For the next two weeks they worked from daylight until well after dark, covering the entire Lazy L range. Clay came to know every nook and cranny of the eight thousand acres that belonged to Jack Lomas.

Many mornings Clay would load a horse in the trailer and haul to one of the remote pastures, while Jack took the Ford and drove around the county roads, checking fences and gates that bordered each one.

At final count Jack had lost forty-one head and was one of the hardest hit in the county. Not that forty-one head was going to break him or even set him back, but he seemed driven to stop the thieves and Clay often wondered at the older man's tireless vigil.

They were into their third week since the rustlers had first struck and Jack was worn and frazzled. He had just returned to the ranch house and was belittling himself for growing old when he saw Clay pull into the yard and unload his horse. The sun had set already and in the dim twilight he watched the young boy wearily lead his tired horse to the barn and unsaddle him. He watched as he rubbed the horse down, feeding him before caring for the other animals. He noticed how slow the boy's steps were and how his shoulders drooped as he went about his chores and it suddenly dawned on him how hard the two of them had been working. But he'd never heard a complaint out of Clay and he smiled as he thought about how the youth seemed as driven as he was to make sure no more cattle were lost. He waited in the chair on the front porch for Clay to finish and join him for supper. They hadn't heard of any more thefts in three weeks now and after talking to Ben the night before, he was pretty sure the rustlers had either moved on or were laying low for a while. Either way there was really nothing more that could be done until they surfaced again. It was time they both took a rest.

Clay was so tired, he didn't see Jack sitting on the porch until he was almost upon him. He gave a start when he saw him sitting there. "Looks to me like you're already asleep," Jack said with a grin as the youth came to an abrupt stop.

Clay didn't smile as he stood looking at Jack. He was worn out and tired to the bone. He didn't mind hard work, but what they were doing now seemed futile to him. How were an old man and a kid going to prevent rustlers from taking the whole herd. All the thieves really had to do was to watch the house to see where he and Jack went and then hit the spots in between, and apparently that's just what they were doing.

Jack must have read his mind. "Why don't you take the Dodge into town and see some of your friends." He paused to see what kind of reaction he'd get but Clay just stared at him. "Go ahead and take tomorrow off too. I don't reckon the two of us are goin' to catch these thievin' rascals anyway. Be back early tomorrow evenin'—we still got a lot of work to do."

Clay nodded, but didn't say anything as he walked into the house. In a few moments Jack could hear the water in the shower running. Thirty minutes later the

screen door slammed as Clay came hurrying out of
the house in a clean shirt and jeans. "See ya tomorrow," he said as he passed Jack, who was still sitting
in the rocker.

"Don't get into any trouble, ya hear?" Jack said to
the youth's retreating back and got no response, not
that he expected one. He continued sitting in the rocking chair until the drone of the Dodge's engine could
no longer be heard, then slowly got up and walked
into the house, looking one more time down the road
in the direction Clay had gone. If anyone could have
seen his face at that moment, they would have seen
the mixture of sadness, regret, and loneliness that
were etched there, but the pain evident in his eyes
was another story that only a few still knew, or remembered, and never talked about.

Jack ate a cold sandwich for supper and went to
bed. Exhausted both mentally and physically, he fell
asleep instantly.

About the time Jack began snoring, Clay was
parked at the Sonic Drive-in talking to Jason Albright
and Scott Hale. He had just wolfed down a hamburger that had cost one-third of his bankroll. Ben
Aguilar had told him he would get five dollars a day
from the county but so far he hadn't seen a dime, and
he wondered if maybe Jack Lomas had got it and was
keeping it from him. But as soon as the thought came
he dismissed it; Jack Lomas may be a cantankerous
old coot, but he was honest and Clay knew he'd
rather die than take anything that he didn't earn or
didn't belong to him.

"You guys want to pool our money and buy some
beer?" Jason asked.

"Sure," Scott said, "but who's goin' to buy it?"

"I can get Harry down at the bowling alley to buy it, but we'll have to give him a couple of beers."

"Sounds good to me," Scott said.

"Count me out," Clay stated.

"You going to wimp out on us again, Tory?" Jason taunted.

"Yeah, you're always woosin' out on us," Scott interjected, "and without you we ain't got enough to buy but two six-packs. That ain't enough to make it worth our while."

"Sorry, fellas, but I ain't got a taste for beer and I ain't about to take a chance on the law catchin' me with any. I reckon I'll head out to the pits and see who's out there. Maybe Shirley's waitin' for me," he said, starting up the Dodge and putting it into reverse.

"We'll see ya later. We're going to find some beer before we head out there. Ain't no fun at the pits without a couple of beers under your belt." Clay shook his head and backed out of the parking place. "Two beers and they'll be so drunk they'll fall in the pits," he said to himself.

The pits were located outside of town in an area where they dug the caliche clay out of the ground, leaving deep holes that filled with water from underground springs and runoffs from the rain. It was a favorite place for the young crowd to gather and as long as nothing serious took place, it was rarely visited by the sheriff's department. Ben understood teens needed a place to gather and had made it clear as long as they kept things under control, he'd leave them alone. But they also knew if things got out of hand too often, he'd close it down.

There were about ten cars parked in a semicircle away from the fire that burned in the circle of rocks. A

Reba McEntire song was blasting from a large portable boom box and several couples were two-stepping in time with the music.

No one recognized the Dodge pickup as it pulled alongside the others. It wasn't until Clay was almost at the fire that several of the others recognized him. "Hey, Clay, we heard you was on your way to the big house," a large youth yelled good-naturedly as Clay approached them.

"Nope. Worse than that—I got hard time with Jack Lomas," he said, smiling.

"You're kidding. You're hitched up with old man Lomas?" the youth asked incredulously.

"Yep, got one year hard labor," Clay said without smiling.

"What's he like? I heard he was hard as nails. Harry Mobbs said he used to have a son but he got killed somehow and ever since the old man has been mean as a snake, spendin' all his time out at the ranch and won't have nothin' to do with anyone else."

"Did Harry say how his son got killed?" Clay asked, interested.

"He didn't rightly know. Said some of the folks around here know what happened but they keep it quiet and won't say. Reckon they're afraid of the old fart."

"Hey, Clay, you seen Joe?" a tall lanky boy standing with his arm around a girl asked as he took another drink from the bottle of beer he was holding.

"Nope, Randy, I ain't seen him, but I sure would like to," Clay answered.

"Well this could be your lucky day, 'cause I ran into him earlier today and he said he'd be here. Ought to be showin' up anytime now."

"Is that so?" Clay asked, smiling.

"Yep that's so."

"Hello, Clay," came a feminine voice to Clay's left. He turned to see Shirley Roberts, the girl he'd been with when Joe had called the sheriff's office.

"Hey, Shirley. How ya been?" he asked, smiling with pleasure.

"Fine, I guess. I'm sorry about what happened," she said. "I told Ben I was sure Joe had loaned you that pickup but since I wasn't there when he did it, Ben said it was hearsay. I'm sorry you got in this fix."

Clay put his arm around her and pulled her close. "It wasn't your fault. It was that lyin' Joe Hanson, and I reckon it was kinda dumb of me to borrow his pickup to come see you."

Shirley smiled knowingly. "He came around the next day after you'd been arrested and wanted to make up. I told him he had to be plumb stupid. I'd already told him we were through before he did that to you, and we are *definitely* through now. He almost broke down and bawled right there. It was so pitiful."

Clay grinned at the thought. "Well no use crying over spilt milk. I need something to drink. Anybody got a Coca-Cola?"

"Yeah there's one here in the cooler," a slim girl with red hair said, digging into the ice chest and bringing out a can that she deftly tossed to Clay.

The music, laughter, and companionship helped ease the tension and weariness from Clay's body, and soon he was laughing and enjoying the night.

"You going to rodeo this summer?" Tom Walker asked, as talk turned to his favorite subject.

"I don't reckon I'll get to," Clay said dejectedly. "Old man Lomas don't know nothin' but that stupid ranch of his. Did you know he's got an arena with bucking and roping chutes and it never gets used."

"You don't say," someone answered. "I heard he used to be hell on wheels as a bronc rider. Might have even been a world's champion."

"Yeah I heard that too," Clay responded, "but that was a long time ago. I doubt he knows what it's like today."

"Well maybe you can work something out with him to let you make a few rodeos. There's one coming up in Ruidoso in about a week. Ought to be a good show. Running H is supplying the stock."

Clay shook his head. "I'd sure like to make that one, but I really doubt old man Lomas will let me go."

"I don't know about the rodeo but if you want a piece of Joe Hanson, he's comin' down the road now," someone said.

Clay looked at the headlights coming down the road and recognized the sound of the truck. It was Joe's all right; he could tell by the sound of the mufflers. "Don't let him know I'm here," he said, stepping away from the group at the fire into the darkness.

Joe Hanson slid his truck to a stop in a cloud of dust that settled over those standing by the fire. Curses and yells went up as Joe walked toward the group, smiling smugly as if he'd done a great deed.

"You're a dipwad, Hanson," someone said as he approached.

"I might be, Willie, but you're worthless as tits on a boar hog," he said with the same smile, reaching into the ice chest and pulling out a bottle of beer.

"You know the rule, Hanson, you don't drink unless you contribute."

"Yeah, well put it on my tab," he said arrogantly.

Joe Hanson stood six feet tall and weighed close to two hundred pounds. Always larger than most of his classmates, he had often used his size to bully and torment most of them.

"I'll put it on your tab," came a voice from the shadows, causing Joe to freeze, the bottle of beer almost to his lips.

Clay walked out of the darkness and into the light, working his way through the group of people until he stood in front of Joe Hanson.

Joe lowered the bottle of beer to his side and stood staring at Clay. "I thought you were in Juvenile Hall," he said in a low voice, which left no doubt he was shaken by Clay's presence.

"Nope, I got time off for good behavior and thought I'd come by and personally thank you for being such a good friend."

"Now look, Tory, you took my pickup without askin' and then you went to my girlfriend's house behind my back. I didn't think they'd send you to Juvenile Hall, neither. I thought they'd just keep you in jail for a night then let you go."

Though Joe stood three inches taller and weighed a good forty pounds more than Clay, it was easy to see he was scared. He had seen Clay fight before and he knew what he was capable of.

"You're a lying snake," Clay spat at him. "You know good and well I didn't steal your truck, and Shirley had already broken it off with you before I went to see her."

Joe Hanson's face turned white. He had not expected this. He knew Clay would come after him when he got out, he just didn't expect it to be so soon. Now he was trapped and everyone was watching to see what he would do. Some would say it was desperation that made him do it, but most agreed it was just plain stupidity and later Joe would admit it was prob-

ably both. Standing there facing his accuser, he felt he
had only one chance and he took it. The full beer was
in his hand and his intent was to bash it against the
side of Clay's head. If he could catch him by surprise,
he might be able to make it to his pickup while Clay
and the others were stunned. Beyond that, he just
knew he wanted away from here and fast.

Clay saw Joe's eyes narrow just before he swung. It
was enough to warn him and he ducked quickly just
barely avoiding the blow as the bottle hit the top of
his hat, knocking it from his head. The momentum of
the swing carried Joe's body past Clay, exposing his
right side. Clay took advantage of it, swinging hard
from a crouching position. He hit Joe full force in the
midsection, causing the air to explode from Joe's
lungs in a whoosh. As he doubled over from the blow,
Clay stepped back and hit him with a right uppercut
to the jaw, sending him sprawling in the gray caliche
dirt.

Joe came to his feet slowly as Clay stood back. He
didn't want this to end too quickly. He was smiling as
he waited for Joe to regain his balance, then he
stepped in and faked a right to the head, then swung
an uppercut to the body. It didn't have the full impact
of the first blow, but Clay still felt satisfaction as he
saw pain cloud Joe's eyes.

He waited again for Joe to regain his composure.
Clay was oblivious to the yells from the crowd as
blood pounded in his ears. He held his hands loosely
at his side and waited for his opponent. Suddenly Joe
ducked his head and charged, catching Clay around
the midsection and toppling both of them to the
ground in a heap. Before Clay could respond, Joe was
astride him, landing blows to his face and head. Clay

brought up his hands to protect his face, partially blocking the blows.

There was a look of triumph on Joe's face as he continued to pummel blindly at Clay's head. Clay waited for an opportunity. Though most of the blows were landing on his arms and hands, some were finding their mark on his head and he was feeling their effects. Glancing between his arms he could see the almost animalistic look in Joe's eyes. As Joe pulled back and prepared to swing, Clay arched his back. The timing was perfect, catching Joe off balance. His forward momentum and Clay's sudden movement caused him to fall forward, reaching out both hands to brace himself. Clay, seeing his opportunity, wriggled out from between Joe's legs and came quickly to his knees.

Joe spun, quickly trying to regain his advantage but Clay had anticipated this and as Joe came around, he looped a hard right to his jaw, knocking him backward.

As Clay staggered to his feet, dazed and reeling from the blows, he shook his head to clear the fog. Joe came unsteadily to his feet and as he did, Clay stepped in and hit him with a straight jab to the mouth, and had the satisfaction of seeing blood explode beneath his fist. Without stopping, Clay waded in, jabbing short vicious blows to Joe's head, closing one of his eyes and opening a cut on his right jaw. When Joe brought his hands up to protect his face, Clay hit him in the body, raining hard blows to his stomach. Joe tried to grapple with him, but Clay stepped easily away from his grasp and hit him another blow to the face.

The fight was all but over. Joe was staggering on his feet, his swings wild and weak, missing their mark

each time. Clay continued to hit him again and again
with short wicked jabs to the face and body.

Clay felt the exhilaration of the fight drain out of
him as he looked at his opponent standing in front of
him, blood pouring from his mouth and nose.

"Had enough?" he asked as Joe swayed unsteadily.

"Go to hell," Joe managed to say between his cut
and bleeding lips.

"Have it your way," Clay said, anger welling up in
him once again. Advancing on his opponent, he faked
another left to the head and swung a roundhouse
blow to Joe's midsection, which landed solidly in the
softness of his stomach. The air whooshed from his
lungs and blood poured from his mouth as Clay pivoted on his left foot and brought his fist in a downward arc landing just behind Joe's right ear. Joe let a
small whimper as he fell to the ground in a heap and
didn't move.

Clay stood back and waited to see if he would rise
again, but there would be no more fight. Joe was out
cold. Somebody walked over and turned him on his
back. Though he was breathing heavily, he was out
like a light.

"Jeez, Clay, you knocked the fool out."

Clay looked at the form on the ground. He felt neither satisfaction nor remorse at what he'd done, just
drained. All the tension and anger from the last few
weeks were gone, leaving only a hollow, empty feeling, a feeling of not belonging, only loneliness.

He turned and walked over to where his hat lay.
Picking it up, he turned without a word and walked
toward the pickup. Shirley hurried to his side.

"Where ya goin'?" she asked in a worried voice.

He gave her a bewildered look. "I don't know," he

said, looking around at the others standing there. "I ain't got no place to go."

"You can stay at my place if you want to. We've got a pretty good couch and I fix a good breakfast."

Clay smiled at her. He knew he didn't want to drive back out to the Lazy L all bruised and battered. "Sounds like a deal to me," he said, putting his arm around her shoulder, more for support than anything else.

Chapter Six

Jack was at the First National Bank the next morning right when it opened. He had some business to take care of and wanted it done early. After spending two hours at the bank, he drove to the store to put in an order for more horse, pig, and chicken feed. While he waited for them to load it in the truck, he talked to Craig Dean, the store's owner, about the weather and beef prices.

"I ain't heard nothin' about those cattle thieves for a spell now. You reckon they done left the county, or just layin' low until things cool down?" Craig Dean asked.

"Don't know, but I sure hope they pulled out and ain't comin' back," Jack said as he chewed on a piece of straw.

"Maybe they have. By my figures they got close to a hundred and fifty head. That makes a pretty good purse, even if they did have to take below market value for them."

"Yep," Jack said, taking off his hat and wiping his forehead with the back of his shirtsleeve, "I reckon those fellas made somewhere between forty and fifty thousand off those cattle. That ain't a bad month's work. But I'll tell you one thing—if I ever get my hands on 'em, they'll regret the day they was born."

"There's several other ranchers feel the same as

you. You reckon these thieves are from around here or just some rovers that hit different places and move on?"

"I don't know, but one thing's for sure—they got someone with 'em that knows the lay of the land. They've hit every large ranch around here and they know the best places to hit, where the chances of getting caught are slim. They couldn't do that unless they'd been around here for a while."

"That's a good point. You reckon the sheriff knows that?" Craig asked.

"If he don't then he ain't got no business bein' sheriff," Jack replied gruffly.

"Your feed's loaded, Mr. Lomas," the dockhand called to him.

"Thanks," Jack said. "Well I reckon I better get on outta here. I still got some things to pick up at the hardware store before heading back to the ranch." Turning, he started toward the front door before quickly turning back. "Hey, Craig, you got any of those *Rodeo News* around here?"

"Sure, just got a supply in yesterday. Here," he said, handing one to the rancher. "You planning on entering a few?"

Jack chuckled. "Not hardly, but I got a young fella that may be interested in reading this."

It was close to lunchtime when Jack left the feed store and drove back down Main Street. He drove to the Cattleman's Café and parked in one of the few empty spots left. As he stepped out of the pickup, he noticed the sheriff's car in the parking lot and frowned to himself.

Entering the café, he saw Ben Aguilar sitting with Clyde Lewis, one of the local ranchers. Weaving his way through the crowd, he made his way to their table and pulled out an empty chair. "Mind if I sit with you fellas?" he asked, sitting down by the time the question was asked.

"Not at all, Jack." Clyde Lewis spoke through his mouth full of chicken fried steak.

Ben nodded. "How ya doin' Jack?" he asked, spreading butter on the steaming roll he was holding.

"I been better," Jack replied, "but I've been worse too, so I guess I better count my blessings."

"I hear you got hit the hardest by the cattle thieves, Jack," said Clyde. "I was just talkin' to Ben about us ranchers formin' a sort of association to help watch each other's places."

Jack looked at him with a guarded expression. "What kind of association?" he asked.

Clyde started to answer but Ben interrupted him. "Clyde thinks it would be a good idea to have more men patrolling the county. He wants to form an association using ranch hands and hired men to help us patrol. I don't think it would be a good idea."

"Why not?" Jack asked.

"Because the last thing I need is a bunch of amateurs running around the county looking for cattle thieves. I'd be spending more time responding to problems with them than I would looking for the thieves."

"Now, Ben, you know that's not true," Clyde interjected. "If we had training for these guys and let the community know what they were doing and had the same people patrol the same areas, I don't see why it wouldn't be a help to you instead of a problem. And if they did spot something they could always radio you and wait till you got there to do anything. I just think we need more people watching the back roads. That's where we're getting hit the hardest."

"Clyde's got something there," Jack stated. "If there were more people watching the back roads, we'd have a better chance of stopping these guys."

"But we haven't even had a theft in three weeks now. These guys may be long gone by now and they may never come back."

"Yeah, and they might be back tomorrow," Jack said.

"He's right," Clyde stated, "and if we got some men ready, we can start patrolling as soon as we hear they're in the area."

"Who's going to pay for all this?" Ben asked.

"The association will. That's what I've been trying to tell you," Clyde said.

"Sounds like a good idea to me," Jack stated.

"I don't know," Ben replied. "I'll have to run this by the judge to make sure it's legal."

"Since when isn't it legal to protect what you've worked for?" Clyde asked hotly.

"I didn't say it wasn't legal. I just want to run it by the judge," Ben said.

"Well you go ahead and run it by him, but I'm going to call a meeting of all the ranchers and present this to them. You and the judge are welcome to attend and give us your point of view, but just remember we're the ones that put you where you are, and we can sure boot you out. Now if you gentlemen will excuse me, I've got to go." Clyde Lewis stood up and laid a dollar on the table for a tip.

"Clyde, don't go off mad," Ben said, trying to placate the rancher.

"I'm not mad, I'm determined and I'm not going to sit by while a bunch of thieves steal all my profit. I'll let you know when the meeting is, Jack." He nodded to Ben and left.

Ben shook his head as he watched Clyde leave the restaurant. "I've never seen Clyde upset like that before."

"He'll calm down," Jack said as the waitress took his order. After she left he turned to Ben. "I think there's some merit to his idea and I'd be willing to contribute to helping catch these fellas."

Ben pushed the half-eaten plate of food away. "I agree it's got some merit, but I'm just afraid if there's a bunch of rowdy cowboys running around out there, it's going to create more problems than it's going to solve."

"Who said it had to be rowdy cowboys?" Jack asked and was pleased to see the look of surprise on Ben's face, "Why can't it be some responsible men that you pick yourself? And why couldn't you be the one to coordinate things and determine which areas need to be patrolled, and who would be patrolling them?"

Ben looked thoughtful, considering what Jack had said. "I reckon that would work. I guess I was so opposed to the idea that I wasn't willing to look at the possibilities." He chuckled. "You reckon I'm gettin' as cantankerous as you in my old age?"

Jack laughed. "Not even on your best day, Ben, not even on your best day."

"How are things going with you and Mr. Tory?" Ben asked, watching as Jack frowned.

"I don't rightly know. He's a hard worker, there's no doubt about it. But it's like he's mad at the world and he's just waiting to explode."

"He hasn't been giving you a hard time, has he?" Ben asked.

"No, no, not at all," Jack hurried to say. "He's a good kid. I just can't understand what makes him seem so angry all the time."

Ben smiled. "I couldn't tell you how many people have said something similar to me about you."

Jack gave him a shocked look. "Me? Now why would people say something like that about me?"

"I don't know, maybe it's that mean expression you wear all the time, or the fact that you stay out at that ranch by yourself most of the time, or that you don't let anybody get close enough to you to know what you're really like. But then again I really couldn't say why folks ask such a thing." He chuckled, watching Jack's face cloud over. "Why don't you consider what it was that made *you* tick when you were that age, and I think you'll come up with the way to reach young Tory. He ain't had an easy road and he's never asked for a handout. He's got so much pride in him that he can't stand to think of anyone doing something for him that he can't do himself. Kinda reminds me of an old hardheaded rancher I know."

"Hmmph." Jack snorted. "I know the boy's had it rough. I know his family and if he ain't gone down the wrong road by now, he's got a lot of backbone and I respect him for it. But I don't know what it takes to reach him. I already failed with one boy. I don't want to make the same mistake with this one."

Ben saw the hurt in the old rancher's eyes and hurried to console him. "Jack, you're not going to make a mistake. You've got what it takes to bring that boy around. All you got to do is stop and think for a moment. What was it that excited you at that age?"

Jack looked puzzled by the question, then as if a light went on he smiled. "When I was his age there were only two things that excited me—women and riding saddle broncs, and not necessarily in that order."

Ben was grinning from ear to ear. "I reckon Clay's just like you. I imagine right now he's thinking he's goin' to miss a full year of riding."

Jack looked stunned. "You're right! I haven't even thought about taking him to a rodeo. No wonder he's so angry. I'd have been like an old grizzly bear at that age if I'd thought I couldn't rodeo for a year."

"I'll bet you would have." Ben laughed. "There's a rodeo at Ruidoso in about a week. Why don't you take him and let him take some of his anger out on the stock. He's already settled the score with Joe Hanson."

Jack was truly stunned. "When?" he asked.

"Last night, out at the caliche pits."

"What happened?" Jack asked.

"Seems like both of them showed up at the pits and Clay called Joe on his lies. Joe swung a beer bottle and Clay whipped him."

"How did you find all this out."

Ben smiled again. "I have a couple of kids that owe me a favor or two and to pay it off they keep me informed about certain things. Helps me keep my finger on what's going on."

"Is Hanson going to cause any problems for Clay?" Jack asked.

"Oh, he tried already. He was at my office early this morning, looking like a Mack truck had run over him, wanting to press charges against Clay. But when I told him I already knew all the details and that I might lock him up for assault since he threw the first punch, he cooled down and left like a whipped puppy."

Jack smiled and sat back as the waitress sat his plate down in front of him.

"Well, I better get back to work before the citizens of Chavez County think all I do is sit in here and shoot the bull with all you ranchers."

"You mean it ain't?" Jack chuckled.

"You have a good day, Jack, and I hope you don't happen to get a flat tire out there in that parking lot."

Jack smiled and turned to his food, his thoughts already on the plans forming in his head.

Jack was sitting at the table in the kitchen when Clay came in. He had been anxiously waiting for him since early evening and the clock on the wall above the kitchen sink showed it to be a quarter to ten when he finally heard the Dodge engine coming up the drive. He waited impatiently for the screen door to open and looked expectantly at the kitchen door to see if Clay would come in to the lighted kitchen or continue straight down the hall to his room. He felt a sense of disappointment as Clay's footsteps started down the hallway, but his spirits rose as he heard them stop and come back toward the kitchen.

Jack waited in anticipation until Clay entered. "Hey," Clay said in way of greeting.

"Howdy," Jack responded. "Did you have a good time?"

A small smile crossed Clay's face. "Yeah I had a pretty good time, I reckon."

"Good," Jack replied. "You ready to get back to work?"

"Sure," Clay said, though the frown on his face contradicted his answer.

"Yeah, I figured you would be," Jack said with the hint of a smile, "but I was just sittin' here readin' the *Rodeo News* and noticed there's quite a few rodeos comin' up in the next few months."

Clay looked curiously at Jack. "Yeah there's usually a lot this time of year. Between New Mexico and west Texas you can usually make two or three rodeos a weekend if you can get drawn in right." Drawing in meant entering in each rodeo on the day you needed to in order to make it to the next rodeo.

"I see Ruidoso is next weekend. Have you ever ridden there?" Jack said.

"Yes sir, I rode there last year. Placed second in the bulls and third in the barebacks."

Jack nodded, clearly impressed. "How's the stock contractor, Running H?" he asked.

"They're one of the best. Their stock is about as even as it can get and they treat everybody fairly—no underhanded stuff to draw the best riders."

"Hmmm, sounds like it might be worth going to," Jack said, feigning mild interest as he noticed Clay perk up.

Clay remained silent, holding his breath, waiting for the other shoe to fall. When Jack didn't say anything more, Clay ventured an offhanded comment. "Ought to be a good show."

"Yep," Jack said, pretending to study the paper before him. He paused for a few moments before continuing. "I don't reckon you'd be interested in entering this year, would you?"

Clay studied Jack's face for a moment to see if he was playing a joke on him or if he was serious, but Jack continued to study the paper before him as if the question wasn't that important.

"Are you serious?" Clay asked, not really trusting this man sitting across the table from him wearing a poker face.

"I reckon I am," Jack replied, looking over the top of his glasses at the young man. "Now do you want to go or not, 'cause if you do I got to make arrangements for someone to take care of the barn stock while we're gone."

Clay smiled, in spite of himself, and Jack felt his heart swell with pleasure. "Yes sir, I want to go!"

"Thought you would," Jack said. "It says the books open tomorrow at one o'clock. Why don't you make sure you call and get yourself entered."

"Uh, there's one small problem," Clay said.

"What's that?" Jack asked looking up again from the paper.

"I'm flat broke and haven't got the entry fees. The county is suppose to pay me five dollars a day but I don't know when I'll get it."

Jack looked thoughtful for a moment. "Well I reckon I could take care of your entry fees, and if you win you could pay me back. How does that sound?"

"Sounds fine to me," Clay responded cheerfully.

"Which performance you gonna try to get into, Friday night or Saturday night?" Jack asked.

"I reckon whichever one you want me to," Clay answered. "Ruidoso's only an hour and a half away. We could leave in the afternoon and be there in time for the rodeo and come back after it's over."

Jack rubbed his chin considering Clay's plan. Then as if making up his mind, he folded the paper and said, "Nope I reckon we'll drive up there early Saturday, get you entered up on Saturday night, then spend the night and come back Sunday. Make it a kinda holiday. Unless you'd rather come back early and start repairing that windmill in the south pasture?"

"No," Clay hurried to answer, "staying over Saturday night sounds fine to me."

"I thought it would," Jack chuckled. "Here's the

paper with the phone number, I'm goin' to bed. I been workin' hard today and haven't been out in the caliche pits havin' fun like someone else I know."

The shocked look on Clay's face made Jack smile as he walked out of the kitchen and down the hallway.

They spent the rest of the week riding through each of the pastures, checking on the cattle. As spring came to New Mexico, the newborn calves had to be checked. Any found sickly or with pink-eye would be roped and doctored accordingly. It was tiring work and each night they returned home weary, but satisfied they had done a good day's work.

Clay had called and entered the Ruidoso rodeo. Thursday evening he drove into town and picked up his bronc saddle, bareback rigging, and bull rope from a friend's house, and spent Friday evening listening to Jack tell him about rodeos in his day while he carefully checked everything over, burning resin into the handle of his bull rope and bareback rigging.

"Well, I reckon I'll hit the hay," Jack said, getting up from the couch where he'd been watching Clay work. "It's going to be a long day tomorrow."

"I'll be along directly," Clay said. "I just want to make sure I've got plenty of resin on this riggin' before I go to bed."

"Don't stay up too late. You've put in a hard week already and you need to be good and rested for tomorrow night."

"I won't," Clay promised as Jack retired to his room.

Chapter Seven

When Jack walked into the kitchen the next morning, he was surprised to see Clay already there. The coffee had been made and he was frying bacon in the old black skillet. "You're up early," Jack noted, pulling out his chair from the kitchen table.

Clay smiled as Jack sat down. "You're just late," he said. "I thought maybe you'd died so I figured I'd make me some breakfast before I started digging your grave."

Jack looked startled at the boy's words. At first he wasn't sure whether Clay was serious or kidding, but one look at Clay's face and the bright grin he wore made him throw back his head and laugh, something he hadn't done in a long time.

"What time are we leaving?"

Jack took a sip of the coffee Clay handed him and replied, "I reckon as soon as we get the chores done."

Clay nodded, and broke another egg into the skillet.

Jack took the plate of eggs and bacon Clay cooked for him and set about doctoring them to his liking, a little salt, a little pepper, and a whole lot of Tabasco sauce. Jack said a little Tabasco sauce in the morning helped get him through the day, but he could never convince Clay of that.

After making arrangements to have Jason Harrison take care of the ranch while they were gone, Jack and

Clay loaded their clothes into the back seat of the
Ford pickup and headed west toward Ruidoso.

The conversation was light as Clay drove, Jack
watching the countryside pass by. They talked about
ranching, rodeos, and the upcoming tournament.

As they entered the outskirts of town, Clay looked
excitedly out the window at the surroundings. They
passed by Ruidoso Downs, where the premiere quarter horse races were held. "Have you ever been to the
races?" he asked.

"I used to years ago," Jack responded but didn't
elaborate. Clay didn't pursue the matter.

Ruidoso, though small, was primarily a tourist
town, especially when there was horse racing in the
summer months. With its cool mountain atmosphere,
it was a favorite of many who came to escape the
southwestern heat. They came from all over Texas,
Arizona, and southern New Mexico, and the winter
snow brought skiers from the same areas. Many of the
seasonal tourists, those who came year after year,
owned homes in the area and rented them out when
they weren't occupying them themselves.

The Mescalero Apache Indian Reservation was located near the town. They owned and operated a
large hotel and gambling casino, which offered a further attraction to the tourist trade.

As they drove through town they noticed the festive atmosphere that prevailed. Though Ruidoso was
always full of tourists and visitors, today it seemed
even more so because of the rodeo. The races were
run during the day and the rodeo was held at night.
That way neither would distract from the other. Jack
and Clay noticed the banners announcing the rodeo,
welcoming all to the annual event.

They pulled into the parking lot of the Kings Arms

Motel. "Let's get our room and store our gear, then we'll head out to the rodeo grounds and see about getting you entered," Jack said.

The room, though not new, was large and comfortable with two large double beds. Clay looked pleased with the sleeping arrangements. "Sure beats sleeping in the front seat of a pickup, or with five guys in a camper," he said as he threw his bag on the double bed.

Jack chuckled as the statement brought back memories. "I can remember when we slept in bedrolls on the ground at the arena and hoped no drunken fool would come tearin' in and run over us."

Clay smiled at the thought and felt a new connection with this old-timer.

The rodeo grounds were a buzz of activity as they pulled through the gate. Stock was being unloaded at the chutes, food vendors were getting their booths cleaned and stocked. A tractor and disk were preparing the ground for the night's events. They headed toward a travel trailer that was set up at the rough stock end of the arena.

There were six other cowboys standing outside the door, waiting to enter the trailer as they walked up. Two of them called Clay by name. He nodded and shook hands with them, but made no move to introduce Jack.

They waited about fifteen minutes for the other cowboys to pay their entry frees, then stepped up into the confined space. There was a small table set up just to the right of the door, and an older woman sat behind it with large ledgers stacked on both sides of her. She looked up as Clay moved forward, and recognizing him said, "You're entered in the saddle bronc, bareback, and bulls, aren't ya, Clay?"

"Yes, ma'am," he replied.

Jack had been standing behind Clay, but now moved to one side, looking around the small trailer. All of a sudden the woman gasped and clapped her hand over her mouth.

"Well I'll be," she spoke loudly. "Jack Lomas in the flesh! I thought you'd have kicked up your heels and died by now."

Jack turned to the woman. He really hadn't paid any attention to her before, but now as he studied her, he noticed she was in her late fifties or early sixties with black-and-gray hair. Studying her features closely, he began to recognize her face, and in a couple of seconds a name came to him. "Dottie . . . ? Dottie Hightower? Is that you?"

"In the flesh," she said, standing and opening her arms wide to hug the old rancher. He stepped forward and the two embraced warmly.

When Jack stepped back, he held her at arm's length, looking her up and down. "You're looking wonderful, Dottie. If you've finally come to your senses and killed off that no-good husband of yours, I'll take you away from all this right now."

Dottie Hightower laughed and gently pushed him away. "If I thought you were serious Jack, I'd kill him right now, but to answer your question he's out in the arena taking care of the stock."

Jack's face registered his surprise. "You mean he's got the stock for this rodeo? When did he go into the stock business?"

"We've been doing this for about six years now." Dottie sighed. "The boys take care of most of it, but you know Will, he's got to be right in the middle of things."

Jack laughed good-naturedly, "I thought he was ranching up around Santa Fe."

"Oh we still got the ranch too, but you know how unstable ranching can be. We got into this to help pay the bills. 'Course things are better now than they were back when we got into this, but you know Will. He's got rodeoin' in his blood and I think he'd rather give up our ranch and home than to give this up."

Jack chuckled again, and began hashing over old times with Dottie when Clay cleared his throat. Both Dottie and Jack looked a little embarrassed as they remembered his presence.

"I hate to break up this reunion but there's several fellas out here that seem to want to enter this here rodeo," Clay said in good humor.

"How much do I owe?" Jack said trying to hide his embarrassment.

"That'll be ninety dollars," she said, reaching for her receipt book.

Jack pulled out a hundred-dollar bill and handed it to her. When Dottie had handed him back his change, she spoke to Clay. "We'll have the drawing this afternoon at four o'clock and they'll be posted by five o'clock."

Clay took the contestant number she handed him. "Make sure that's pinned on your back before your ride."

"Yes, ma'am," he said politely.

"You better go see Will before you leave," she said, turning to Jack. "He'll be mad as one of those bulls of his if you don't."

"I will," Jack promised, stepping down to the ground, "and I'll see you again too. So have your bags packed for a quick getaway."

Dottie laughed. "Forget the bags, I'm ready now.

You can buy me all new clothes when we get to Hawaii."

Jack waved good-bye. As he left he got winks from the other cowboys standing in line.

Clay was standing outside, waiting for him. "Ben said you couldn't give me any money. Won't that get you into trouble, paying my entry fees?"

Jack smiled. "The blazes with Ben Aguilar. Besides, I didn't pay you, I paid Dottie so what Ben don't know won't hurt him. And if he does find out I'll take care of it. Don't you worry about it. Now let's go find Will Hightower. I want to introduce you to him."

Walking down the alleyway that led into the arena, Jack stopped at the gate and waited until the two cowboys inside moved a bull into the holding pen. Once that was done they opened the latch and stepped inside. He had already spotted Will Hightower sitting on a large gray horse by the bucking chutes. He was talking to the cowboys behind the chutes, instructing them as to which pen each animal should be held in. Jack waited until he was through with his instructions before moving up to the chute. Keeping his head down, he walked up to the gray horse's head and leaned against the chute. With his back to Will Hightower, he spoke in a loud, clear voice. "This is about the sorriest excuse I've ever seen for a rodeo company. Why, those horses ain't had a decent meal in at least a month, and I doubt if those bulls have enough strength to make it into a bucking chute, much less throw a cowboy."

Clay had been watching the reaction on Will Hightower's face and saw irritation begin to narrow his eyes, but Jack continued to look out over the animals in the holding pens. "I think I see a couple of horses that were stolen from a friend of mine a while back.

Probably the only way this two-bit outfit can stay in business is by stealin', cause I know the owner ain't never had two nickels to rub together," Jack chided.

Clay could see anger replace the irritation on Will's face and he thought for a moment he might force the big gray horse to run Jack down. Jack slowly turned around and Clay could see Will peering at the old rancher's face as he tried to recognize his antagonist. Suddenly, Will beamed as he recalled who it was standing before him. "Jack Lomas, you old scoundrel! I figured you'd be dead by now. How come somebody ain't done a public service and shot you?"

Will stepped down from his horse and the two old cowboys heartily shook hands. "How you been?" Jack asked, looking his old friend over.

" 'Bout as well as can be expected I reckon." Will said, sizing Jack up. "You've gotten old, Jack."

Jack laughed. "You ain't no spring chicken yourself."

"That's the truth," Will said. "Every time I finish one of these shows I tell myself I'm going to retire. But these boys couldn't get along without me and Dottie wouldn't have anything to complain about, so I just keep sacrificing myself and coming back for more."

Jack cocked an eyebrow. "Yeah that's about what I figured. You're still the biggest liar this side of Mississippi. You haven't changed a bit."

Will feigned a hurt look. "Now, Jack, is that any way to talk about your old ridin' partner?"

"Dottie's still lookin' good," Jack said, changing the subject, "though I can see she still ain't no smarter if she's still hangin' with you."

"I reckon she's been with me so long now, she

couldn't stand the thought of breakin' in another one," Will said with a belly laugh.

Clay had been standing off to the side, letting the two old friends get reacquainted, but now he walked up and stood quietly beside Jack. Jack noticed him and said to Will, "I'd like you to meet Clay Tory. He works for me."

Will took Clay's hand. "I know Clay, or know of him. He's ridden my stock on several occasions and done a pretty good job of it too." Turning to Clay, he winked. "You'd do yourself justice, son, if you found another job and got yourself as far away from this old coot as possible. He's a bad influence and he'll steer you down the wrong road."

Clay enjoyed the easy banter between the older men. "Thanks, Mr. Hightower, I'll keep that in mind." He was grateful to Jack for not saying he was working for him because he was a ward of the county.

"How long has it been since we last crossed paths?" Will asked Jack.

"What's it been now, eight, nine years?" Jack asked.

Clay climbed up on the chute and looked out over the stock, letting the two old friends talk. He knew most of the bulls and horses by reputation and had already ridden several of them. They were as good a string as there was and he knew he wouldn't get a bad draw with any of these animals.

Will and Jack talked for another twenty minutes before Jack said it was time to go, but not before promising to have supper with Will and Dottie after the performance that night.

Clay and Jack drove back downtown and looked in some of the local shops, acting like tourists and enjoying the day. They ate lunch at a local restaurant and after doing a little more shopping Jack suggested they head back to the motel and get some rest before the rodeo began. Clay didn't argue and fifteen minutes after lying down, he was fast asleep.

Jack waited until he was sure Clay was asleep before slipping quietly out of the room, truck keys in his hand. He returned two hours later and was relieved to see the boy still asleep. He crept slowly into the room and set several boxes he was carrying on the dresser by Clay's bed and then lay down on his own, a long forgotten feeling of peace flowing within him.

Jack had been asleep for an hour when he felt someone nudging him. "Mr. Lomas," someone whispered above him. Jack closed his eyes tightly, hoping it was a dream. "Mr. Lomas," came the whisper again, a little more strongly now and accompanied by a gentle shake. He opened his eyes slowly and saw Clay standing above him.

"Hmmph," he grunted, still groggy.

"It's almost five o'clock and the draw will be posted soon. Do you mind if I take the pickup and drive out to the arena and see what I've drawn?"

Jack fought the cobwebs of sleep from his mind. "Wait just a minute and I'll go with you," he said, sitting up and swinging his legs over the edge of the bed.

Clay was looking in wonder at the packages on the dresser. "I took the liberty of buying you a few things," Jack said.

Clay was perplexed as he walked over to the packages on the dresser. "Why did you do this?" he asked, lifting the top off a box and revealing a new Resistol hat.

"Well, that hat you're wearing looks like it needs an oil change and a burial, and those jeans have more holes in 'em than a hunk of a Swiss cheese. I figured if you was gonna ride tonight you ought to at least look presentable."

"Were you worried that I might embarrass you?" Clay asked a little suspiciously.

"No," Jack replied, "I wasn't worried about being embarrassed. I just figured you needed some new jeans and a new hat. I'm sorry if I offended you. I'll take 'em back if it upsets you that much," he said almost angrily, grabbing the packages from Clay's hands.

"I'm sorry," Clay said, taking hold of Jack's arm to prevent him from leaving the room. "I'm just not used to people doing things for me unless they want something in return." He kept a hold of Jack's arm as if he were afraid he'd leave forever if he let go. "Nobody's ever given me anything."

Jack set the boxes on the bed. "Well if it'll make you feel better you can pay me back out of your winnings."

Clay smiled. "How 'bout I just say thank you and try these on."

Jack gave him a serious look. "Na, I think I like the idea of you paying me back."

Clay was taken aback until he saw the corners of Jack's mouth curl up into a smile. "Get changed or we're going to be late," he said, the smile now stretching fully across his face.

Chapter Eight

The parking lot at the arena was starting to fill as they pulled in. Clay showed the gate manager his contestant number and they were waved into the contestant parking area. While Clay went to locate the posted draw, Jack wandered over to the grandstands and found himself a seat.

Clay found the sheets hanging on a board by the alley leading into the arena. In the barebacks, he'd drawn number two eighty-nine, Copenhagen, a good horse with lots of try in him. Number fifteen, Bold Caliber, was his draw in the saddle broncs and he smiled with appreciation. But he was most pleased with his draw in the bull riding, number z-six, High Cannon. He'd drawn this bull twice before. He'd been thrown once and ridden him to a first-place finish the second time, so now the score stood tied between them. Tonight would be the deciding ride.

He was turning away from the board when Will Hightower walked up. "Hey, Clay, looks like you drew pretty good."

Clay smiled and glanced back at the board. "I don't think I could have done better if I'd handpicked 'em myself."

"Well, that's the luck of the draw. Sometimes you get the good ones and sometimes you don't. Where's Jack?"

Clay glanced around, trying to locate him. "I think he's in the grandstands, but I don't see him."

Will nodded and said, "I'll go see if I can find him. I've got a set of box seats down by the arena. I was going to see if he wanted to sit there."

"I'm sure he'd like that," Clay commented, then bit his lip, struggling with himself over whether to ask the question that had been burning in his mind for a long time. Finally, he forced himself to ask. "Uh, Mr. Hightower, you've known Mr. Lomas for quite a while and I was wonderin' if I could ask you something?"

Will Hightower saw the troubled look on the boy's face and wondered what was on his mind. "Sure, son," he said with concern. "What is it you're needin' to know."

"Well, sir, it's just . . . uh," Clay began, not really knowing exactly how to approach the subject. "I've been with Mr. Lomas for over a month now and he ain't never mentioned anything about ever having a family. But I know from the pictures in his house that he had a wife and a son. He just never talks about them."

Will scrutinized Clay closely before speaking. "I wish I could tell you what you want to know, but it's really not my place. All that I can say is that he did have a family, and as a father he had to make a decision that would have broken most men I know. It took a lot out of him and he had to fight hard to survive afterward, so if he's a little hard around the edges or a little short with you sometimes, just give him a little slack and try to be patient. He's the best man I've ever known, and he'll never do ya wrong on purpose."

Clay felt a lump come into his throat as he heard

the honesty and sincerity in Will Hightower's voice. "Yes sir," he said.

Will patted him on the shoulder and turned away. Clay watched him walk toward the grandstands to find Jack. He considered what Jack's friend had told him and though Clay knew little more now than he had before, his suspicions had been proven right. Jack had once had a family and something had happened that caused him to withdraw and turn bitter. But in the last few days he had seen a change in the old rancher, a glimpse of what he must have once been. He would try to remember what Will Hightower had told him.

Clay wandered around the rodeo grounds talking to friends about other rodeos they'd been to. It was always interesting to find out who was laid up due to injuries or who couldn't make it because of financial straits. He also learned who the competition was and reveled in the news of great rides that had been made by one cowboy or another. He even told a few stories of his own.

He found Jack in Will's box seats just before the rodeo began and sat down next to him. "Good seats," he exclaimed as he sat down. "It just goes to show it's not what you know but who you know," he said with a grin.

"This is about the only thing other than a headache I ever got from Will Hightower," Jack replied with a chuckle.

"Ya'll go back quite a ways don't you?" Clay asked, looking thoughtful.

Jack looked at the bucking chutes where Will was supervising the loading of the horses. "Yeah we go way back. We used to travel the rodeo circuit together back when we were both young and full of fire. I can't tell you the number of times we had to pool our money just to buy one hamburger so we could split it."

Clay could see the memories well up in his eyes. "Jack and I both started our ranches about the same time, and between working sixty and seventy hours trying to get our places going and traveling to rodeos, we still found a little time to get into trouble." He smiled as their old revelry came to mind.

"We even got married about the same time. Actually, I dated Dottie first, but since she lived closer to Will than she did to me, he started seeing her during the week. Stole that girl plumb away from me."

Clay's mouth dropped open. "You mean he stole your girl and ya'll are still friends."

Jack nodded. "Yep. Oh, we had our words about it, even got in a fistfight."

Clay's eyes were wide in astonishment. "Who won?"

Jack chuckled. "Neither one of us. We fought for about twenty minutes, swinging at each other and cussin'. I'm not sure either of us did any damage. Finally we just wound down until we couldn't swing anymore. We just both sat on the ground and pretty soon we started laughing and that was the end of it."

Clay sat spellbound, hardly believing what he'd heard. "That's by far the strangest tale I've ever heard. Are you pulling my leg?"

Jack laughed at the boy's question. "It's the honest truth. We decided we were too good'a friends to let a woman come between us. Later I found Marie and married her, and Will and I have been close friends ever since."

"Marie was your wife's name?" Clay asked hesitantly.

Jack nodded and his face grew sad. "Yep, we were married twenty-eight years. She died several years ago."

Seeing the sadness on Jack's face, Clay was sorry he'd mentioned it. Wanting to take Jack's mind off his misery, he hurriedly asked another question. "If you and Mr. Hightower are such good friends, how come you haven't seen him for so long?"

"I don't know," Jack answered slowly. "I reckon we both just got wrapped up in our lives and forgot to stay in touch. I haven't been to a rodeo in a long time, and I guess Will's been so busy he hasn't had time to come down my way. It's a shame when you think about it. I mean, the best thing in life is your friends and a man shouldn't forget about 'em."

Clay nodded, not knowing what to say, then looking toward the chutes he spoke. "I reckon I'd better get down there and get ready. Looks like they're about ready to get this thing going."

Jack nodded. "You ride the hair off 'em."

Clay smiled. "Count on it," he said, and with that he jumped over the rail of the box seat section and landed agilely in the arena. Jack smiled as he watched him walk to the bucking chutes. Memories of an earlier time flooded his mind, a time when he was young and ready to conquer the world and feared nothing but failure. His mind clouded at the thought. Failure; it came in a variety of packages, and his had come unexpectedly and from the last place he'd ever imagined, and it would have devastated him, but Marie had saved him and then he'd lost her too.

After she'd pulled him out of his depression and was sure he was going to make it, she had given up herself and passed on. After her death he hadn't wanted to go on, and he had hoped each day would be his last, until finally the weeks turned into months, and months to years, and he found that he was managing to keep going on. His solace was the ranch and he lost himself in the day-to-day work it provided him.

The announcer's welcome brought Jack out of his reverie. The grand entry was about to begin. The crowd quieted as a voice boomed out of the speakers located around the arena.

The grand entry featured many of the contestants mounted on horses as well as the Ruidoso rodeo queen and the runners-up. They were all preceded by riders carrying the flags of the United States and New Mexico, and every person stood as they came by. Jack removed his hat and held it over his heart as he watched the colors flutter in the breeze.

As the riders exited the arena, the announcer's voice boomed out over the public address system. "Ladies and gentlemen, please remain standing for our invocation." The microphone was handed to one of the town's local clergy, who asked the Lord to protect those who were participating and gave thanks for His good blessings.

The first event was bareback riding, and as Jack sat down again he saw Clay adjusting his rigging on the back of a horse in chute number three. There were three chutes on either side of the alleyway leading into the arena and all six chutes had horses in them. Each had several cowboys working to help the rider get his rigging on, giving him last-minute advice.

The crowd grew quiet as they waited for the first rider to come out. The announcer called his name and a few seconds later the gate on chute number one swung open and a mouse-colored horse came charging out. He ran about four lengths before stopping hard on his front feet, and burying his head between his legs, leapt into the air. The cowboy on his back had one hand in the rigging, which was similar to the handle on a suitcase, while his other hand was held high in the air to prevent him from slapping the horse. His spurs were in the points of the horse's shoulders, and as the bronc lunged again the audience could hear the rowels on his spurs rake across the horse's flesh.

The trick to bareback riding was to stay in time with the horse, keeping your spurs in the points of his shoulders when his front feet hit the ground and raking them back as he lunged away. If a rider didn't have his spurs in the horse's shoulders on the first jump out of the chute he was disqualified. This was called "missing him out." Both horse and rider were scored separately by two judges, on a point rating system from one to twenty-five. Their combined totals would be awarded to the rider and the top four scores took home the prize money.

The first rider successfully rode to the whistle, which was an eight-second ride, before being helped off by the two pickup men. His score totaled sixty-six, and the crowd applauded loudly as he walked back to the chutes.

The next rider had drawn a long-legged sorrel named Red's Nightmare and it certainly turned out to be a nightmare for the rider. Two jumps out of the chute, the rider's hand was jerked loose from his rigging. He was catapulted over the horse's rump and shot into the air. The rider hit the ground in a heap and the air was forced hard from his lungs. He lay unmoving for several moments as men worked over him to ensure he had no major injuries. After a few seconds he was helped groggily to his feet and was led from the arena.

Jack sat watching the episode and wondered how it affected Clay. He remembered how disconcerting it was to have an injury just prior to a ride, and he hoped Clay could put it out of his mind.

Clay watched as they helped the injured cowboy, then turned his attention to Copenhagen. The horse stood tense in the chute, quivering with the excitement, his ears flicking forward and backward as he sensed his performance was about to begin. Clay forced his gloved hand into the handle of the rigging, gripping it hard and beginning to rotate his hand. The friction of the movement caused the resin on the glove and the rigging handle to heat up and become sticky, giving him a tighter grip. It was like gluing yourself to the horse. Satisfied he had the grip he wanted, Clay eased himself onto Copenhagen's back and extended his legs until his spurs touched the horse's neck. Pulling his hat down with his free hand, he gritted his teeth and nodded to the gate man.

Jack watched as the gate swung open and Copenhagen exploded from the chute. The horse reared slightly on his hind feet, and pivoted toward the open gate. Then, using the mighty power in his back legs, he pushed himself high into the air. Clay's spurs were perfectly positioned over the points of the shoulders and as Copenhagen lunged, Clay raked his spurs backward, only to return to the shoulders as the horse's feet came in contact with the ground. Jack was on his feet yelling as Copenhagen shot into the air again, this time turning his feet out to the side in midair in what was called a sunfish move, but Clay stayed centered on his back and raked the big horse again. This time when the horse's feet touched the ground, he lined out in a straight line, bucking hard and high. Clay rode him in a true classic bareback style until the whistle blew and the pickup men moved in to help him dismount.

Clay was grinning widely as he slid to the ground. Jack was still on his feet cheering loudly with the crowd. As he walked back toward the bucking chutes, Clay listened to the announcer, eagerly waiting to hear the judges' score. "Ladies and gentlemen, we have a new leader in the bareback riding. Clay Tory has just turned in a score of seventy-six!"

The crowd roared as Clay took off his hat and waved it in the air.

Jack was the last one to take his seat after yelling and applauding. He wore a proud smile on his face as he watched Clay walk through the gate to retrieve his rigging.

Clay's score held and he placed first in the bareback riding. It was hard to tell who was happier, Jack or Clay.

The next event was steer wrestling. It was called "the big man's sport," but Jack knew there was more to the sport than just size. It took strength, all right, but it also took agility and he had seen men of smaller stature consistently win in this sport.

As the crowd watched the opposite end of the arena, two men on horseback entered the three-sided boxes on either side of a chute, which held a coriente long-horned steer. These cattle were specially bred for their lanky form and wide horn base. The mounted rider on the right side of the steer was called the hazer. His job was to make sure the steer ran in a straight line while the other mounted rider, the steer wrestler, rode alongside on a dogging horse and dropped down on the running animal. Once the dog-

ging horse and the hazer moved past the steer, the
steer wrestler would plant his feet in the ground and
pull the steer around, throwing him to the ground. If
timed perfectly, the steer's back feet would be in the
air as the dogger twisted his neck, using the steer's
momentum to help throw him.

Jack loved to watch this event, and as he waited he
thought about how this event had changed since he
used to participate. The steers were somewhat smaller
than the rangy longhorns he had thrown, the horses
were faster, and the technique had been improved
considerably.

The first steer wrestler nodded for his steer and
with the clang of the opening chute gate, the two
horses and a steer surged forward with a burst of energy. The two riders caught up with the steer fifteen
feet from the chute and the dogger quickly slid down
on the steer's back. In a cloud of soft dust he brought
the steer around and twisted him down in a time of
six point three seconds. It was a good time, but Jack
didn't think it would hold. His attention was brought
back to the bucking chutes as they began loading
horses for the saddle bronc riding. He saw Clay setting his bronc saddle on the fence, working resin into
the swells. The saddle bronc riding would be the next
event and Jack felt his excitement rise as he watched
the men run the horses into the chutes. This had been
his specialty in his younger days and he still felt his
heart quicken when he watched the heated contest between man and horse. He made himself turn back to
the steer wrestling and realized he'd missed two contestants and their times.

There were six more steer wrestlers. Jack watched
with half interest, glancing from time to time toward
the bucking chutes to watch Clay. He hadn't saddled

any of the six horses loaded in the chutes, which meant he'd be further down in the bucking order. This was both good and bad, Jack knew, since he'd have a chance to see what the other riders were doing, but it could also be hard on the nerves, if others posted scores that would be difficult to beat.

The last steer wrestler threw his steer in five seconds flat to place third. A four-one and a four-five took first and second, and five-two took fourth.

The announcer was soon calling the crowd's attention back to the bucking chutes for the beginning of the saddle bronc riding as the first rider climbed into the saddle and nodded to the chute man.

The horse, Lucky Seven, came out of the chute head down and bucking hard. The cowboy on his back held the woven rope rein in his right hand and kept his left hand in the air, using it for balance. He pulled himself into the saddle and tried to lock his thighs its the swell. He had his spurs over the points of the horse's shoulder, but rather than spurring up like the bareback riders, he went from the shoulders back to the cantle of the saddle, as was the proper form. Again the secret was to get in time with the horse and let his bucking action dictate the spurring action.

The first rider made it almost five seconds before he lost his seat and landed in the dirt, unhurt but disappointed. The length of the ride was the same in each of the rough stock events, eight seconds, and to many a cowboy that was a lifetime when you considered what hinged upon that short span of time.

Jack watched intently as the next five riders came into the arena. Only two made qualified rides, scoring a sixty-eight and a seventy-two respectively. He looked at the chutes and saw Clay had saddled a horse in chute number two, and was adjusting his

rein and halter. He was amazed at the pride he felt for
this young man, though he'd only known him a
month. If anyone had told him two months ago he'd
be swelling with pride watching him ride, he would
have laughed and called them crazy. But here he was,
and he hadn't felt this much excitement in years, as
was evidenced by the smile on his face.

Chapter Nine

Clay felt the nervous tension build in him as adrenaline pumped through his body. He loved this moment, loved the way he felt just before he rode, but it was nothing compared to the thrill he felt when he was in the arena on a good bronc. The crowd, the announcer, and the other cowboys disappeared. It was just him and the horse, and he never felt as free as he did for those eight seconds. It wasn't the same with the barebacks or the bulls as it was with the saddle broncs. There was something primitive about saddle bronc riding. Maybe because it was the first event dating back to the early cattle drives that made it somehow more real, more important, and he often wondered if those cowboys from long ago were up there watching and cheering him on as he rode.

The rider in chute number one nodded that he was ready. Clay watched as he marked the horse out, which meant having his spurs in contact with the points of the horse's shoulders when his front feet touched the ground, and continued to ride to the whistle. As the pickup men moved in, Clay stepped across the chute and eased himself down into the saddle, placing his feet in the stirrups and gently easing them over the points of Bold Caliber's shoulders. The big black horse lunged slightly in the chute but quickly settled down. Clay checked his rein one more time to make sure he had it at proper length. Too long and he wouldn't be able to use the rein to pull himself into the saddle. Too short and Bold Caliber wouldn't be able to get his head down to buck, or he'd pull the rein from Clay's hand.

The rider was off the horse and in the arena now, and the announcer called his score—a sixty-nine, which moved him into second place. As the rider moved to the side of the arena, the arena director called Clay's name. "You're up, Tory, let's ride." Clay nodded to the gate man and the large gate swung outward.

Bold Caliber reared on his hind legs and lunged forward with such a surge of energy that Clay would have been thrown backward had he not anticipated what the big horse was going to do.

As the horse's front feet hit the ground he let out a bellow and straightening his flexed knees, shot into the air, leaving almost six feet of daylight between his hooves and the ground.

Clay spurred the horse from his shoulders to the saddle cantle, and had his feet back at his shoulders when he hit the ground. His thighs pressed into the swells of the saddle as he pulled hard on the buck rein.

Jack sat mesmerized, watching the performance before him. Bold Caliber was a fine bucking horse and Clay was doing an admirable job of riding him. He was silently giving the boy pointers, as if by telepathic means Clay could hear his thoughts.

Bold Caliber was giving it all he had. Six seconds into the contest he crashed broadside into the arena fence in an attempt to knock the stubborn rider from his back. Clay's right leg banged into a board rail. He winced in pain, his concentration broken for a moment. At that moment, Bold Caliber made his move. As he felt the shift in Clay's weight, he ducked his head and reversed ends in a move that would have made a cutting horse proud. Clay felt the move coming and gripped hard with his right leg, but he was too much out of balance. As Bold Caliber came around, Clay felt himself slipping from the saddle. With one more powerful lunge the horse planted his feet and swung to the right as the whistle blew, satisfied to feel the unwanted rider thrown from the saddle.

Clay hit the arena dirt on his side and rolled, coming to a stop unhurt. He pushed himself up to his knees and stood up, disappointed in his ride.

Jack watched him walk dejectedly from the arena as the announcer gave his score. It was a sixty-nine—a tie for second place as it stood right now. Jack smiled to himself. The boy had ridden well and with a little practice and some coaching, he'd make a great bronc rider. As he mused over the ride, a thought came to him. He reminded himself to talk about it with Will at supper.

Clay got his saddle and carried it to the pickup before joining Jack in the box seats. "You put on a good ride," Jack said, seeing the dejection on the boy's face.

"I should have won it. If that sorry rascal hadn't run me into the fence, I'd have scored a seventy-five."

"That's rodeo, son. You take your draw and you make your ride, and when it's over you take what you got and be happy, or figure out what went wrong and how to do better next time. But you don't dwell on the things that might have been, or that's what you'll become, a might-have-been."

Clay listened to the old rancher's words, and

though he knew they were true it didn't make him feel any better.

As they watched the calf roping and barrel racing, Jack noticed the gleam in Clay's eyes as Cathy Richland ran the barrel pattern. Though Clay remained aloof during her performance, his eyes didn't leave her until she disappeared out of the arena. Jack remained silent, smiling to himself.

Since there were thirty-three bull riders entered in the event, the bull riding was divided into two sections. They bucked out the first sixteen riders before the team roping, and the last seventeen after. Since bull riding was the biggest crowd pleaser, it was always the last event. Known as the most dangerous sport in the world, it always drew the most contestants eager to test their mettle. Jack wondered why anyone would want to tie themselves to a ton of angry flesh bent on doing bodily harm to them. He had tried it one time himself and found it wasn't to his liking. He was too tall and his legs were too long for the event, but he had to admit he thoroughly enjoyed watching a good bull rider in action. The problem was there were too many wanna-bes who were there just for the glory and the bragging rights, and weren't serious about it. Those were the ones who more often than not got themselves hurt.

Jack felt if a fella wasn't going to keep himself in shape mentally and physically, he'd better forget about bulls and take up cross-stitching. Another thing he didn't like about bull riders was most of them were cocky loudmouths. They'd swagger around talking about the great rides they'd made and rough bulls they'd been on, trying to impress everyone with their skills, when most of the time it was mostly their imaginations that made those rides. The great bull riders were the ones usually more modest about their achievements.

Jack and Clay watched the first section of bull riding together, talking about the rides and the riders. They would analyze each ride to determine what had gone wrong and what had been done right. At the end of the first section, Toby Martin was leading with a score of seventy-three. Second place was a seventy, third was a sixty-eight, and fourth a sixty-seven. As the team ropers came into the arena, Clay left to get his bull rope ready. He would be the sixth rider in the second section. Jack wished him luck and offered a silent prayer for his safety.

Jack watched the team roping without interest, lost in his own thoughts. Team roping, as its name implies, is done by a team of mounted cowboys. One, called the header, ropes a coriente steer around the horns, the other, the heeler, comes in from behind and ropes the back heels. Between the two of them the steer is stretched out and time is stopped when they turn and face each other. It's a precision event that requires skill, timing, and teamwork. Jack was still deep in thought when Will Hightower suddenly sat down beside him. "Clay's done pretty well so far. He won the bareback riding and split third and fourth in the saddle broncs." Clay had been bumped out of second place by the last rider.

"Uh huh," Jack said, not revealing his concern for Clay's next ride.

"He's got the makings of a top hand. He just needs some experience under his belt and someone to coach him."

Jack smiled at his friend. "I was just thinking the same thing earlier. He's got barebacks down, but he needs some work on the saddle broncs and I don't know as much about bull riding as he does."

"No, but you know the important things, like the physical and mental side of the sport."

Jack remained thoughtful for a moment, considering what Will had said. "It's funny you should mention that. I was going to talk to you about getting a couple of good broncs for him to practice on. You happen to know where I could buy any?"

"Nope, sure don't. But I know a fella that's got three he'd be glad to loan you for as long as you need 'em."

Jack looked at him in surprise and couldn't say anything.

"I don't believe it," Will said, chuckling, "Jack Lomas is speechless. That's got to be a historical event."

"Hmmph," Jack snorted. "You offering something for free is a bigger historical event. That's what threw me. Are you sure you're feelin' all right? Do I need to call a doctor?"

Both men laughed. Jack felt elated as he thought about what this would mean to Clay.

"I'll be coming down your way next Thursday on our way to Pecos. I'll put them on the truck with the others and we'll drop them off."

Jack offered, "Why don't you come early and spend some time with us?"

Will thought for a moment and answered, "I think we could arrange that. I better get back to the bucking chutes right now, though. They're about through with the team roping. I'll meet you and Dottie by the trailer after the bull riding and we'll go eat."

Jack nodded. "Will, don't say anything to Clay about this. I want it to be a surprise."

Will smiled. "Sure thing," he said as he turned and walked away.

The bull riding began with the usual excitement as the first cowboy rode for about four seconds before being thrown. As he hit the ground the rodeo clowns, or more precisely bullfighters, moved in to draw the bull's attention away from the cowboy. Dressed in bright clothes, and made up in clown's face paint, they put on a show of agility and speed for the crowd as the bull tried to hook them.

The next two cowboys met with the same fate and each returned to the chutes unhurt, but the fourth cowboy hung up in his bull rope and was tossed about like a sack of potatoes tied to a tornado. The bull fighters moved in and were finally able to free the cowboy, but not before he'd been stepped on and butted. Fortunately, he sustained no serious injuries. Jack felt beads of perspiration form on his brow, though it was a cool evening.

Clay had his bull rope around High Cannon, who got his name from his famous leap out of the chute. The bull rope consisted of a heavy braided rope with a loop in one end. The "tail," which is the other end, is run through the loop and pulled tight around the bull. There is also a flat plaited handle woven into the rope and it's this handle that the bull rider runs his hand through. When the rope is pulled tight, the tail is then laid across the palm of the cowboy's hand. By clenching his hand into a fist, the rider holds both the handle and the rope. The tail is then run around the back of his hand and brought around again through his palm. Some cowboys keep a little slack in the loop behind the hand, while others pull it down tight and even run the tail between their little finger and ring

finger. This is called a "suicide hold" due to the fact
that the cowboy is literally tied to the bull's back.

Clay waited until the rider before him nodded for
the gate to open before easing down on High Cannon.
As he stood astride the large animal, he felt adrenaline course through his veins. Taking the tail of the
rope, he worked his resined glove up and down to
heat the resin, making it tacky. He eased down on the
bull's back and ran his hand through the handle.
Since he rode right-handed he set the handle just
slightly to the left of High Cannon's spine, nodding to
the cowboy helping him when it felt right. The cowboy began to pull the rope, tightening it down on
Clay's hand until he nodded again. Too tight and
High Cannon would rip the rope loose from his hand.
The rope was then laid across his palm. Clay wrapped
it around behind his hand then brought it through his
palm again, leaving little slack as he clenched his fist.

The fifth bull rider made it to the whistle and was
off safely.

In bull riding, the rider wasn't required to mark the
animal out in any fashion by spurring the bull over
the points of the shoulder on the first jump out of the
chute. But spurring would increase their score. Riders
usually used tied-down rowels on their spurs to better grip the bull's muscular sides.

Clay waited tensely for the bull to be cleared from
the arena. The arena director then indicated it was his
turn. "Let's ride, Tory," came the call and Clay pulled
his hat down tighter and scooted up on his rope.
"Let's go!" he yelled, and the gate swung open.

Jack's breath caught in his throat and there was an
audible "Ooh" from the crowd as High Cannon
leaped into the air, twisting his body into the arena as
he came. This move had unseated many a cowboy

due to the bull's quickness and power, but Clay remained seated in the middle and was in good position as the large beast came back to earth.

High Cannon was unimpressed with the fact that Clay had remained on his back, and as he touched down he immediately lunged to his left and began a bucking spin.

Clay felt the big bull start left, and he dug his left spur into the bull's tough hide, leaning slightly into the spin and waiting for his chance to gain points. As High Cannon's spin picked up speed, Clay began to use his right spur to rake up the bull's side.

As quickly as he'd gone into the spin, High Cannon came out of it, hoping to throw Clay off balance. But Clay anticipated his move and when the bull leapt into the air, he had his spurs dug in and was sitting up on his rope.

High Cannon turned to his right, then switched quickly to his left. He dropped his right shoulder, trying to throw Clay down into the well, but Clay leaned back and kept his balance. Finally, he heard the eight-second whistle and grabbing the tail of the rope with his free hand, he flipped it through his hand and threw his left leg over the bull's shoulder, stepping off and running for the chutes.

As if upset over being ridden to the whistle, High Cannon turned, looking for the man who had been on his back. He spotted him racing for the chutes and turning quickly, the bull charged after him, head down and hooves churning, intent on running him down.

Clay sensed rather than saw the bull coming for him. He was a good thirty feet from the safety of the bucking chutes and knew he could never outrun the large beast, but he was determined to give it his best shot.

High Cannon had closed the distance between him

and his quarry. The bull had him in his sight, and in the next instant it looked as if Clay would fall victim to the massive animal. Someone in the audience screamed as it looked certain Clay would be run down. At that instant, one of the bullfighters moved between the narrow gap that separated bull and cowboy. High Cannon, seeing the movement close to him, changed direction to pursue this new target, but the swiftness of the man proved to be too much for the bull as he ran around behind him. High Cannon stopped, head high and nostrils flaring, looking for any human upon whom he could vent his anger.

Clay cleared the first three boards on the chute gate and stood on the third, turning to see what took place only after he was safe. He breathed a sigh of relief as he saw the big bull attacking the barrel man. The barrel man is the bullfighter who remains in an open barrel during the bull riding. Essentially he is the fixed target in the arena, used to draw the bull's attention. Clay made a mental note to thank the bull fighter after the event.

Jack sat back weakly in his seat, his heart beating much faster than it should have. He didn't know if he'd be able to stand too much of this, but when he turned and saw the smile on Clay's face after hearing his score, a seventy-eight, he forgot about his fright and applauded with the rest of the crowd. Clay had just taken over first place, and chances were he'd hold on to it.

Jack watched the rest of the bull riding from his seat and grinned as the last rider made it only three seconds before hitting the dirt. Clay's score had held, giving him two first-place finishes and a split for third and fourth. He knew the boy would be excited, practically walking on air. Jack was very proud of him.

Chapter Ten

It was almost ten-thirty when Will finished giving his final instructions on loading the stock for their ride back to the ranch. He met Jack and Dottie by the trailer. Jack had been watching for Clay and was beginning to get worried, when he finally came running up, out of breath and excited. "Do you reckon I might be able to go to the rodeo dance tonight?" he asked.

Caught off guard, Jack stammered for a response. "Well—I—uh, I don't—"

"Oh, come on, Jack, let the boy go to the dance. Don't you remember when you were young and could work all day and dance all night and then work again the next day?" Dottie chastised.

Jack smiled. "Yeah I remember. Do you two mind dropping me at the motel?"

"No problem," Will chortled as Jack handed Clay the keys to the truck.

"Thanks," Clay said, taking the keys and hurrying off. "Wait a minute," Jack yelled and walked stiffly after the young man. Taking his billfold from his back pocket, he took out two twenties and handed them to Clay. "Here, you have a good time."

Clay looked from Jack to the money in his hand. "I'm not supposed to take any money from you, Mr. Lomas. Sheriff Aguilar made it real plain to me about that."

"I don't give a frog's rump what Ben Aguilar said," Jack said gruffly. "You take this money and go have a good time and I don't want to hear another word about it."

"Yes sir," Clay said with a smile, taking the two twenties.

"And one more thing, young man," Jack said, putting emphasis on his words. Clay looked at him, expecting to hear a lecture. "That was some mighty fine riding you did out there tonight." A beaming smile broke across his face, and he looked around quickly to cover the obvious embarrassment of one who wasn't used to giving compliments. "I was mighty proud of you."

It was Clay's turn to be embarrassed. "Thanks, Mr. Lomas."

"I think it's about time you called me Jack. This Mr. Lomas stuff is starting to make me feel old."

Clay smiled and Jack motioned with his hand. "Go on, get out of here and have a good time. And don't wake me up when you come in, you hear?"

"Yes sir," Clay said brightly as he headed toward the pickup.

Supper was a festive affair as the three old friends reminisced about old times. Jack couldn't remember the last time he'd laughed so hard as Will reminded him of the stunts they'd pulled in their younger days.

"You remember that time we were down to our last two dollars and hadn't eaten for two days?" Will asked.

"Yeah," Jack answered with a chuckle, "we were both so hungry we would have eaten the leather on our pickup seats, if there'd been any left."

Will smiled. "We had just pulled into Phoenix and

saw this small café with a sign in the window: ALL THE
SPAGHETTI YOU CAN EAT 75 CENTS. We almost wrecked
the truck trying to get turned around and into that
café."

"Sure did, and that was the best tasting spaghetti
I'd ever eaten. And you ate enough to sink a ship,"
Jack said.

"I can't argue that with you," Will said, "but I didn't
eat as much as you did."

"I don't know, I think it was a draw. But it was definitely you that tossed your stomach first."

Will burst out laughing. "We ate so much we both
got sick and threw it all up. If we hadn't been able to
borrow that ten dollars from Lucy Taylor the next day
to buy food, I don't think either one of us would have
been able to ride that night."

Both men laughed as Dottie shook her head in disbelief. "I don't see how you two managed to stay
alive long enough to make anything of yourselves.
And I sure don't know how I was lucky enough to get
saddled with the two of ya," she said.

Will put his arm around her affectionately and
pulled her close. "I don't know, babe, but I'm sure
glad ya did. If it weren't for you I'd have never
amounted to a hill of beans. I'd have ended up like
old Joe Waskom, a broken rodeo bum hanging around
rodeos looking for a handout."

Dottie pushed him away gently, a blush filling her
cheeks. "You're full of it, Will Hightower. I don't ever
remember a time when you weren't working to get
yourself a ranch. You'd have gotten along with or
without me."

Will shook his head. "Nope. I did it all for you, Dottie. I wouldn't have wanted it without you."

She blushed again when she noticed Jack smiling at

them. "I think it's about time we called it a night," he said. "I'm gettin' too old to stay up until dawn."

"I agree," Dottie said. "It's been a long day and we got stock to load in the morning."

"I remember when we used to dance all night and work all day and go dancin' again the next night," Will said, "and it don't seem like it was that long ago."

"It's been longer than I care to think about," Jack replied.

"I reckon it has," Will said reflectively. "Well, I don't know about you two but I'm ready to hit the hay."

"I second that motion," Dottie said wearily. "I'm just about done for."

They left the restaurant and dropped Jack at the motel. "We'll see you next week," Will called out as Jack got out of the truck. "I'll ring you when I know what time we'll be there."

"I'm lookin' forward to it," Jack said with a smile.

It was one o'clock in the morning when Clay came into the room. Jack had tossed and turned in bed since shortly after Will and Dottie had dropped him off, but he pretended to be asleep when Clay came in. He indeed fell asleep a short while later.

Little was said between the two the next morning until they were well on their way back to Roswell. "Where'd you get that bruise on your cheek?" Jack asked, referring to a dark purplish mark on Clay's cheekbone.

With a small grin Clay felt his bruised face gingerly, wincing as he did. "I had a disagreement with Cathy Richland's ex-boyfriend. Seems he didn't appreciate me takin' her to the dance last night and decided to rearrange my face."

"Looks like he almost succeeded," Jack noted wryly.

Clay turned and looked out the window, but not before Jack caught the angry look on his face. "What happened?" Jack asked in a quiet voice.

"Ah, shoot," Clay finally said. "Cathy asked me to go to the dance with her last night. Then her supposedly ex-boyfriend Kyle Linson shows up and starts creating a scene. I tried to get him to calm down and back off but he started pushing me, telling me he was going to whip me if I didn't get out of there, so I invited him to step out into the parking lot." He stopped there and Jack wondered if he was going to finish on his own or if he was going to have to ask what happened. Just as he started to state his question, Clay continued. "We both went out into the parking lot and when I turned around to face him, he sucker-punched me. I guess I kinda lost my temper."

"What happened?" Jack asked with concern.

"I whipped him all over the parking lot. By the time they pulled me off of him he was begging me to quit, or so they told me, I don't remember. Anyway after I whipped him Cathy ran to him and started crying, telling him how sorry she was. Then she called me an animal and told me she never wanted to see me again." Shaking his head Clay looked at Jack. "I don't reckon I'll ever understand women."

Jack chuckled. "Welcome to man's biggest dilemma, son. I don't reckon there's a man alive that understands women, and if one tells you he does, he's either crazy or the biggest liar in the world."

"I really thought she liked me, but she was just using me to make Kyle jealous."

"That happens sometimes, son. But believe me when the right one comes along, you won't have to worry about her motives. It'll be as clear as a bell."

"Just as long as it doesn't hit me like one." Clay smiled.

"It might just do that, son, it might just do that."

Jack called Ben Aguilar as soon as they returned to the ranch. There had been no other reports of cattle being rustled, much to Jack's relief. He told Ben about their time in Ruidoso, leaving out the part about Clay's fight. Ben was delighted to hear of Clay's success and was silently thankful the two of them were starting to get along so well. Jack invited him out to the ranch next Thursday and told him about the horses Will would be delivering. Ben said he would try to stop by.

When Clay came in from checking on the stock, Jack told him there had been no more cattle thefts, but they would have to keep a watch since the thieves could start up again at any time. "We'll ride fences tomorrow to make sure there's none been cut that we don't know about."

Clay nodded and started toward his room. "Wait a minute," Jack called to him. "I almost forgot something." Pulling his billfold from his back pocket, he pulled out four one-hundred-dollar bills and three twenties and handed them to Clay.

The boy stood there looking questioningly at the money. "It's your winnings. Will and Dottie gave it to me last night."

"But Ben told me I couldn't have any money. Except what the county gives me," he said, standing back and looking at Jack.

"I don't care what Ben said. You won this money

and it belongs to you." He could see the worry on the boy's face and understood the problem. One infraction on the terms of his release and he could be back in the county jail.

"Tell you what, why don't I take this money and open up a savings account for you at the bank. That way when your time's up you'll have a nest egg to fall back on."

Clay's eyes lit up in surprise. "You mean you'd do that for me?"

It was Jack's turn to look surprised. "Of course. It's yours—you earned it."

Clay stood there, confusion written plainly on his face. His own father would never have let him keep the money. He would have taken it and bought liquor, then laughed and thanked him for being so generous.

As if reading his thoughts Jack continued. "Whatever you earn while you're here with me is yours to keep. Is that understood?"

Clay nodded hesitantly. "Yes sir."

Jack smiled. "Good, we'll go into town Wednesday and open you up a savings account and while we're there we'll stop at the feed store and get the new *Rodeo News* magazine. I don't know about you but I'd like to make another rodeo or two."

Clay smiled. "I reckon I could handle makin' one or two more."

The next two days were spent riding to each section of the ranch and checking all the cattle. They roped and doctored several calves with runny noses. Jack was impressed with Clay's roping skills, noting the natural rhythm he had.

Jack thought about Clay's talent. He knew the boy had the ability to become a world champion just as

Ben Aguilar had said, but he also knew it would take practice to hone his skills to the level it would take to compete on the professional circuit. He also knew the boy needed expert tutoring that he wasn't sure he could provide. After all, it had been twenty years since he'd been involved in rodeo and he wasn't too sure he'd be able to coach Clay properly, but at least he could provide him with the horses to practice on and maybe even a bull or two. They'd worry about coaching as the need arose.

Wednesday found them in town and while Jack went into the bank, Clay walked down Main Street to the drugstore. He needed more tape for his glove, and liked the medical adhesive they sold there.

He was nearing the door, lost in thoughts of future rodeos, when a large hand grabbed his shoulder from behind and almost jerked him off his feet.

"What the—?" Clay sputtered, jerking free and spinning around, ready to strike out at the person who had grabbed him. As he came around his mouth opened in surprise but the anger remained as he turned to find his father standing there, an insolent sneer glued to his face.

"Hey, runt, where ya headed in such a hurry?" Jason Tory asked his youngest son.

Clay looked around uncomfortably, not liking the look in his father's eyes. It was obvious he was looking for trouble and Clay wanted no part of it.

"I was just going in to buy some tape," he answered, his head downcast, not daring to look his old man in the eyes. He had learned at an early age that the easiest way to get the back of a hand was to stare directly at the old man.

"Tape, huh? I reckon if you can afford tape you can afford a few dollars for your old man."

Clay fingered the five-dollar bill in his pocket. It was all he had with him and he needed the tape, but he also knew his father wouldn't hesitate to slap him around right here on the street.

"Sure," Clay responded. "Let me get my tape and I'll give you the change." He turned to start into the store but the big man's hand reached out in a steely grip on his arm, stopping him.

"Let me see what you got," Jason Tory said, squeezing the boy's arm until he saw him wince in agony.

Clay reluctantly removed the five dollars from his pocket and held it close to his jeans, not willing to hand it over so easily. "This is all I got and I need some tape. Tape's only a dollar and a half and I'll give you the rest," he said, looking at the sidewalk as his father stood there squeezing hard on his arm.

Jason Tory reached down and ripped the bill from his son's grasp. "Tell you what, I've got a powerful thirst right about now so I'm goin' to buy me a beer or two. Anything I got left I'll let you have to buy your tape." He threw back his head and laughed.

"So how's things goin' with you and old man Lomas?" he asked, his grip now lessening a little. Clay looked up, surprised by the question but more surprised by the tone of his father's voice. He almost gasped at the piercing gaze and the anger he saw there.

"F-f-fine," Clay stammered.

"Yeah, well, see that it stays that way. We may need you in the near future." He released Clay's arm and turning on his heel, walked away, leaving Clay with a puzzled frown on his face. He wondered what his father had meant when he said they may need him. What could they possibly need him for? And why was he interested in Jack Lomas?

He walked back toward the bank, hoping Jack wouldn't ask him about the tape. For some reason he couldn't explain, he didn't want Jack to know about the meeting with his father. Clay could see the pickup still parked in front of the bank. He was leaning on the front of the truck when Jack finally walked out. "Did you get everything taken care of?" he asked before Jack could say anything.

"Sure did," he said handing him a folded bank book made of imitation leather. "That's your savings account book. Hang on to it and keep your deposits recorded. I've set the account up in both our names so neither of us can draw any money out without the other's signature. You'll have to fill out a signature card next time you make a deposit."

"Sure," Clay said, opening the book and looking at the amount printed in the deposit column. He couldn't help but smile. "How come it always looks like more when it's typed?"

Jack smiled. "I don't know, but I think it's a secret that only banks know."

"Where to now?" Clay asked, walking to the driver's side of the pickup, an arrangement that suited Jack just fine.

"First to the courthouse and then to the feed store."

Clay drove to the courthouse and parked in the spot marked DEPUTY SHERIFF as Jack instructed. Clay smiled to himself as he switched off the engine. He was beginning to like Jack Lomas more and more. He waited in the pickup while Jack went in, entering through the door marked SHERIFF'S OFFICE. Fifteen minutes later Jack came out and got in on the passenger's side, handing Clay an envelope.

"What's this?" Clay asked, looking surprised.

"The money the county owes you. Five dollars a day. That'll give you a little spending money."

"Thanks," Clay said, stuffing the envelope into his pants pocket without even looking inside.

"Let's go by the feed store then we'll get a bite to eat," Jack said.

Clay backed the truck into the street and noticed Ben Aguilar standing at his window, watching them as they pulled away. He couldn't swear to it but it sure looked as if the sheriff was smiling.

After stopping by the feed store, where they picked up the new *Rodeo News* and ordered a load of mineral blocks, they had lunch at the Cattlemen's Café and poured over the paper, looking at upcoming rodeos within driving distance. By the time their lunch arrived they had agreed on four rodeos that were close enough to make without having to leave the ranch unattended for long periods of time. Every rodeo they chose had to meet certain criteria, such as an acceptable stock contractor, added money for each event, and a certain number of performances. They also considered the distance they had to travel and the time the rodeos began.

"We can make Seagraves and Pecos this Friday and Saturday and Lubbock and Carlsbad next weekend," Jack said, pushing the paper back to Clay's side of the booth.

"Sounds like a plan to me," Clay said. "We can drive back here after the Lubbock show and rest until Saturday afternoon before driving to Carlsbad."

"That'll work," Jack agreed, "except you'll have to do most of the driving on the way home since it'll be past my bedtime."

Clay grinned as he bit into his cheeseburger.

After lunch Jack directed Clay to drive south of

Roswell. Though Clay gave a questioning glance, he asked nothing as he followed the directions given him. Jack looked out the window at scenery as the road they were traveling on wound through rolling prairie hills. They left the blacktop and drove on a caliche road for several miles until Jack directed Clay toward a drive to a ranch house that appeared over a rise.

Pulling the truck up to the chain-link fence that encircled the yard of the ranch house, Clay switched off the engine and watched a lanky man about Jack's age come out the screen door and down the steps toward them.

"Ya'll get out and come on in," the man said, pushing open the gate.

"How ya doin, Clyde?" Jack called out as he closed the pickup's door behind him. Clay noticed that Clyde did not seem the least bit surprised to see them and he wondered what Jack was up to. He also knew it wouldn't do any good to ask—Jack would let him know whenever he was ready, if at all.

As they walked through the gate that Clyde held open, Jack introduced him. "Clyde, I want you to meet Clay Tory. Clay works for me."

Clay smiled and held out his hand. "Clay, this is Clyde Jones, an old friend of mine," Jack continued.

"Old is right," Clyde said, taking Clay's hand in a firm grip. The man might have a little age on him, but he certainly wasn't soft. There didn't seem to be an ounce of fat anywhere on him.

"Pleased to meet you, Mr. Jones," Clay said.

"It's Clyde, son. My dad's Mr. Jones."

Clay smiled at the old cliché.

"Come on in. Mary's got some iced tea fixed."

As soon as they entered the house, they were greeted by a short robust lady who moved toward them in a rush. "Jack Lomas, it's been ages since you've been out to visit us!" she said, standing on her tiptoes and hugging his neck. "And who's this good-looking young man you've got with you?"

Mary Jones was a bundle of energy, and trying to keep up with her constant movement and chatter almost took your breath away. As soon as she turned from hugging Jack's neck, she was wrapping her arms around Clay as if she'd known him for years.

"Mary, this is Clay Tory."

She stepped back, holding him at arm's length and looking him up and down, "You need some meat on your bones, young man." Clay smiled at her, not knowing how to respond, but Mary Jones didn't wait for a response. "Ya'll sit down and I'll fix you some iced tea. Have you two had lunch?"

"We ate at the Cattlemen's before coming out," Jack replied.

"You'll eat a piece of peach cobbler and some ice cream, won't you?" she asked, already taking the bowls down from the cabinet.

"I wouldn't pass up your peach cobbler for the world, Mary," Jack said kindly.

"Which you couldn't if you wanted to," Clyde added.

Mary was already busy spooning ice cream into the bowls and acted as if she didn't hear.

Jack and Clyde were soon talking cattle, range conditions, and rustlers between mouthfuls of peach cobbler and ice cream. As the last of the dessert was scooped up and eaten, Clyde reached for his hat. "If you're ready we'll go have a look at them bulls."

"I don't know if I can move after eating all that delicious cobbler," Jack jested.

"That sure was good, Mrs. Jones," Clay said, putting a flush to her cheeks.

"I'm glad you boys liked it. It would have gone to waste if ya'll hadn't eaten it. Clyde won't hardly eat desserts."

Clay and Jack thanked her again and Jack promised not to take as long getting back to visit her as they made their way outside.

Clyde led them out of the yard and down to a tin Quonset barn. Sliding open the large door, he led them through the barn and out into a large corral. There they saw eight head of bulls standing around, chewing on large round hay bales. Clay noticed the bulls were of different breeds. There were three Brahma bulls, one Brahma cross, two large Angus bulls, and two brintle bulls that were impossible to tell what breed they had come from.

Jack stood with his foot on the bottom fence rail, studying the animals, looking over each one carefully. "These are all good-looking bulls, Clyde. What's the history on 'em?"

"That big Brahma standing over there next to the gate is one of the best. He'll make it to the top. That brintle over on the other side is a little less active and is probably more what you're looking for. Him and that Angus over on the far side," he said, pointing to black bull standing on the far side of one of the hay rings, "would probably suit you for the time being, and neither bull is mean. If you want to take 'em and try 'em, I'll trade 'em down the road if you find you need something with a little more power."

Jack studied the two bulls and then pointed to a large Brahma standing off by himself. "What about that one?" he asked, nodding in the bull's direction.

"That's a good tough one there. A bit more bull than the other two."

Clay looked at the beast and wondered why it would be important for a herd bull to be tough, but kept quiet and didn't ask any questions.

"I'll take him and the brintle, if you'll deliver 'em tomorrow morning," Jack said, turning to face Clyde Jones.

"No problem. I'll have them out at your place around ten o'clock."

Jack smiled and turned back to look at the bulls quietly grazing.

Chapter Eleven

Clay woke the next morning to the sounds of pots and pans rattling. Wiping sleep from his eyes, he stumbled into the kitchen and looked at the clock over the sink. It read four-thirty. Clay rubbed his eyes and stared incredulously at Jack. "What in the world are you doing?"

Jack turned at the sound of Clay's voice and saw him standing in the doorway in his underwear. "Oh, did I wake you? Sorry," he said as he pulled a large pot from under the counter. "I'm cooking some stew for lunch and I wanted to get it on early."

Clay looked at the size of the pot he was setting on the stove and asked, "What army are you planning on feeding?"

Jack chuckled. "I figured as long as I was making stew, I'd make enough to freeze so we can thaw it out to eat later."

"Looks like we'll have enough for the next year if you fix that whole pot. I sure hope it's good."

"Best stew you've ever eaten," Jack said, cutting up chunks of sirloin. "Why don't you get dressed and help me peel some potatoes and carrots."

Clay turned and walked back to his bedroom, shaking his head in wonder as he went.

"I want you to ride over to the north pasture and check the cattle over there," Jack said later when Clay was helping peel the large spuds, cutting them into chunks as Jack requested. "I want you to check on those two windmills while you're there and make sure they've got plenty of water."

"We were just over there three days ago and they were fine," Clay responded.

"I know," Jack said, "but the south windmill has been acting up and if it quits, the north one won't be enough to take care of all the cattle in that pasture."

Clay nodded. "I'll make sure I check both."

"Make sure you're home by lunch. I want to drive over and check on the cattle in the southwest pasture, and I know you want to get back before I eat all this stew."

Clay chuckled. "Yeah I'm worried there won't be any left if I'm late."

Jack cooked them both breakfast while continuing to add ingredients to the stew. When they had both eaten, Clay went to the barn and saddled his horse. Jack met him as he came out of the corral, saying, "Make sure you check on that Hereford cow. She should have dropped that calf by now. This is the second year in a row she's been late calving. I'll probably take her to the sale barn this fall. Also, check on that black bull and see if he's still lame in that front hoof. He should be all right after that shot of antibiotics we gave him but if he's not we'll have to give him another shot tomorrow."

"Gotcha," Clay said, stepping into the saddle. "I sure hope that stew's as good as you say it is. I'm going to be mighty hungry by the time I get back."

Jack looked taken aback. "I can't believe you'd even question my stew. Why, there's famous chefs around the world that would pay good money to have my recipe."

Clay laughed and touched spurs to his horse. "I can't wait."

Jack watched him ride off, a smile on his face as he thought about the events that were due to take place that day. "I do love surprises," he said to himself as he turned back to the house, humming a tune as he went.

Clyde Jones showed up a little after ten o'clock. There were two bulls in the large gooseneck trailer pulled behind his one-ton Ford pickup. He and Jack quickly unloaded the bulls, putting them in one of the holding pens behind the arena. Just then a tractor trailer with RUNNING H STOCK CONTRACTOR painted on the side in large letters pulled into the drive, followed closely behind by Will and Dottie Hightower in their pickup.

"Where do you want these broncs?" Will asked, parking by the barn.

"Have your driver back up to the loading chute over there and we'll put 'em in the pen," Jack said, pointing.

With little trouble there were soon three bucking horses standing in the holding pen, eating the bales of hay Jack had placed there earlier.

"I got coffee on the stove," Jack announced as they closed the gate and walked out of the arena.

"Let me get my driver on his way and I'll be right in," Will said.

When Clay rode back to the house, he was surprised to see all the vehicles parked in the yard. Riding to the barn, he unsaddled and fed his horse before walking up to the house, failing to notice the new animals behind the arena. As he walked into the house he heard voices raised in laughter.

"What's going on in here?" Clay asked, stepping into the kitchen.

A hush fell over the group sitting around the table as they all turned to look at him.

"We're having a party," Jack said. "Come on in and join us. We're waiting on you so we can eat."

Clay greeted the group. "Hey, Mr. Hightower, Mrs. Hightower, what brings ya'll out this way?"

"We were on our way to Pecos and thought we'd stop by and see how you two were gettin' along," Will said with a sheepish smile.

Clay shook hands with Will and Clyde across the table. "I reckon you brought those bulls out but I didn't see 'em. Where are they?" Clay asked.

"Uh, we put 'em in the upper trap behind the house," Jack said.

"You turned two bulls out in a strange trap without keeping them in a pen for a few days?" Clay asked incredulously.

"I had some work to do on the pen before we put 'em in it. We're going to move 'em back in right after lunch. Hopefully they won't get into too much trouble."

Clay looked at him in amazement. Something was going on, but what, he didn't know, though he had a feeling he'd soon find out.

"Well I don't know about the rest of you, but I'm starving and I can't wait to try some of Jack's beef stew," he said.

Dottie Hightower came to her feet. "You go wash up, Clay. I'll fix you a bowl while you men clean up your mess on the table. Jack, where are your bowls?"

Clay could see she had everything under control so

he headed to the bathroom. When he returned a few minutes later, the table was set and Dottie had the men fixing glasses of iced tea and getting the soda crackers and hot sauce. He marveled at how well she mobilized these tough ranchers into action without the slightest hint of objection.

Dottie had filled the bowls with stew and placed them on the table, telling the men to sit down. When they were all seated, Jack uttered grace and the meal began. Dottie Hightower was soon rolling her eyes skyward at the noisy slurping sounds around the table.

"Jack Lomas, I hate to admit it but this is some of the best stew I've ever eaten," Clyde said, taking another bite. "What's your recipe?"

Jack Lomas smiled slyly. "Choice beef is the secret," he said, "and from there it's just a matter of seasoning until you get the flavor right." Clyde gave him a questioning look but just smiled and nodded. He knew he'd never get the ingredients. There's just some things that a man held sacred and he could tell Jack Lomas's stew recipe was one of those things.

After they'd eaten their fill and pushed back away from the table, Jack asked nonchalantly, "You fellas want to see what I've done down at the arena?"

Will was leaning back in his chair, his feet stretched out in front of him. "I reckon I need to walk off some of this lunch anyway." He sighed.

Clyde Jones was leaning on the table with his arms crossed in front of him. "I guess we need to get them bulls penned up before they decide to take off on their own."

Clay sat listening to the exchange and felt like it was a play that had been rehearsed and staged just for him, but he didn't know why.

The three older men got up and walked outside without saying a word to Clay. He sat at the kitchen table for several moments after their departure, watching Dottie wash the dishes, then stood and walked to the screen door, watching the backs of the three men as they approached the barn. He slowly pushed open the door and stood there hesitantly before following.

Jack, Will, and Clyde walked through the barn and exited the other end, walking a few feet to the gate that opened into the side of the arena. Clay entered the barn and saw them turn toward the bucking chutes and wondered again what was going on. Picking up his pace a little, he walked through the barn and entered the arena, hurrying to catch up with the men in front. He was only steps behind when they halted at the gate leading into the alleyway between the bucking chutes.

As Clay neared, the older men moved to one side so Clay would have space at the gate. Moving up and looking in the same direction, Clay's face registered surprise before a questioning look furrowed his brow. He turned to look at the three men, each with a knowing grin on his face, and suddenly it dawned on him what the stock in the holding pens meant. His expression turned to shock and disbelief. He opened his mouth to say something but promptly closed it again as he looked from the grinning men to the bulls and horses in the pens. Clay began to grin himself.

"Well, boy, you reckon these critters'll be enough for you to practice on?" Will Hightower asked.

Clay looked once more at the horses and bulls, the smile slowly fading from his face. "I don't know what to say," he said in awe and gratitude.

"You don't got to say nothin'," Jack said. "All you

got to do is be willin' to listen to some instruction and practice every day."

Clay swallowed hard to clear the lump in his throat, then let his eyes roam over the arena. "This is a dream come true. I never thought I'd have an opportunity like this."

Will Hightower put his hand on Clay's shoulder. "Son, you got as much talent as anyone I've ever known, and if you'll listen to Jack and do like he tells you, you'll make a world champion like he was."

Surprise showed on Clay's face and he looked up into Will's face. Will glanced at Jack then back to Clay. "He didn't tell you, did he?" Clay shook his head.

"Now don't go fillin' the boy's head with a bunch of nonsense," Jack Lomas said. "That was a long time ago and it don't mean nothin' now."

"It may have been a long time ago, but that don't mean you've forgotten what it took to become a worlds champion. Now it's time for you to pass that information along to Clay here."

"I'd be proud to have you coach me," Clay stated.

Jack looked hard into the young man's eyes and saw he was being sincere.

"If I'm going to coach you, you have to promise to follow my instructions to the letter, without question."

"I'll do it," Clay responded with enthusiasm.

Clyde stepped forward and said, "There ain't none better than Jack when it comes to bronc riding, and if you listen to him and take his advice, he'll turn you into a champion bronc rider. I happen to know a couple of top bull riders that owe me some favors, and I'm sure I can get 'em to come out and give you some instruction too."

"I'd appreciate that, Mr. Jones."

They stood there for the next hour discussing the qualities and particulars of each animal.

Clay was surprised to learn that Clyde bought bucking bulls and sold them to several stock contractors. Will Hightower had bought many a bull from him in the past and much of the conversation was about which of his bulls had performed well and which ones hadn't.

Clyde left shortly after, saying he had to get back to his ranch work. He promised Clay he would be calling him in the near future to let him know when his friends could help him with the bulls. Clay, eager to know who they were, was simply told not to worry, and was assured they were champion bull riders.

After Clyde left, Jack turned to Clay. "We might as well get started on your training right now."

Excitement gleamed in Clay's eyes. "Should I get my saddle and bull rope?" he asked.

Will turned away so Clay couldn't see the grin on his face. "Whoa there! I got something for you to do first." Jack chuckled, motioning for him to follow. Clay was not able to hide his surprise when Jack led him into the hay barn, stopping beside the stacked bales on one side.

"I want you to take these bales of hay and stack them on the other side of the barn. Start from the top and work your way down to the ground. Don't throw them down."

"Stunned" was hardly the word to describe Clay's state of mind as he stood there with his mouth open. "You want me to move this whole stack of hay from here to over there?" he asked, pointing at the empty side of the barn, which had been cleared of the hay that was used as feed through the winter.

"Well I doubt you'll get it all moved before we get back, but you ought to make a pretty good dent in it."

Clay looked astonished. "I thought we were going to practice. How come I got to move this hay for you?"

"I didn't say you were going to practice. I said we were going to start your training, and that's just what we're doing. Anybody can crawl on a bronc or a bull and they might even make a decent ride on one from time to time, but to become a world champion you have to be both mentally and physically prepared, so that every time you get on one of those animals you're pitting the best you got against him. So now we start gettin' you physically ready. Will, Dottie, and I are going to drive over and look at the cattle in the lower east pasture. We should be gone for about two hours, and when we get back we'll go into town and eat supper. You get as much of that hay moved as you can."

Clay nodded grimly and picked up the pair of gloves lying on the bale of hay. He wasn't sure he was going to like Jack's training program, but he wasn't about to say anything.

When Jack and the Hightowers returned from their tour, they found Clay soaked with sweat, still moving hay from one side to the other. Jack was impressed by the number of bales he had moved. "Go on in the house and take you a shower. I'll do the chores," Jack offered.

Clay plodded up to the house, wiping grimy sweat from his brow with his shirtsleeve as he went. Will, helping Jack with the chores, said, "I hope you didn't overdo it with the hay. You know he's got two rodeos this weekend. You get his muscles too sore and he won't be able to ride worth a dime."

"I thought about that," Jack said, "but Clay's already in good shape. He just needs toning up. He'll be in good shape for this weekend."

Will shrugged. "I'm sure you're right. It's just that I see so much potential in that boy that it would be a crying shame if anything ruined it."

Jack laid a hand on his friend's shoulder. "I know how you feel, but there's more to that boy than just his talent. Right now I'm more concerned about properly developing his character and spirit than I am about his riding. So if I push him a little hard, or I make him a little sore and it causes him to lose one rodeo, he'll know he wasn't in the best shape he could be in. Hopefully he'll want to work a little harder so he can be the best, but it has to be what he wants."

Will smiled. "I never would have believed you were that smart, Jack."

Jack chuckled. "If I were that smart I would have shot you years ago and swear you committed suicide 'cause you were too contrary to live with yourself."

Both men laughed as they started back toward the house.

Chapter Twelve

Will and Dottie left early the next morning on their way to Pecos. Since Clay was entered at Seagraves on Friday night and Pecos on Saturday, he and Jack would have to leave around noon, make the Seagraves show, then drive on to Pecos, where Dottie had reserved them a room in the same motel she and Will were staying in.

Jack let Clay sleep in that morning and didn't wake him until eight o'clock. Clay was surprised at the time but kept quiet, grateful for the extra rest. He took his shower and ate the breakfast Jack prepared. "Will and Dottie get off all right?" he asked between ravenous bites.

"They left about six this morning," Jack said. "How'd you sleep?"

"Like a log. I didn't even hear 'em leave."

"Are you sore?"

Clay raised his arm shoulder high and moved it around, testing his range. "A little," he said, "but I reckon it'll be gone by the time we get to Seagraves."

Jack looked at him with a frown. "Clay, I want you to understand something. If you want to be a world champion you have to be in top shape both mentally and physically."

Clay nodded, saying, "I know."

Jack shook his head. "I'm not sure you do. You see,

it took me a long time to realize just what that meant. I wasted a lot of years chasing the same thing you're after now and all the time I thought I knew how to do it, but it took me too many years to find out what it *really* took."

Clay sat silently waiting for Jack to continue. "The reason I'm telling you this is because you may wonder at some of the things I do, but I want you to understand I'm going to do everything within my power to make you the best you can be. Do you understand what I'm saying?"

Clay nodded. "I think so. I think what you're saying is that if you ask me to stack hay all day it's for my own good, not just so you can get your hay moved so you'll have room for this year's hay when it comes in."

Jack grinned and stood up. "I think you got it. Now hurry up and finish your breakfast so we can hit the road."

They rolled into Seagraves around five o'clock, after stopping in Hobbs, New Mexico, for two hours. Jack contracted for two semiloads of alfalfa hay to be delivered to the ranch sometime during the summer. They had driven out to look at the fields of freshly cut hay so Jack could see the quality for himself. Clay breathed in the aroma of alfalfa, smiling at the delicious scent. "We need to make an air freshener that smells like this," he told Jack. "We could spray it in the house to kill the odor of your feet."

Jack feigned a shocked expression. "I'm not so sure my feet are the ones that stink. I saw a couple of spiders keel over dead the other day when they walked within two feet of your boots."

Clay laughed. "I don't reckon either of us have feet

that smell too good, but if we had a way to bottle the smell of this alfalfa, I bet we could make enough money to wear a new pair of boots every day and wash our feet in rosewater."

"You're probably right. We'll start workin' on it just as soon as we get caught up on all the other things we got to do."

"That should be in about fifteen or twenty years," Clay joked.

"At least," Jack said. "But right now we got a rodeo to make, so let's get going."

Seagraves is hardly more than a wide spot in the road but it looked like everyone from fifty miles around had shown up for the rodeo, and they'd all come early to get a good seat. The parking lot was jammed full and there was no area for contestant parking. They found themselves parking further away from the arena than they liked. "I'm going to go ahead and take my gear up to the chutes so I don't have to make three or four trips to the pickup," Clay said.

"Good idea. I'll give you a hand."

"Thanks. If you'll get my saddle, I'll carry my gear bag."

Jack wouldn't admit it, but it gave his heart a thrill to be able to be behind the bucking chutes where the cowboys were getting their saddles, riggings, and ropes ready for the night's events.

"I'm going to check in and see what stock I've drawn," Clay said, setting his gear bag down in a clear space next to the fence.

Jack laid the saddle down next to the gear bag and took out his wallet. He pulled three fifty-dollar bills from within and handed them to Clay.

Clay took the money hesitantly. "I don't feel right taking this. I know it didn't come from my savings account."

"I'll get it back from your winnings. Now go and get checked in."

Jack remained behind the chutes, talking to several of the young riders getting their gear ready. It was fun to analyze each of the young men to determine which were serious about their events and which were there merely to impress their girlfriends, family, or themselves.

He was listening to one such young man telling another of his great riding abilities when Clay returned. "How'd ya draw?" Jack asked.

"Good in the saddle broncs and pretty good in the bulls, but not so good in the barebacks."

Jack raised his eyebrows in a questioning look.

"I drew Calico. I drew him last year and he ran halfway down the arena before he started bucking. I scored a fifty-eight and the judge wouldn't give me a reride."

"Luck of the draw," Jack said.

"Yep," Clay said dejectedly.

"Who knows? Maybe he'll buck better than he did last year."

"Maybe," Clay agreed, albeit halfheartedly.

"Who'd you draw in the saddle broncs?"

"Crying Shame. He's that big black horse standing over there," he said, pointing to a large black horse standing in the pen behind them.

"Looks like a stout horse," Jack said with approval.

"He's stout all right, and he bucks like nobody's business."

"And I reckon you're going to ride him like nobody's business?"

"You bet I am," Clay said with a grin. "I'm going to cowboy up and ride hard."

"I like that, cowboy up and ride hard," Jack chortled.

The rodeo was due to begin at seven o'clock and Clay had drawn the fifth position in the bareback riding. He was rubbing resin into the handle of his bareback rigging when the announcer began his oration by welcoming everyone to the rodeo.

Jack and Clay stood on the platform behind the chutes and took off their hats as the American flag was carried around by a pretty girl on a beautiful palomino horse.

As the arena cleared of contestants and grand entry participants, Jack told Clay he was going to find a seat in the grandstands.

"But I was hoping you'd stay and help me pull my riggin' and give me some advice."

Jack was taken aback by the request. "Sure," he managed to stammer.

The first bareback rider out of the chute was bucked off in three jumps and Jack couldn't help but smile as he remembered his evaluation of the young man earlier. The next rider made a qualified ride but was weak in his spurring. The judges gave him a sixty-four.

As the next rider climbed down on his horse, Jack remembered watching him earlier. He was curious to see what kind of performance the young man turned in, for he expected it to be a good one.

The announcer's voice was booming out over the PA system, "The next rider out of chute number three is Jason Lambright from Midland, Texas. He's mounted on number sixty-seven, T.R. Now ladies and gentlemen you may wish to know that T.R. stands for

Teddy Roosevelt, and why, you may ask, is he named after Teddy Roosevelt? Well Jim Atkins, owner of Atkins Rodeo Producers, tells me it's because he's earned the reputation of being a rough rider."

Jack watched as Jason Lambright took his seat and worked his hand into the handle of his bareback rigging. Once he was seated with his feet resting on the boards of the chutes, on either side of the points of the horse's shoulders, he reached up and pulled his hat tighter on his head. He then nodded quickly.

The chute gate swung open and the big horse raised his front feet and pivoted on his hind legs, pushing off and into the air as he burst into the arena.

Jason's spurs were locked into the horse's shoulders when his front feet hit the ground. As the horse lunged, he raked his spurs along T.R.'s shoulders and had them back over the points when the beast's feet hit the ground again.

Jack knew he was watching a good ride and was pleased to see his knack for appraising riders was still sound.

Jason Lambright completed his ride in the same fashion he'd begun and was helped to the ground by the pickup men. His score was very good—a seventy-five.

There was one more rider before Clay, and they moved the horses up in the chutes. The bucking chutes were portable, brought in by the stock contractor, and there were only three, so as soon as the first two bucked out they would move the third animal up to the first chute and load two more. That way it enabled the next riders to get their riggings or saddles on while the rider in the first chute rode out.

Calico was herded into the second chute, and Jack helped Clay get his rigging set in place.

"Even if he comes out running, dig your spurs into him and let him have it. I got a feeling if you show good form you'll either get a reride or score high enough to place. I don't think there's enough good riders here to fill all the places, and if tomorrow night is the same, you might take some money home."

Clay nodded as he pushed his hand into the rigging, working the resin until it became hot and sticky on his glove. He sat astride Calico and placed his feet on the boards on either side of the horse's shoulders.

The rider in chute number one had come out and immediately put his feet into the horse's sides, missing him out and receiving a no-score. If the cowboy's spurs aren't in the points of the horse's shoulders when his feet hit the ground on the first jump, thus "missing him out," he receives a no-score.

"See what I mean?" Jack asked.

"Yep," Clay responded, gritting his teeth. "Cowboy up and ride hard."

The pickup men herded the horse out, and the arena director stepped up to the chute saying, "Let's go, son."

Clay eased his spurs into Calico's shoulders and nodded. The gate swung open and Calico stood in the chute, rolling his eyes. Suddenly he turned and bolted, running two full lengths before stopping hard on his front feet and dropping his head between them. He bucked straight for two jumps then ducked back to the left.

When Calico started to run, Clay had expected him to continue. When the horse stopped short Clay was thrown forward on his rigging, and only by sheer strength did he prevent himself from being thrown over the horse's head. Using his right arm as leverage, he pushed himself back behind his rigging and re-gained his balance.

As Calico cut back to his left, Clay was back in con-trol and dug his spurs into the horse's shoulders. As Calico lunged forward he raked his spurs upward.

Calico wasn't a top-ten bucking horse but he had definitely improved since Clay was last on him. After the sudden turn back, Calico bucked straight into the air, turning as he bucked, a hard move to stay in time with. After four such moves he lunged forward and kicked out with his hind feet, stretching himself out fully while still in the air, flexing his muscles in a way that made it hard for any cowboy to maintain his bal-ance. As he hit the ground, he bucked right then sud-denly switched and bucked back to the left.

Clay had managed to stay in time through most of Calico's moves and had raked the horse's shoulders with each jump. As the whistle blew he lowered his feet to the D rings and grabbed the rigging with both hands as the pickup men moved in to help him off.

Clay scored a seventy-two, good enough to move him into second place. Jack slapped him on the back as he came to stand beside him. "He almost lost you there on that first jump, but you recovered real good and made a great ride. Looks like ol' Calico's learned a few moves since you last rode him."

"He sure did," Clay said, shaking his head. "I was expecting him to pull a runaway again and he sur-prised me. I guess it would have served me right if he had. That's what I get for underestimating him."

Jack looked at the young man standing next to him. He had expected excuses, and was proud of him for not making any.

They watched the five remaining bareback riders from behind the chutes. Clay held on to his second-place standing but wouldn't know until after tomorrow night whether it would hold or not. They would call Monday to find out.

They walked over to the concession stand and got something to drink. Jack ordered a Coke while Clay got a bottle of water. They walked around the outside of the arena and watched the people. Several cowboys called Clay by name and girls smiled at him as he spoke to them. They made their way back behind the chute and waited through the calf roping. The saddle bronc horses were soon run into the chutes and stood waiting like patient professionals, having been through the routine many times.

There were nine saddle bronc riders entered and Clay had drawn the last position. Cowboys were busy behind the chutes getting their saddles ready. The first three horses were already saddled when the last calf roper exited the arena.

Jack resumed his evaluation of each of the riders and had to admit there were more dedicated cowboys in this event than there were in the barebacks. The announcer introduced the first rider as he was let into the arena. He had drawn a good horse but didn't spur well and received a low score. The next rider was thrown six seconds into his ride, the horse he'd drawn one of the best in the string.

Jack stood out of the way and watched the riders, mentally noting the things they did right and the things they did wrong. He felt exhilarated just being behind the chutes where the action was. The next three riders rode to the whistle with the best score being a seventy. The next rider failed to mark his horse out while the next was thrown three jumps out of the chute.

Crying Shame was in the chute and Clay, with

Jack's help, was cinching down his saddle as the last horse was driven from the arena. There was one rider to go before him and Clay stood behind the chute, doing deep knee bends to loosen up his legs and hips. When the gate opened, Clay moved astride the big black horse and eased down into the saddle. He reached down and eased the stirrups on his feet, holding them up on the sides of the chute.

The rider in the arena was on the ground and the horse was being moved out as the arena director moved up to the chute. "We're ready to go," he said. "Arena's clear."

Clay picked up on his rein and leaned back, nodding to the gate man. Crying Shame didn't hesitate but turned and sprang into the arena, pushing off with his back feet and leaping into the air. Clay's feet were positioned over the points of his shoulders, his toes turned out. He kept them in place as the black horse came down and when he lunged again Clay brought his spurs along the horse's sides and all the way back to the cantle, his spur rowels singing as they traveled the distance.

Crying Shame bucked straight but hard. Each time he launched into the air his feet cleared the ground by at least six feet. He came back down in a bone-jarring hit and Clay was making a good showing until Crying Shame planted his front feet and pivoted his body, swinging his hindquarters in midair over his shoulders. When his back feet came down, he was heading in almost the opposite direction and Clay lost his left stirrup. It was only a matter of time after that. Without the use of his stirrup he couldn't maintain his balance. The next jump sent him flying through the air, landing on his side in the soft dirt. Unhurt, he got to his feet, retrieved his hat, and started the long walk back to the chutes.

Jack was waiting for him behind the chutes when he got back, but said nothing as they retrieved his saddle. Clay's mood was somber as he climbed down off the fence. "He pulled a good one on me."

Jack remained silent and Clay looked at him, apparently expecting him to say something. But Jack held his tongue.

"I'm going to take my saddle to the truck and then get something to drink," Clay said.

"I'll meet you by the concession stand," Jack said, handing him his bronc halter.

Chapter Thirteen

Clay remained sullen and angry as they sat in the grandstands, watching the steer wrestling. He was still gloomy all the way through the team roping. Though Jack noticed, he said nothing until the pickup rolled into the arena and began setting up the barrels for the women's sport of barrel racing. "How many times you gonna make that ride?" he asked innocently, noticing Clay's faraway look.

Clay glanced at him, knowing exactly what he was talking about but refusing to be drawn into conversation.

Jack placed his hand on Clay's knee, and spoke softly. "If you can't get that ride out of your mind you better drop out of the bull riding."

Clay's face immediately registered anger, but slowly it drained and he nodded his head. "I just can't believe I let that horse throw me."

"It won't be the last time you'll get thrown if you want to keep riding. You remember what I told you in Ruidoso? If you dwell on what might have been then that's what you're gonna be."

Clay let out a deep breath. "I know. It's just that I get so mad when I don't make a ride that I know I can make."

"Getting mad 'cause you got bucked off is all right. You just have to quit dwelling on it, getting yourself all worked up. You've got another ride to make and if you don't get out of the mental state you're in you might as well forget it and we'll head on back to the ranch." Jack's tone had taken on a stern warning which wasn't lost on Clay.

"You're right," he said. "What I need to do is put it out of my mind and start concentrating on the bull riding." He smiled. "Or maybe I could concentrate on her," he said, nodding in the direction of the arena where the barrel racing was taking place.

Jack grinned. "I think you'd do better to concentrate on your ride for now and concentrate on her later."

Clay looked at him in mock surprise. "Jack, you must be getting old if you'd rather concentrate on a bull than a good-looking woman."

Jack burst out laughing. "At my age I probably got more use for a bull."

Clay laughed with him. "I hope I never live to be that old."

Clay had drawn a bull called 007, a Brahma with a wide horn spread. Clay watched as they ran him into the chutes. He was not impressed with the fact that the big bull had to turn his head sideways to get his massive horns through the gate.

"I'm not familiar with this bull," Clay said, "but they say he's a bad hooker," which meant once he had a cowboy on the ground he'd do his best to hook him with his horns.

"That's why I always liked saddle broncs and bare-backs," Jack said. "They don't try to get you once you're on the ground."

"Yeah but the girls don't chase bronc riders," Clay said with a grin on his face.

Double-Oh-Seven was loaded in the second chute and Jack helped Clay hook his bull rope by using a long wire hook to reach beneath the bull's stomach and pull it through the open slat of the chute. As the first rider turned out into the arena, Clay eased down onto 007's back and adjusted his rope to the left of the bull's backbone. Once he had it set where he wanted it, Jack took hold of the tail of the rope and began pulling, taking up the slack and tightening the rope around Clay's hand. When the rope was tight enough Clay nodded, gripping the rope firmly. Jack then laid the end across Clay's open palm, waiting for him to close his fingers again in a tight fist before wrapping it around behind his hand and into his palm again, running the tail between his little finger and ring finger.

Clay moved up on his bull rope as far as he could, almost sitting on his hand. He was ready when the arena director called his name and nodded tensely to the gate man.

As the gate swung open, 007 crouched and his leap into the air was spectacular, causing a stir in the audience.

Clay pulled hard on his rope and dug his spurs into the bull's tough hide. He knew he was in for a ride.

As the big Brahma started to the ground, his front feet hit first and he pivoted to the left, swinging his tail end around. From there he went into a dizzying left-hand spin.

A cowboy that rode right-handed preferred a left-hand spin, as it meant the bull was spinning away from his hand and allowed him more leverage, and Clay was taking advantage of it. He lifted hard on his bull rope and dug in with his left spur, using his right spur to rake the bull's side.

After three spins, 007 switched back and jumped into the air, a move that had unseated a lot of cowboys. But Clay was well seated and able to retain his balance, and he stayed in the middle and dug in with his spurs as 007 slung his head in a backward motion. This was a move designed to intimidate the rider on his back and break his concentration as the massive horns swung toward the man on his back.

Clay ignored the horns and concentrated on his position. He was still seated in the middle of the bull's broad back when the buzzer sounded. Waiting for the bull to move to the left he swung his left leg forward over 007's neck, a move that helped force his hand from the rope as he jerked free. He hit the ground on his feet and dashed for the chutes fifteen yards away.

Double-Oh-Seven had been turning to the left as he felt the rider leave his back, and with the agility of a cat, he swung quickly back to his right, spotting the figure running for the chutes. With head down and horns ready, he charged his victim, rapidly closing the distance between them.

Clay heard the pounding of hooves but didn't turn to look. Straining for all he was worth, he raced for the safety of the bucking chutes as all those standing on the ground climbed quickly to the top rail.

Double-Oh-Seven was only yards away from his quarry and gaining fast. He was like a dive bomber, concentrating only on the target before him and bent on destruction. His entire focus was on Clay's back when something suddenly crossed in front of him and reached out to slap his horns. A new and closer target presented itself and the bull slowed his forward progress to turn after his new target. That move allowed Clay to reach the safety of the chutes.

The rodeo clown, a seasoned bullfighter, moved

nimbly out of 007's way and jumped the arena fence. Jack's heart had been in his throat, and he breathed a large sigh of relief as Clay climbed over the chute and came to stand beside him on the platform.

"You got bull snot on the seat of your pants," Jack said as Clay smiled.

"Clay Tory's score on 007 is a seventy-seven," the announcer said, causing Clay's smile to grow broader. "That makes him the leader in the bull riding."

They stayed until the end of the rodeo, until the last bull rider made his ride. Clay's score held through the first performance but they would have to wait until they called Monday to see if it held throughout Saturday's as well.

Leaving the rodeo grounds at ten-thirty, they found a fast-food restaurant and bought hamburgers and fries before heading off to Pecos.

Driving south on Highway 385, they talked about the rides that were made that night. Jack expounded on what each of the riders did and did not do well. The conversation eventually got around to Clay's saddle bronc ride.

"What did I do wrong?" Clay asked.

"What do you think you did wrong?" Jack asked in return.

"I got bucked off," was Clay's answer.

"Sure did, but let me ask you this: how come you made such a good bull ride, but got bucked off a horse that you should have ridden?"

Clay thought for a moment before answering. "I don't know, except that on the bull I felt in control. I didn't feel that on the bronc."

Jack nodded. "That was evident. How come you didn't get thrown when the bull pulled that switchback on you?"

"I was ready for it. I knew it was coming."

"Uh huh, and how did you know it was coming?"

Clay pondered the question a few moments before answering. "I saw his head move in that direction."

"Exactly," Jack replied, "and I'll bet you didn't see it coming on the bronc."

"Nope, I didn't," Clay admitted.

"If you'll learn to watch the horses' heads the same way you do those bulls' you'll find you can stay with 'em when they make sudden moves. I suspect you try to ride saddle broncs the same way you ride barebacks, just hanging on and riding."

Clay nodded, understanding Jack's point.

"You can't ride saddle broncs the same way. On a bareback you're relying on strength and spurring. Your center of balance is always in the riggin' handle and that doesn't change, 'cause your arm remains fixed to that handle and the handle remains in one place on the horse's back. But with a saddle bronc, your center off balance is in the buck rein, and it's not stationary—it moves, so your center of balance will move too. You have to control that with the saddle swells and by positioning your feet. If the horse changes direction with his head it throws off your center of balance. So you have to anticipate when the change is coming so you can compensate for it."

"That makes sense," Clay said. "I reckon you're right—I have been trying to ride saddle broncs the same way I ride barebacks. I just wish you'd told me this before I got thrown."

"It wouldn't have made as strong an impression if I'd done that."

Clay grinned. "Like letting someone hold my horse while I get on, huh?"

Jack smiled and leaned back in the seat, pulling his

hat down over his eyes. "Yep, now try to keep this thing between the ditches. I'm going to catch a little sleep. It takes a lot out of an old man having to train hardheaded youngsters."

"I'll try to miss the potholes. I wouldn't want to jar your poor old bones too much," Clay said.

"See that you do that," Jack replied, and five minutes later he was snoring softly.

It was almost one-thirty by the time they found their motel and checked in, so it was no wonder they didn't wake up until ten o'clock, when Will Hightower knocked on their door. "I was beginning to think you two had died in here," he said when Clay opened the door, yawning and blinking in the bright sunlight streaming into the room.

Jack sat up in bed and wiped the sleep from his eyes. "What time is it?" he asked gruffly.

"Ten after ten," Will said. "Why don't you two get dressed and Dottie and I'll meet you in the café."

"I got to have a shower," Jack said. "I smell like I've been dead for three days."

"I wondered what that odor was," Clay said, wrinkling his nose. "I kept looking around in the truck last night. I thought maybe some varmint had crawled under the seat and died."

Jack threw a pillow at him, hitting him upside the head. "You don't smell so good yourself, junior. I've smelled dogs that've been left out in the rain that smell better'n you do."

Will laughed at their banter, saying, "I'd appreciate it if you'd both take a shower before coming to the café. We don't want to chase away all their business."

"We'll be there in about thirty minutes," Jack replied. "Make sure they got plenty of hot coffee."

Once they were ready, they made the short walk to the café where Will and Dottie were waiting for them. "You two look a whole lot better and you even smell human," Will said as they took their seats.

"I don't know how I look, but I feel like I've been rode hard and put up wet," Jack said as the waitress filled his cup with steaming coffee. "I think I'm getting too old to pull these all-nighters."

"Nah, you're just not used to it," Dottie said, patting his hand. "In a couple of months you'll be staying out all night and still be rarin' to go the next day.

Jack groaned. "I'm not sure I'll even last a couple of months."

While Jack and Clay ate, they filled the Hightowers in on Clay's rides the night before. Will told them about Friday night's performance and which horses and bulls would be in tonight's rodeo.

Some stock contractors hold their best stock for the Saturday night performance when the crowds are usually larger, trying to make sure that their ticket sales stayed high. This puts the cowboys that enter on Friday night at a disadvantage. But Will Hightower, along with most of the other good contractors, didn't do this. Will had name tags for all his bucking stock, which were put into a hat and drawn for each night. The stock that bucked on Friday night was held out of the Saturday night draw in order to give them a rest.

They all spent the rest of the day driving around Pecos and seeing the sites of the town. They saw the saloon where Judge Roy Bean held court, and walked the streets, window shopping and enjoying the summer afternoon.

They returned to the hotel around three o'clock. Clay and Jack went to their rooms to rest, while Will and Dottie drove out to the rodeo grounds to check on the stock and make sure things were ready for the night's event.

Jack dozed off while Clay resined his bareback rigging and bull rope in front of the TV. He watched a movie until he too fell asleep. They both awoke around five o'clock and went to supper. Jack ordered a chicken fried steak and Clay ordered a salad, not wanting to eat a heavy meal before riding.

They drove to the rodeo grounds around six-thirty. Clay stared at the sign over the entrance: WELCOME TO PECOS, HOME OF AMERICA'S FIRST RODEO.

"Is that true?" he asked Jack.

"Supposedly," Jack answered. "I think Phoenix claims to have had the first one also, but I think theirs was the first to charge admission."

They pulled into the contestant lot and parked the truck. Clay pulled his gear bag from the back and carried it straight to the bucking chutes. Jack marveled at the number of cowboys already there preparing their riggings and bull ropes. It was the same at every rodeo as it had been in his day. The area behind the chutes was a meeting place for bronc and bull riders, a place where they could find their friends and talk about broncs and bulls they'd ridden and rodeos they'd been to, not to mention swapping stories about the women in their lives. It was a haven that had an exclusive membership, and you had to be willing to pay your dues to gain entrance.

The contestant board was located in the alley between the bucking chutes, and they walked over to it to find out which stock Clay had drawn. In the bareback riding he had drawn a new horse called Ragin' Red. In the saddle broncs he'd drawn Bloody Marey, and in the bulls he'd drawn Triple L, named for the brand on his hip.

"Bloody Marey is a pretty good horse," Jack noted. "I watched her in Ruidoso and she bucks hard. I don't remember Triple L, but Will said Ragin' Red was a new horse he'd picked up at a bucking horse sale in Clovis."

"I've never drawn Triple L, but I've seen him several times. He turns back to the right out of the chute. He's not hard to ride and usually places if you make a qualified ride."

Jack took three fifty-dollar bills out of his billfold and handed them to Clay. There was no protest this time when Jack told him, "Go pay your entry fees. I see Will over at the roping chutes. I'm going to go give him a hard time. I'll meet you back here before the rodeo starts."

"Don't get into any trouble while I'm gone," Clay jested.

Jack turned with a grin. "I don't make any promises I might not be able to keep," he said, then walked away humming.

Will and his two sons were busy separating the calves and steers. "If you'd get out of there and leave them alone, your boys would get this job done a whole lot faster," Jack said, leaning on the fence.

"Hey, Mr. Lomas," Carl Hightower greeted, "you're right, but you know Dad, he's got to be in the middle of everything except the real work, like feeding and doctoring."

"Watch it, young man," Will Hightower warned, but his voice carried no severity.

"Could you find something for him to do and get him out of our way for a while so we can get this finished before the rodeo starts?" Terry Hightower, the youngest son, asked, grinning at his father.

"Hmmph, I know when I'm not wanted," Will

Hightower said, climbing over the fence and jumping to the ground beside Jack.

Both of the young men laughed and winked at Jack. He grinned back at them. "Come on, old man, I'll buy you a cup of coffee," Jack said.

"A cup of coffee sounds good right about now. If I have to keep putting up with ungrateful whelps like these two, I might just put something stronger in it."

"I know what you mean," Jack replied.

The rodeo kicked off promptly at seven-thirty with the usual grand entry. Jack was behind the chute to help Clay set his rigging. He was the ninth rider, so they would be able to watch most of the bareback riding.

"I talked to Will about Ragin' Red. He said he's bucked him out three times at home. He threw two of the riders. He belonged to a rancher that got tired of him throwing all his hired hands so he sold him to a contractor that furnished stock for high-school rodeos. He turned out to be too rank for those boys, so he took him to the bucking stock sale where Will bought him."

"Sounds like he might be a good draw."

The bareback riding began with Charles Grayson from Lubbock on Cold Outlaw. He rode to the finish and scored an even seventy, which held first place through the sixth rider when Mickey Tyler scored a seventy-two on Double Barrel.

Ragin' Red was run into chute three and Clay set his rigging on the big sorrel's back, waiting for the man on the ground to hook his latigo—the leather strap used to cinch the saddle tight—and pass it back up to him.

The eighth rider turned out into the arena as Clay

stood astride Ragin' Red with his feet on either side of the chute. As soon as the ride was over and the pickup men drove the horse from the arena, Clay worked his hand into the handle of his rigging and eased down on the horse's back. As he placed his feet on the rails on either side of the horse he leaned back and nodded to the gateman.

Ragin' Red bolted from the chute, ducking his head between his legs and flexing his knees, shooting into the air, bellowing loudly. Upon landing he instantly repeated the move, going higher into the air this time, twisting his body and kicking out with his hind feet.

Clay's spur rowels were ringing out as he raked the points of the horse's shoulders. He was stretched out on the horse's back as he spurred, the bucking motion of the horse snapping his neck each time the beast lunged forward.

Six seconds into the ride, Ragin' Red hit the ground hard, jarring every bone in Clay's body. He then lunged forward with all his eleven hundred pounds of strength and Clay's hand was torn from the rigging. He tumbled backward off Ragin' Red's rear in a complete somersault that would have made a circus tumbler proud, except for the landing, which was a facedown slide in the dirt, which added to Clay's humiliation.

Jack winced as Clay landed hard on the dirt of the arena, then got up and kicked at a dirt clod in anger.

Clay came back behind the chute, his anger under control but still evident. "I know . . . don't dwell on it," he said as he came to stand beside Jack.

Jack nodded. "You'll beat him next time."

The calf roping and steer wrestling passed without conversation. They were both lost in their own thoughts. As the horses were run into the chutes Clay turned to Jack. "What kind of advice do you have for me?"

"Ride the hair off her," Jack simply said.

Clay looked at him as if he'd lost his mind. "Is that all you got to say? Ride the hair off her?"

Jack chuckled. "Yep, right now you're not on your horse yet. When you get in the saddle I'll give you my advice. It'll more likely stay with you that way."

Clay nodded, agreeing with the older man's logic.

Bloody Marey was run into chute number four. Clay set his saddle on her back, moving it up on her withers and positioning it just to his liking. The chute man hooked his latigo and passed it up to him. Clay ran the latigo through the D ring on the girth, which was a wide belt made of braided cotton with a large metal ring attached to the end. He ran the latigo through the D ring again and pulled it tight. Bloody Marey reared and tried to climb the gate in front of her that separated the chutes. Clay quickly grabbed a handful of her mane and pulled her back into the chute. Like other athletes, it isn't unusual for horses to get nervous before performing. Cowboys are as much at risk during the time they're in the chutes as they are while riding.

Clay finished adjusting his latigo while Jack soothed Bloody Marey by holding her mane and talking to her in a calming voice.

The first three riders rode out, with one getting thrown, one missing his horse out, and the other scoring a sixty-nine.

"Your turn," Jack announced as Clay climbed down on Blood Marey's back. He felt her tremble beneath him, but she made no other move as Clay eased into the saddle and placed the stirrups on his feet.

"You're up, Clay," Will Hightower said from his seat on his gray horse.

As Clay reached up and pulled his hat tighter on his head, Jack bent down close to his ear, "Watch her head and remember your balance is in the buck rein. Don't let her get you out of balance."

"Gotcha," Clay said as he nodded to the gate man.

It was the best ride Jack had seen him make. Bloody Marey swung out of the chute and reared on her hind legs. Clay's spurs were over the points of her shoulders when she hit the ground, and moved to the saddle cantle as she leapt into the air, lunging forward.

Clay kept his eyes on the big mare's head. When she swung to the left he was ready for her, using his left thigh against the swell of the saddle and pulling hard on the buck rein.

Bloody Marey bucked first left then right in rapid succession, a trick that had thrown many a rider. But Clay had seen each move coming and had used the saddle and buck rein for leverage. He kept his seat as he raked his spurs from shoulder to saddle cantle.

When the eight-second whistle blew, Clay knew he'd made a good ride. The smile on his face showed his pleasure as he waited for the pickup men to move in and help him off.

"*That* was a saddle bronc ride," Jack beamed when Clay joined him.

"It felt real good," Clay admitted.

"Once we get you in shape and get your balance improved, you might just make a bronc rider."

Clay grinned. "You reckon I might?" he asked with mock sincerity.

"You just might if you listen to what I tell ya," Jack said, smiling back.

Clay scored a seventy-three and won the saddle bronc riding.

Chapter Fourteen

Clay had his rope ready as the bulls entered the chutes. Triple L was the first bull in and as Clay dropped the tail of his rope down beside the animal, it jumped forward and kicked the chute behind it. The chute man hooked Clay's rope and passed it back up to him.

The last barrel racer exited the arena as a pickup truck drove in to remove the barrels.

"Get him ready, Clay," Will Hightower said.

Clay eased down the chute, carefully placing his legs on either side of the Triple L. As he did, the bull lunged forward in the chute, squeezing Clay's legs against the chute rails. Helping hands reached down and lifted him out. Even though each cowboy competes against the other cowboys, they never hesitate to help prevent injury to another.

When Triple L settled down, Clay eased down on the bull's muscular back. Though he flinched, the bull quickly settled down. Clay set his hand in the handle of the bull rope and Jack began pulling it tight.

Ready to ride, Clay moved up on his rope, held his left hand up, and nodded for the gate.

As Triple L burst out of the chute, Clay set himself for the move to the right. Sure enough, two thousand pounds of bull dropped his shoulder and started right, but with a twist of his body, quickly turned back to the left.

Clay had already set himself for the move to the right by shifting his weight to the left, so when the bull turned back to the left his feet were pulled behind him and he was lurched to the side away from his hand. One more lunge by Triple L had Clay off his back, but his hand was still wound tightly in the rope. The one thing all bull riders fear is being hung up on a bull, and Clay was now in that exact predicament. He knew his best chance to prevent injury was to remain on his feet as long as possible; once down, the chance of going beneath the bull was almost certain, and being stepped on by a ton of bull was to be avoided at all costs.

The rodeo bull fighters moved in quickly when they saw Clay was in trouble. One moved to the head of the bull, waving to keep its attention away from Clay, while the other moved in to help free his hand from the rope.

Triple L was still bucking against the flank strap. Clay was finding it difficult to keep his feet under him, but he managed to remain upright as the bull fighter grabbed the tail of his bull rope and pulled in an attempt to loosen Clay's hand. When that failed, he moved in closer and grabbed Clay's hand, trying to jerk it free. Both the bullfighter and Clay were locked in an awkward dance with Triple L, one on each side of the large animal, each trying to keep time with the bull's lunge and turns. The other bull fighter kept working to keep Triple L following him, ducking and weaving to prevent being hit by the bull's angry head.

Clay was yanking his hand, trying to free it from the handle of the bull rope, but felt no give. Suddenly Triple L tired of the bullfighter in front of him and turned his attention to the man hanging on his side. As he turned sharply to his left, Clay felt himself slipping down. His legs buckled under him and Triple L's back hoof came down right on his foot. When it lunged forward again, it jerked Clay beneath him, pulling the arm still hung in the bull rope until it stretched all the muscles and tendons to the point of tearing.

Between the agony of being stepped on and the pain in his arm Clay felt himself close to blacking out. Suddenly his hand was pulled free by the sheer force of Triple L's weight and he fell beneath the animal. The big bull pushed off with his back feet, releasing Clay's trapped foot, but as his hoof came up it caught Clay in the side of the head. It was like being hit with a hammer. Clay went down in the soft dirt of the arena.

Turning on his front feet, Triple L lowered his head and charged the inert form on the ground, burying the knubs of his horns into the small of Clay's back. Both bullfighters moved in to draw Triple L away but not before he managed to grind his head into Clay's back and ribs.

The bullfighters finally managed to draw the big bull away and mounted cowboys rapidly moved in between Triple L and Clay. Once the bull was at a safe distance, several cowboys rushed over to Clay. He was semiconscious when they reached him. The paramedics hurried into the arena, carrying their medical bags. The crowd parted to let them attend to Clay.

He moaned as one of the paramedics gently rolled him over and pulled open his eyelid, shining a penlight in his eye.

"Can you hear me?" one asked.

Clay managed a weak, "Yes."

"What's your name?" he asked.

"Clay," came the hoarse reply.

"Do you know where you are?"

"On the ground," Clay answered.

Though the paramedic didn't laugh, several of the cowboys hovering over him did, relieved that Clay didn't seem to be critically hurt.

"What town are you in?" the paramedic tried again.

"Pecos, Texas," Clay replied.

"Okay," the paramedic said, satisfied that Clay still had all his faculties about him, "can you tell me where you hurt?"

"All over," Clay said, trying to sit up.

"Just lie down and let us check you out," the other paramedic said, pushing him gently back down.

Clay groaned and closed his eyes.

The paramedics checked him out thoroughly, making sure there was no spinal or neck injury before finally helping him to his feet. Jack was right beside him, worry etched on his face, though he was trying hard not to show it.

Leaning on Jack and another cowboy, Clay limped from the arena. Jack promised the paramedics he would take him directly to the emergency room for X rays on his arm, back, foot, and head. "He definitely has a concussion, so make sure he gets thoroughly checked out," the paramedic instructed him.

Dottie was waiting outside the arena gate. As they came through, her maternal instinct took over. "Let's get him into my pickup. It's right over here. Will can drive yours when he comes."

They drove Clay to the emergency room, where they spent four hours getting X rays taken. It took the emergency room doctor, who wasn't the least bit fond of people who took what he called unnecessary chances, two hours to get around to reading the X rays and diagnosing Clay's condition. He ran Jack and Dottie out of the examining room while performing his examination on Clay. In the waiting room it was all Dottie could do to keep Jack from storming back in and choking the daylights out of the arrogant young doctor. When he finally did come to talk to them, Jack was fit to be tied. Dottie held on to his arm to make sure he didn't do anything rash.

"He has a mild concussion and a sprained ankle," the doctor explained in a tone that left no doubt about his frigid feelings. "The ligaments in his right arm are damaged but they'll heal. He doesn't have any broken or cracked ribs and there doesn't appear to be any damage to his spine, but he is badly cut and bruised and he'll be sore for several days. I'm giving him some pain pills to hold him tonight and tomorrow, and I'll give you a prescription so you can pick up some more on Monday when you get home. If he has any trouble with his vision or has any dizzy spells tonight, bring him back in."

Jack nodded, but said nothing, not trusting himself to speak. The doctor hurried away after delivering his curt message.

Dottie had called the hotel and gotten them rooms for the night, as there was no way she was letting them drive home.

Will came in just before they released Clay, having to take care of loading the stock and getting it headed back to New Mexico before he could leave. He had collected Clay's gear and driven Jack's pickup to the hospital.

The pain pills they'd given Clay at the hospital had taken effect by the time they got to the hotel, and he required assistance getting in the room and into bed. He was fast asleep before the Hightowers left.

Jack sat down on the edge of the bed, exhausted, watching Clay sleep. He wondered if he'd be able to stand much more of this. He also wondered for the thousandth time how he'd gotten into this. He smiled wearily as he looked at the sleeping figure in the bed next to his. "I reckon the Good Lord knew how much we needed each other, but I swear if you ever scare me again like you did tonight I'll wring your neck," he chuckled and reached down to pull off his boots, sighing as he did.

Clay woke up at nine o'clock the next morning, groaning as he sat up. Jack was already dressed, sitting in the only chair the room provided, drinking a cup of coffee and reading the Sunday paper. "How do you feel?" he asked watching Clay's slow movements.

"I hurt in places I didn't know I had. Even my hair hurts."

"Next time you pick a dance partner make sure it's one that won't step on your feet." Jack chuckled.

Clay tried to grin, but even that hurt. "Where's Dottie and Will?"

"They left about an hour ago. Dottie didn't want to, but Will and I finally convinced her you were going to live."

"Are we absolutely sure about that?" Clay asked, gingerly rubbing his head.

"I imagine right about now you feel like you have to get better to die, but take my word for it, you'll survive. If you feel up to it, we'll get you dressed and get something to eat, then I'll drive us home."

It took them half an hour to get Clay dressed and almost that long to make the short walk to the café.

The three-and-a-half-hour drive home went without incident. After eating, Clay took another pain pill and was asleep before Jack turned onto Highway 285 heading north toward Carlsbad.

When they arrived home, Clay groggily stepped from the pickup and walked straight to his room. He was asleep in a few moments, and Jack went about doing the chores. He made two phone calls, the first to Ben Aguilar.

"We've had two more reports of stolen cattle in the southern part of the county. It sounds like the same bunch—they move into a pasture at night, drive the cattle into a makeshift chute, and load them into a trailer, leaving very few clues. We have tracks from the pickup, trailer, and horses. The tires on both the pickup and trailer are the most common type sold and there's nothing unique about the hoofprints, but if we ever catch 'em, hopefully we can make a match."

Jack wasn't cheered by the news, but at least the thieves were working in the south part of the county for the time being.

The second call was to an old friend Jack hadn't seen in years. They talked for a long time, catching up on each other's past. When they finally hung up Jack felt a little better.

It was a full week before Clay was able to do anything. Jack had insisted on taking him to see his own doctor, saying he didn't trust that quack in Pecos. However after examining him, Dr. Johnson said almost the same thing but with a little more finesse and understanding. "It'll just take time for everything to heal. You've been banged up pretty bad," he said to Clay, "and fortunately you're young and you'll heal fast. But don't try to hurry it. If you push too hard, you'll just delay the healing process."

By the end of the week Clay was moving about with little pain. He had called and withdrawn from the Lubbock and Carlsbad rodeos and entered in the Artesia and Alamagordo rodeos for the following week. He and Jack had agreed that Clay would not ride bulls for a few weeks. Though Clay had argued he would be ready, Jack requested that he give it some time, and Clay honored his request.

By Monday, Clay was back in the saddle, riding the pastures and checking fences, counting cattle and monitoring the water tanks at the windmills. The summer rains had been good and the grass was plentiful in all pastures. Each morning Jack and Clay sat at the kitchen table discussing what needed to be done and dividing up the tasks between them.

Tuesday afternoon Jack was waiting for Clay when he rode up to the barn. "How you feeling?" he asked, noticing Clay wasn't stiff as he dismounted.

"Fine," he replied. "My ankle's still a little sore but it doesn't hurt and my arm's good. It doesn't ache when I move it anymore."

"Good," Jack said. "It's about time to start your training."

Clay moaned. "Come to think of it, my head still hurts quite a bit and my back's been killing me."

Jack cut his eyes at him in a disbelieving look. "Well, we'll just have to work that out of you."

"Oooh," Clay moaned, "you're not going to make me move hay again, are you?"

Jack chuckled. "Nah, this won't hurt you a bit. I've been working on this for several days," he said, leading him to the side of the barn.

Clay followed close behind and as they rounded

the corner, what he saw surprised him. There were three two-inch pipes each twenty feet long, set at different heights. The first was set up on wooden blocks about a foot high. The second one was about two feet off the ground on short sawhorses, and the third was three feet off the ground. Each pipe had ears, welded and nailed down so they couldn't move.

"What in the world is this?" Clay asked, walking around the contraption.

"This, young man, is the first stage of your training," he said, pointing to the lowest of the pipes.

"How does it work?"

Jack walked to the end of the lowest pipe. "I'm glad you asked. Step up here and the training will begin."

Clay stepped cautiously up on the block and stood there looking at Jack.

"Start walking," Jack said.

"Walking where?" Clay asked, looking around.

"The pipe," Jack said. "You walk the pipe down and back without falling off."

Clay's eyes registered surprise. "How is this going to help me ride?"

"By working on your balance. Strength and knowledge are important parts of riding, but balance is critical. You can be as strong as an ox and know everything about riding, but if you don't have balance you can just forget it. Now you have reasonably good balance but you don't have *great* balance, and that's what you're going to work on here. You'll start on the one-foot rail first. When you've mastered it, you'll move to the two-foot rail. When you've mastered that one you'll move to the third and when you've mastered that one you'll move to the rail around the arena."

Clay was dumbfounded. He'd thought he'd heard

of everything but this was a new one on him. "Are you sure this will improve my balance?"

"It worked for me," Jack said, "except I started out on rails five foot high. The falls were harder but I think it was more incentive for me to try harder. I don't want to add to your injuries so we'll just start out easy and work our way up."

Clay moved tentatively out on the pipe, getting only two feet from the end before stepping off. He started to step back on where he fell off but Jack stopped him. "Nope, you start over at the end, it'll give you more incentive to try harder to stay on."

Clay sighed and his shoulders slumped, but he walked back to the end of the pipe and started over. "I'm going in to start supper. You keep working, I'll call you when supper's ready," Jack said.

Clay nodded and fell off the pipe again.

Jack whistled as he walked to the house, looking back when he reached the door. He saw Clay make it halfway across the pipe before falling off, and noted the frustration in his face. He hummed "Tumbling Tumble Weed," an old song sung by the Sons of the Pioneers, and turned back into the house.

The next few days the two of them settled into a routine. Jack would wake Clay up at five o'clock in the morning so he could work on the balance rails for an hour before eating. Over breakfast they would discuss what needed to be done that day. After washing the dishes they would leave for their day's work, meeting back at the ranch house by five o'clock to work on Clay's training.

Jack went to town one day and came home with a set of training weights, including devices that would help increase the strength of Clay's grip. By Thursday, he had Clay on a light workout, making sure he didn't aggravate any of his recent injuries.

By Friday, Clay was walking across the one-foot rail and back, seldom falling off.

"Keep it up and you may graduate to the two-foot next week," Jack said.

"Yeah, or go to work for the circus as the tightrope walker," Clay lightly responded.

The Artesia rodeo, though not big, had good stock, and after the first night's performance Clay was sitting second in the barebacks and winning the saddle broncs.

He had placed third in the barebacks and third in the saddle broncs in Alamagordo. By the time they started home, Clay was feeling the strain on his body. Not fully recovered from his injuries, Clay's arm felt like a leaden weight and ached badly. He refrained from taking any more pain pills, realizing how easy it would be to get addicted to them, physically and mentally. He also knew he could do more damage to his arm by always removing the pain.

Sunday morning they went to church, giving Jack a chance to talk to several of the other ranchers and catch up on local happenings. He was pleased to find that Ben Aguilar had been working with the Chavez County Cattlemen's association to use extra men to patrol the local roads. Ben was now in the process of working up plans for communication and area coverage.

"We've got three extra men hired through the association," Clyde Lewis told him, "and Ben will be coordinating the whole thing. He's really come around."

"I'm glad," Jack said. "I think if we all work together on this, we'll eventually catch these thieves and put an end to this."

"There's an association meeting tomorrow night here at the church. You going to be here?" Clyde asked.

"I should be," Jack answered.

"Good. We need as many members as possible present. We have several items on the agenda that need to be discussed and voted on."

After a leisurely lunch at the Blue Bonnett Café, they went back to the ranch and spent the afternoon planning the next month's rodeos. Jack talked Clay into playing a game of gin rummy. He hadn't played cards since his wife died and playing now with Clay brought back peaceful memories of a time long past.

As dusk settled in, Clay went down to feed the saddle horses and barn stock while Jack prepared them a light supper. He fixed them each a bacon, lettuce and tomato sandwich and waited for Clay to return. After waiting for twenty minutes he walked to the screen door to call the boy, but just as he opened the door he noticed Clay sitting on the arena fence, staring out over the horizon. Closing the door silently behind him, he walked down to the arena and leaned on the top rail next to Clay. "Anything bothering you?" he asked.

Without looking at him, Clay answered, "Nope, I just wanted to watch the sunset and enjoy the evening."

"It is beautiful." Jack commented. "I used to spend a lot of time watching sunsets and pondering my life. It was some of the best times. I came up with some of my best ideas sitting right here on this fence. Of course, I didn't always use them or put them into practice, but I sure had some good ones."

Clay smiled. "I know what you mean. Sometimes at the end of the day, when things are really peaceful and the pressures of the world all seem insignificant, I can come up with some ideas that seem to be almost brilliant, at least to me. Then when a new day comes and the pressures are back, those ideas don't seem so brilliant anymore."

Jack looked at the young man, knowing exactly what he was talking about. "Have you come to any brilliant deductions this afternoon?"

Clay looked out over the horizon again. "Only that I can't believe I'm here. I can't believe that there's horses and bulls for me to practice on and I can't believe we were just sitting in there planning rodeos we're going to next month."

"I find it pretty hard to believe myself," Jack said. "If someone had told me four months ago that I'd be traveling to rodeos with a kid that has a bad attitude, won't listen to advice, and almost gives me a heart attack by trying to do the two-step with a one-ton bovine, I would have told them they were crazy. But that's what I'm doing and I couldn't think of doing anything else."

"Do you really mean that?" Clay asked.

Jack put his hand on Clay's arm and looked into his eyes. "I really mean it. I haven't felt this young in years."

Clay laughed. "It has been some kind of trip, hasn't it?"

Jack nodded. "It sure has."

They stayed there in silence watching the sun descend behind the mountains. As darkness closed in on them, Jack pushed away from the fence. "I'm going in to get something to eat."

Clay swung around on the fence and jumped to the ground, falling in beside Jack. "What do you mean bad attitude?" he asked.

Chapter Fifteen

The routine started over again Monday at five-thirty in the morning. Clay worked on the balance beams for an hour, then came in for breakfast.

"I think we'll drive over to the south pasture this morning and finish that windmill. We should have it finished by noon. I need to go into town this afternoon and pick up some parts for the hay baler, and I got an association meeting tonight. You want to see a movie or something while I'm at the meeting?"

"I think I'd rather go see Shirley Roberts, if that's all right."

Jack laughed. "Isn't that the girl you went to see when you got into all the trouble?"

Clay blushed. "The same," he replied, "but it wasn't her fault. She and Joe Hanson had already broken up, and that's why I went to see her. If they'd still been going together I wouldn't have gone close to her."

Jack recalled a time when he might not have believed him, but now he knew without any doubt Clay was telling the truth.

"Well I sure wouldn't want to stand in the way of your love life," Jack said. "The meeting will probably last till about ten o'clock. You reckon that'll give you enough time? If not you can take the Dodge."

Clay smiled. "That should be enough time. We'll

probably get a burger and run out to the caliche pits for a while."

Jack's eyebrows raised slightly, but he just nodded.

The windmill took longer than expected, as is generally the case. It was after two when they finally rolled into Roswell. They went to the bank first, where Clay deposited his winnings from the rodeos. Jack had him keep fifty dollars for expenses, though Clay argued against it.

"If Ben finds out we'll just say I gave it to you to buy groceries," Jack said.

Clay smiled and put the money in his billfold.

They went by the John Deere store and picked up the parts Jack needed for the hay baler and put in an order for hay twine. As they left the store Clay asked, "If you bale your own why did you buy hay in Hobbs?"

"Because the hay I cut is just prairie hay. It's a good filler but it doesn't have the protein alfalfa has. I feed the prairie hay first as a supplement when the grass starts dying, then I feed the alfalfa during the winter along with cake." Cake was what they called the hard molasses cubes of cattle feed.

They went to the feed store and picked up some horse feed and mineral blocks, then stopped by the courthouse to talk to Ben Aguilar.

"How you doin'?" Ben asked as they stepped into his office.

"Great, Ben. Any breaks on our cattle thieves?" Jack asked.

"None yet. There hasn't been another robbery since I talked to you last time."

"You going to the association meeting tonight?" Jack asked.

"I was planning on it," Ben responded. "You going to be there?"

"Yep," Jack replied. "I think if we all work together we can catch these thieves."

"It could be," Ben replied. "Thanks to your suggestion I think this could work if we all coordinate together."

"That's the secret," Jack replied, "but I didn't come here to talk about catchin' cattle thieves. We'll get enough of that tonight." Ben chuckled and nodded.

"I wanted to know if there were any other young men like Clay here that wanted to ride saddle broncs or bulls." He glanced at Clay and wasn't disappointed to see the look of shock on his face. "As you know we got three broncs and two bulls out at the place, but we need some help bucking them out, and we need some bullfighters and pickup men to help. I figured if there were some boys around who wanted to practice we could get them and their fathers to help out for the opportunity to practice."

Ben leaned back in his chair, reflecting on what Jack had just said. "I think I know a couple of boys that would jump at the chance to get some practice and I can probably round you up a couple of good bullfighters to help out, too."

"That would be great," Jack said. "Why don't you have them get in touch with me."

"I'll talk to them this week and have them give you a call," Ben replied.

They talked for a while longer before leaving. "I'll see you in a little while," Jack said as they left the office.

Clay dropped Jack at the church at six-thirty. Instead of going directly to Shirley's house he decided he would first run by the discount store and pick up a few things. Pulling into the parking lot, he drove into one of the marked spaces. He was starting to step out when someone suddenly grabbed him and pushed him back in the seat. At the same time another person opened the passenger door and climbed in. Clay was pushed to the middle, sandwiched in between the two interlopers. He felt his spine tingle as he heard the harsh laugh. It was his father. He turned to look at him, then at the sneering face of his older brother Warren.

"What do you want?" he asked in anger.

"Now just settle down, little brother. Daddy's got something to say to you and we wanted to make sure we got your full attention."

Clay felt the sweat begin to run down his back. "What do you want to talk to me about?" he asked, turning toward his father without looking directly at him.

Jason Tory snickered, giving Clay an involuntary shudder. "Eager little snot aren't you?" the elder Tory asked. "Well, Junior, we got plans and we need your help."

"I don't want any part of your plans," Clay said, looking from one to the other.

Warren Tory reached over and slapped Clay's face with the back of his hand. It wasn't hard enough to do any physical damage, but the humiliation of it caused Clay's hackles to rise.

"Now, Warren, there's no need to be hittin' your little brother like that. He's going to be real cooperative. He just hasn't heard all the facts yet."

Clay, rubbing the side of his face, knew when his father spoke in that tone of voice, nothing good was coming.

"What do you want?" he asked again.

"Well now that you asked," Jason Tory said, putting his arm around Clay's shoulders, "we need you to find out what's going on at the association meetings."

"Why don't you just go to them and find out yourselves?" Clay asked sarcastically and instantly regretted it as Jason's arm tightened around his neck.

"Because, Junior, we ain't been invited. Besides, we don't just want to know what's goin' on tonight. We want to know what's goin' on with these men they're hirin'. We want to know where they're patrollin' and when."

Clay struggled against the crushing arm around his neck. "Why do you want to know that?" he asked.

Jason Tory laughed again. "Why, so we can help them, of course."

Warren Tory laughed too. "Yeah, we want to help them catch those sorry cattle thieves."

"You'll get us that information or we'll take away your meal ticket," Jason Tory said.

"What do you mean?" Clay asked, suddenly frightened.

"What I mean," Jason said, as if disgusted with the question, "is that if you don't do what we tell you, we'll make sure Mr. Jack Lomas meets with a bad accident, and if that happens they'll throw you back in the county jail."

"You do anything to Jack and I'll make sure you spend time in jail," Clay said vehemently.

Jason Tory laughed once more. "And how are you going to prove it?" he said, tightening his armhold on his son's neck, his rancid breath strong in Clay's face.

Clay was as scared as he'd ever been in his life. He knew now that his father and brother were somehow involved in the cattle stealing. Why else would they want to know about the patrols that were being set up by the association?

"Now you're going to tell us what they're up to or, like I said, Jack Lomas is going to have trouble he can't handle. If you tell anybody about our conversation, I promise you they'll find Mr. Lomas by following the buzzards to his carcass."

Clay shuddered again at the thought. "But I don't know anything about what's going on. I wasn't invited to the meeting either," Clay spoke, trying to convince them.

"No, but Jack Lomas will tell you," Jason Tory said.

"What if he doesn't?" Clay asked. "He doesn't tell me everything."

"Maybe," Jason Tory replied mockingly. "But a smart boy like you can find a way to get him to tell you, and you better hope for his sake that he does. Now I'll be expecting a call from you by Wednesday night, telling me about these patrols the association is footing the bill for."

"Is that all?" Clay asked.

"Not hardly, Junior. I want to know exactly where these patrols are being placed and what times they'll be patrolling."

"But Jack won't know that," Clay protested. "That will be handled by Sheriff Aguilar."

"Like I said, a smart boy like you can come up with a way to find out, and find out you will," Jason Tory said, giving his son another brutal squeeze before releasing him.

"We're going now, but you heed my warning. You don't come through you'll be responsible for what happens." Warren got out of the truck, slamming the door behind him, but Jason Tory turned back to his youngest son. "Oh yeah, if you're thinking of telling

Jack about our visit tonight, I wouldn't. Any hint that Jack knows about it and we'll make sure he finds out you were a part of it all along. And if Jack Lomas wouldn't side with his own son you can bet your hide he won't side with you." With that, he got out of the truck and was gone.

Clay sat where he was, his mind in turmoil. He didn't move for thirty minutes, but replayed the scene over and over in his mind, going over what his father had said and wondering what he was going to do.

He finally got out of the pickup and walked into the discount store. Finding the pay phone, he called Shirley to tell her he wouldn't be able to come by, giving a lame excuse that he had to help Jack with some errands. He knew there was no way he could be with her tonight with this trouble on his mind. She'd know something was up and he didn't want to tell her what had happened, not right now anyway.

He drove around the streets of Roswell trying to come up with a solution to the situation. He still hadn't come up with anything by ten o'clock when it was time to pick up Jack.

Clay talked very little on the way home except to ask about the meeting and how it went.

"Fine," Jack said. "I think we've got all the bugs worked out and everybody seems to be in agreement about what we're going to do."

Clay started to question him about their plans but caught himself. He still hoped there was another way out of this without having to betray Jack's trust.

He tossed and turned all night, getting very little sleep. When Jack woke him at five-thirty the next morning, Clay was tired and irritable. Jack noticed his sullen attitude. "Anything wrong?" he asked.

"No nothin's wrong," he snapped, "why do you ask?"

"No reason," Jack said as he watched him walk out the door and head to the barn. *Must be girl troubles,* Jack said to himself and shrugged, turning back to the kitchen.

Clay remained silent during breakfast, only nodding as Jack outlined the day's work ahead of them. He saddled his horse after eating and rode out without saying anything. Jack watched him go, a frown creasing his face.

That afternoon wasn't much better. Jack had Clay work on the balance pipes and lift weights, but he could tell Clay's mind wasn't on his training. He continually fell off the pipe and only half attempted to work with the weights. Finally Jack had enough. "Something's eatin' you. What is it?"

Clay gave him a furious look. "Nothin's eatin' me! I'm just tired of all this silly nonsense. I don't believe any of this is going to help me ride any better." He stomped off toward the arena and left Jack standing there with his mouth open.

The mood at supper that night was tense. No words were spoken between the two as they ate. After dinner, Jack washed the dishes, something Clay usually did, but tonight he had retreated to his room after eating very little of his meal.

The phone rang and Jack, drying his hands on the towel tucked into his belt, answered it, expecting it to be for him. He was surprised when a male voice, one he didn't recognize, asked for Clay. Not wanting to eavesdrop, he called Clay and handed him the receiver, and walked back to his bedroom.

"Hello," Clay said, wondering who would be calling him.

"Hey, Junior." The slippery voice made Clay stiffen. "You find out anything I need to know?"

Clay glanced down the hallway to make sure Jack wasn't close enough to hear. "I haven't had time to find out anything," Clay responded in a whisper.

"You've had time. You rode home with him last night," Jason Tory hissed.

"I didn't want him to get suspicious. It's going to take me some time to find out what went on."

"You got until Friday," the elder Tory said. Clay could tell there would be no bargaining.

Clay had made up his mind he would make something up to tell them, hoping it would buy him some time until he could figure out what to do.

As if reading his mind, Jason Tory said to him, "Don't think you can feed us a bunch of bull and get by. We got ways of checking on your information. You lie to us and Jack Lomas is history, and it'll be on your head. By the way you look real good trying to walk across them pipes."

Clay gasped. "What do you mean?" he asked, but the phone had already gone dead. He hung up and walked unsteadily to his room.

Jack heard his door close and came out of his room, hesitating by the closed door. For a moment he considered going in and confronting Clay, but thought better of disturbing the boy's privacy, and went on to the kitchen.

Clay heard Jack's footsteps slow as he approached the door. While one part of him dreaded the thought of him coming in, another part seemed to scream for him to open the door. He knew if Jack came in, he would tell him everything. So Clay willed Jack not to open the door.

His thoughts turned to his father's parting words.

How could they know about the balance rails unless they were watching them? If they were able to watch Clay and Jack without being noticed that meant they were close enough to carry out the threats they'd made. It made his skin crawl just to think about it.

Jack sat at the kitchen table, a worried frown on his face. He didn't know what to make of Clay's change. At first he suspected he had had a falling-out with his girlfriend, but after thinking about it, he knew Clay would never let a girl affect him in this manner. No, whatever it was, it was eating away at Clay and he wouldn't tell him what it was. And what about the phone call tonight? What was that about? Clay had a few phone calls since moving in, but none had been secretive. Something was going on and apparently Clay was in some kind of trouble, but until he was ready to talk about it there was nothing Jack could do but be patient and understanding, something, he admitted to himself, he had never been real good at.

Jack finally turned out the kitchen light and went to his bedroom.

Clay lay on his bed, still fully dressed. He'd been watching the light underneath his door. When he saw the light go out and heard Jack's footsteps padding down the hallway, he let out a weary sigh. He knew he was causing Jack to worry and it made his stomach knot up to think about it, but he didn't know what to do. He had no doubt about his father carrying out his threat and now that he knew they were watching him it made him even more afraid.

He lay there in the dark wondering what to do, and for the first time he could remember, he prayed for an answer.

Watching the hands on the illuminated clock, he saw midnight come and go. He was still worrying when a plan suddenly started to form. What if he were to gather the evidence against his father and the others and turned that evidence over to Ben Aguilar? Ben could arrest them without them ever knowing who had uncovered their illegal acts. That way, he could protect Jack and still do what his father asked. As the plan began to come together in his mind, he smiled. That was the solution, the only solution. Lying in the dark, Clay allowed himself to smile. "I can do this," he thought out loud.

Chapter Sixteen

Jack was sitting in the kitchen the next morning when Clay walked in. The clock over the sink showed it was five forty-five. "How come you didn't wake me up?" he asked, pouring himself a cup of coffee.

Without looking up Jack spoke dryly. "Because you don't seem to think my training plan is helping you, so I didn't figure you wanted to get up early."

Clay dropped his eyes, feeling ashamed. "I'm sorry about what I said. I was just having some problems and they were making me crazy."

"Anything you want to talk about?" Jack asked, looking at him.

"Nah, it was just something personal. I got it worked out." He sat down at the table across from Jack. "I know I was in a bad mood yesterday, and I'm sorry I took it out on you."

Jack looked up at him with understanding. "I reckon we all have bad days. I seem to recall having a few of my own."

Clay chuckled. "Yeah I bet you have."

Jack looked up, feigning anger. "I'll have you know I'm one of the most even-tempered men around."

Clay laughed again. "Yeah I heard you're the most even-tempered person around. You just stay mad all the time."

"Hmmph," Jack blurted out. "Rumors. All rumors."

They both laughed as the tension between them passed.

Clay gulped the last of his coffee. "I guess I better get out there and work on those pipes—we've got rodeos this weekend," and with that he hurried out, leaving Jack sitting there with a smile.

Later in the day they loaded the Dodge with tools and sucker rods, which were the twenty-foot lengths of pipe used to pump water from the wells. One had broken in the east windmill and had to be replaced, an arduous task. While Clay drove, Jack lost himself in his thoughts. Clay looked tentatively at him, then mustering his courage he asked, "Has the association hired the new men to patrol yet?"

Jack looked up from his reverie. "We've hired three of them and we're going to hire four more."

"Have they worked out the areas where they'll be patrolling?"

"Not completely, but we figure they'll start on the south end of the county first, since that's where they hit last."

"That makes sense, but doesn't that kind of leave us unprotected?" Clay asked.

"For the time being it does, but as soon as we get the other men hired they'll be working the north section."

"Are these guys going to carry guns?" Clay asked.

"No," Jack said with emphasis, "that's one of the stipulations Ben made us agree to. No guns. They'll be given radios and cellular phones so they can stay in contact with the sheriff's office."

"Will they have regular routes to patrol?" Clay asked.

Jack hesitated, looking at him, and Clay wondered

if he'd gone too far. He didn't want to make Jack suspicious. "No, they'll vary their routines. All of that will be st up by Ben."

"Sounds good," Clay said. "I just hope they catch 'em real soon," and nothing he'd said was more true.

Late that afternoon while Jack was in the barn, Clay went to the house and dialed his father's number. When the elder Tory answered the phone, Clay told him everything he'd found out, which wasn't that much and Jason Tory said as much. "I could have found all this out by reading the paper."

"Look," Clay said vehemently, "this thing is just beginning. That's all I know. That's all Jack knows."

"It had better be. If I find out you're holding anything from me, Junior, our next meeting will be at Mr. Lomas's funeral. You got that?"

"Yeah I got it," Clay said bitterly and hung up the phone.

Clay was entered in the Clovis rodeo Friday night and La Mesa, Texas, Saturday night. Since both rodeos were close, there was no need to spend the night away from the ranch.

Clovis was only seventy miles from Roswell so they didn't have to leave until three o'clock in the afternoon, but Clay asked to leave early so they could stop in Roswell and buy a few things. They stopped at the local discount store and Jack remained in the pickup while Clay ran in, saying he would only be a moment.

He hurried to the electronics section and quickly found what he was looking for. It took him longer than he'd expected to find someone who could explain the operation of the device, and even longer to get through the checkout. He was almost dancing with impatience by the time he paid for his purchase and walked out. He had bought some tape as well, and opening his gear bag in the back of the truck, he placed all the items inside.

"Did you get what you needed?" Jack asked, with impatience in his voice.

"Yep." Clay smiled. "I'm all set."

"Good," Jack replied. "I thought I was goin' to have to send the law in to get you out."

"There were long lines at the checkout, that's what took so long," he explained.

"Can we go to the rodeo now or do you need to stop for something else?"

"You sure are impatient, aren't you?" Clay said with a smile.

"Putting up with hardheaded bad-tempered children makes me that way," Jack said, pulling his hat down over his eyes and leaning back in the seat.

Clay turned onto Highway 285 and headed north, and by the time he turned onto Highway 70 Jack was snoring softly.

Though Clay was almost fully healed, he hadn't entered the bull riding at either rodeo. He had refrained from entering because, though he didn't say it, Clay knew Jack didn't want him to ride. But he also knew that he loved riding bulls too much to stay off them very long.

Clovis is a town of about thirty thousand people. It hosts one of the best horse auctions in the Southwest. "Yep, I've bought many a horse right here in this town," Jack said as they came to Clovis's outskirts. "I bought the best horse I ever owned right here. He was a six-year-old gray gelding that came off the Chapman ranch. They sold him because he'd gotten caught up in some barbed wire and cut his back leg. The cut wasn't that bad, and I bought him for a hundred and sixty-eight dollars. Took him home and doctored his leg every day. Washed it with a water hose twice a day. It took me six weeks to get him healed. He was the best cow horse I ever rode. He could go to a cow like nothin' I'd ever ridden, and I'm tellin' you, that horse could cut on a dime and give you back seven cents' change. I could rope fifty head off of him in a day and he'd work the rope on the last one just as good as he did the first."

"What happened to him?" Clay asked.

Jack's face went blank and Clay noticed a tightening of his jaw. "He got killed," was all Jack said.

It was only five o'clock when they pulled into the rodeo grounds, but things were already a beehive of activity. The stock was being cordoned off in the holding pens while cowboys and cowgirls were exercising their horses in the arena. They found the contestant board and looked at the horses that Clay had drawn. General Jackson was his draw in saddle broncs and Bay Watch was his bareback horse.

Since Circle C was the stock contractor, Clay knew little about the horses, only what he'd heard from other riders. He'd never seen the horses that he had drawn perform.

"At least I won't be anticipating their moves," he said.

Jack raised his eyebrows. "That's true, but it is kinda nice to know how a horse bucks. Let's see if we can find the contractor and talk to him a little."

"Sounds like a plan to me," Clay said.

By asking around, they found out the owner was a man named Gary Taylor, and he was at the roping chutes, sorting calves.

When they got to the roping chutes, they asked for Gary Taylor and were pointed in the direction of a

large man about forty years old. They waited by the
roping boxes until Gary was through with his work,
and climbed over the fence before they walked up to
him. "Gary?" Jack asked, waiting for him to turn.

"Yeah," he said, "what can I do for you?"

"This is the first time for Clay here to ride your
stock and we were hoping you could tell us a little
about the horses he drew."

"Who'd you draw?" he asked, looking at Clay.

"Bay Watch in the barebacks and General Jackson
in the saddle broncs."

"You drew pretty good," he said. "Bay Watch is a
real good horse. He has a brand on his hip, number
fifty-six, the bay over there with one white stocking.
He comes out of the chute hard and comes out bucking. He never bucks the same way twice. One time
he'll come out and buck to the left, throwing his feet
out to the right, the next time he'll buck straight and
jump high."

"What about General Jackson?" Jack asked.

"He's not the best I've got, but he'll give you a good
ride. He bucks hard and straight. If you get in time
with him and spur, you'll score high enough to place.
We have some good judges here and they're fair."

"We appreciate the information," Jack said. He had
been watching Gary Taylor and noticed something familiar about him. "Have we met before?" he asked.

"I don't think so," Gary said.

"My name's Jack Lomas," Jack said, introducing
himself.

Gary Taylor smiled and extended his hand. "I was
wrong—we have met before, Mr. Lomas. But I was
only ten or twelve then."

Jack looked at him curiously. "I'm sorry, son, but
I'm afraid I don't remember."

"I wouldn't expect you to," Gary Taylor said. "My dad is George Taylor; does that ring a bell?"

Jack broke into a big smile. "George Taylor! Well I'll be," he said, "I haven't seen George in twenty, twenty-five years. What's he doin' now?"

"He's living in Arizona. He moved down there 'cause of his arthritis," Gary said.

Jack turned to Clay, saying, "George Taylor was one of the best calf ropers and steer wrestlers going down the road. We used to travel together some in the old days."

Gary Taylor smiled. "Dad still tells stories about you and him and Will Hightower. I used to watch you and Mr. Hightower. You two are probably what made me want to ride saddle broncs."

"If memory serves me right," Jack said, "you did all right for yourself for a while."

"I made it to the finals a couple of times," Gary said, "but I never could win the world championship. Finished third one year, and that's as close as I got."

"That's not bad," Jack said. "There's a lot that don't make it that far."

"Yeah, but my dream was to open a saddle bronc school and it's hard to do without that title."

"Looks like you've done all right here," Jack said, impressed.

Gary looked around. "Yeah, if I can't rodeo or teach, this is the next best thing."

They had walked back to the bucking chutes while they were talking. "Well, I guess I better get back to work so we can get this rodeo put on. I'll see ya'll later."

As they walked back to the pickup, Clay turned to Jack. "I swear I can't take you anywhere."

Jack looked at him questioningly. "What do you mean?"

"I mean for some reason you just can't seem to get along with people. You really need to learn how to loosen up and make friends."

Jack smiled. "I think you're just jealous, youngster."

"I might just be," Clay said. "I might just be. You know when I first met you I thought you didn't have any friends at all, but I'm finding out you got a lot of friends, and they're the good kind of friends, ones that will always remember you. You're a lucky man, Jack Lomas."

Jack remained silent, thinking about what Clay had said. He hadn't thought about it before but now he realized he *did* have a lot of friends and that was something to be thankful for.

They left the rodeo grounds and drove into town. Jack wanted to look at some new hay balers and since they had tractors there as well, he looked at what they had to offer. The implement dealer was closed but that didn't stop Jack from looking. "My old baler has about had it and I'm going to have to replace it, but I don't know whether to replace it with a new one or a good used one."

"I've always heard that buying used ones is just buying a headache that someone else got rid of," Clay said.

"There's some truth to that," Jack said. "I once bought a used baler at the beginning of summer. That thing had so many problems I lost all my hay that season because I couldn't get it to work. But I've bought some good used balers, too. The last one I bought was new and it's lasted twelve years. I've probably baled a million bales of hay with that thing. I just don't think I'll be around to bale another million."

"Ha," Clay said, "you're too mean to die. You'll be around for another fifty years just so you can make people's lives miserable."

"You might be right. Especially if you're the one I'm making miserable."

"That works both ways," Clay said.

"You're too late, youngster, you've already made my life miserable," Jack said, grinning.

"Yeah and I've only just begun."

Jack groaned. "You mean I can expect more from you?"

"You bet you can," Clay said, laughing.

They drove back to the arena, both in a better mood. Clay had forgotten all about his problems, his mind now on the two rides he had for the night.

They carried Clay's gear bag and saddle behind the chute and once again Jack felt the exhilaration of being behind the action. The smells that drifted to his nostrils might have upset some sensitive noses but to him they were the greatest smells on earth. The smell of horses, bulls, leather, tobacco, and resin came wafting to him and he breathed it in, reveling in the earthy odors.

The bareback horses were loaded into the chutes and the grand entry began. After the announcer welcomed the audience, there was the national anthem and the invocation, then the action began.

The arena had six bucking chutes and Clay would be coming out of number four, so he had his gear bag ready when his horse was run in. Bay Watch was standing quietly in the chute when Clay eased his rigging down on his withers and waited for the chute man to hook his latigo strap. Jack stood beside him and helped him set his rigging. Bay Watch lunged forward as Clay began tightening the cinch.

The first rider was already in the arena, and Clay
and Jack stood back and watched. The horse was a
good one, bucking hard and using several tricks that
made him hard to ride. The rider was trying to spur
but he was overmatched and soon had his spurs in
the D rings of the girth instead of over the horse's
shoulders, squeezing hard with his knees. He barely
made the whistle and hit the dirt soon after. His score
was a sixty-two.

The second rider scored a seventy on a horse that
wasn't nearly as good as the first, but he rode hard
and spurred well. The third rider was making a winning ride but lost his grip just before the whistle and
was thrown over the rear of the horse.

Clay was straddling the chute when they drove the
horse from the arena. He worked his way down on
Bay Watch's back and reached for the handle on his
rigging, just as Bay Watch reared and lunged forward.
Clay had no hold and as the horse reared he felt himself slipping down into the chute. Fear clutched him
as he grabbed for a handhold. His mind flashed back
to Pecos, feeling the same terror he did when he got
hung up on Triple L. Sweat beaded his brow. Going
under a horse in the chute was the worst nightmare
for any cowboy.

Just as he felt himself slipping off the horse's back
strong hands grabbed him and pulled him up and
over the chute rail. As Clay regained his feet he
looked up into Jack's face, his arms still around him.

"Thanks," Clay said earnestly, standing up straight.

They had Bay Watch settled down and standing
quietly in the chute again. Clay eased down on the
horse's back and worked his hand into the rigging.

He positioned himself without further incident, and
when he was finally ready, nodded to the gate man.

His feet were turned out and his spurs were over the points of Bay Watch's shoulders when his front feet hit the ground on the first jump.

Just as Gary Taylor had said, Bay Watch charged out of the chute and began bucking. He turned left and bucked high into the air, swinging his feet to the right side, leaving Clay's back parallel to the ground.

Laying along Bay Watch's back, Clay made sure his spurs raked in time with every lunge the horse made.

Bay Watch tried several different maneuvers to lose the stubborn rider aboard him. After coming back to the ground after several sunfish moves, he tried rearing on his hind legs and switching directions by pivoting on his back legs. Being unsuccessful with that move, he bucked up next to the chutes, trying to rub his passenger off on the rough boards.

After moving away from the chutes, he bucked down the arena, kicking high in the air as Clay's spurs continued to rake his shoulders.

When the whistle blew, Clay was still laid back and spurring. The pickup men moved in and he grabbed hold of the saddle and slipped to the ground. The crowd was applauding his ride, and Jack was smiling.

When the announcer called out Clay's score, he waved to the crowd in appreciation as they applauded his seventy-seven.

Clay retrieved his bareback rigging. After putting it in the pickup, he and Jack found seats in the grandstands and watched the calf roping.

The object of calf roping is to use a rope measuring approximately thirty feet to rope the calf. The calf is given a head start by using a barrier rope, which is stretched across the roping box and tripped by the calf when he leaves the chute. The length of the barrier is based on the length of the arena—the longer the

arena, the longer the barrier. If the roper breaks the
barrier by leaving too soon, he is given a ten-second
penalty, which usually puts him out of the money.
Most ropers practice hitting the barrier just as the calf
releases it. The same barrier is used in the steer
wrestling.

Once the calf is caught, the roper dismounts and
runs down his rope to where the calf is waiting, usually not patiently. Grabbing the calf by the flank and
holding the rope, he has to throw the calf to the
ground. Using a short rope called a pigging string,
which is carried in his teeth, the roper ties three of the
calf's legs together with two wraps and a half hitch.
The clock is stopped when his hands release the pigging string. While the roper is on the ground, his
horse has to keep the rope tight by backing up against
it. A good calf horse works the rope and keeps it just
taut enough to hold the calf without pulling it too
tight. That's the reason good calf roping horses sell for
a premium.

The calf ropers were in rare form that night. The
first three ropers roped and tied their calves in over
ten seconds. The next two missed and the next two
tied their calves in under ten seconds.

The leading time in the calf roping before the last
four calf ropers was a nine point three. The next calf
roper roped and tied his calf in nine point one, electrifying the already stunned silence. The next calf roper
tied his calf in a nine flat and the arena exploded in
noise, with people cheering, stomping and whistling.

The tension was thick in the arena as the next-to-
last calf roper entered the box. Nodding, his calf was
let out, and he hit the barrier just as it released. Two
swings of his rope and he threw down at his target.
The loop settled neatly around the calf's neck and the

roper pulled his slack and stepped off his horse. The horse slid to a stop and the rider was propelled down the rope toward the calf. Reaching the calf, he flanked him easily, and with the smooth motion that only comes from hours of practice, he wrapped the three legs and finished them off with a half hitch to hold them in place.

His horse had worked with him beautifully, keeping just the right amount of tension on the rope. Once the roper had successfully tied his calf, the horse had to step forward, allowing the rope to slacken. The calf had to stay tied for ten seconds after he's ridden forward. If the calf got up during the ten seconds, the roper was disqualified.

The crowd waited in anticipation for the roper's time. "Ladies and gentlemen, we have a new leader in the calf roping," the announcer stated. "Jim Hayes has just roped his calf in eight point nine seconds!"

The crowd stood up applauding and whistling in a deafening roar. "This is one of the best calf ropings I've seen in a long time," Jack said.

"It's been exciting," Clay agreed, "and we've still got one to go."

The next roper was settled in the box and a hush fell over the crowd. He nodded for his calf and the race was on. He made his catch just out of the chute and was down the rope in short order, flanking his calf and unpending it to the ground. Two quick wraps and a half hitch, and his hands flew into the air. He walked back to his horse and after mounting rode forward to allow slack in his rope.

Once more, tension mounted in the grandstands as they waited for his time.

"Folks, you're not going to believe this but we have a new leader once again in the calf roping. Carl Jenkins has just turned in a time of eight point eight seconds. Now, I don't know how anyone is going to beat that but you can bet the ropers tomorrow night will be doing their best, so don't ya'll miss it." The crowd, going wild now, wouldn't dare.

Chapter Seventeen

After the calf roping they walked back behind the chutes. Six horses were loaded, and cowboys were busy placing their saddles on their backs. Clay was the tenth rider, so he would get an opportunity to see most of the other bronc riders before his turn. His rig was ready so he and Jack stood on the platform behind the chutes and watched the rides.

The first two riders bucked off, the third rider made a qualified ride and scored a sixty-nine. The next rider failed to mark his horse out and was disqualified. The next two were qualified rides, one scoring a sixty-seven and the other tying the leader with a sixty-nine.

General Jackson, a broad red horse with a blazed face, was run into the number three chute. Clay picked his saddle up and eased it down on the large horse's back. Other than a slight quiver, the big horse stood quietly as his latigo was hooked and passed up. While Clay was cinching his saddle, Jack slipped his bronc halter over the horse's head and buckled it on.

Two more riders had ridden out; one had bucked off and the other scored a sixty-three. Only one rider remained ahead of Clay, and when he went out the gate, Clay gripped hold of his rein and climbed down into the saddle. The rider in the arena rode the eight seconds but missed his horse out, receiving a score of zero.

"Get ready," the arena director called as the pickup men herded the bronc out of the arena.

Clay was in the saddle and ready, his feet over the points of General Jackson's shoulders, his rein held at a predetermined length. Pulling his hat down, he held his left hand high and nodded.

General Jackson pivoted on his back feet and tore into the arena. Clay's feet were over the points of his shoulders when his front feet touched the ground. Clay's spurs raked all the way to the saddle cantle as General Jackson jumped into the air.

Clay was watching the horse's head as he rode. He felt in balance with the animal and knew Jack's training had improved his skills. His timing was in perfect rhythm and he almost felt as if he were one with the big animal.

General Jackson was bucking hard and straight, his back legs kicking way up into the air. It was a classic ride, Clay spurred from shoulders to cantle, with each jump his seat firm in the saddle. Six seconds into the ride Clay knew he was going to make it to the whistle. He'd never before felt as confident on a saddle bronc as he did now. He felt in control, as if he could ride forever. Pulling hard on the buck rein and using his thighs against the saddle swells, he kept himself centered on the big horse.

The whistle blew and Clay smiled. Even if he didn't win he knew he'd ridden this bronc to the best possible ride and that meant almost as much. On the ground, Clay's smile broadened as he walked the short distance back to the bucking chutes.

"We have a new leader in the saddle bronc competition," the announcer's voice rang out over the speakers. "Clay Tory's score is a seventy-one!"

Clay basked in the applause and accepted congratulations from the cowboys on the ground. "Good ride," several said appreciatively as he walked by.

Jack was stone-faced when Clay came up to him. "Well?" he asked, waiting for Jack to say something.

"I reckon you did all right."

"All right?" Clay said in astonishment. "It was the best saddle bronc ride I ever made!"

"It probably was," Jack agreed, "but a good bronc rider would have scored at least a seventy-five on that horse."

Clay shook his head, not believing what he was hearing. "What could I have done to score any higher?"

"Oh, I reckon you could have done your nails out there or polished your boots," Jack said with a grin.

Clay realized he'd been pulling his leg all along. "Dad burn you, Jack Lomas, I thought you were serious!"

"You rode real good. You get to where you can ride that way consistently and you'll be ready to go pro."

Clay beamed at the compliment. "I could tell there was a difference in my riding. It was like I had control the whole time and knew what was coming before it happened."

"That's the way it goes when you have it all together," Jack said.

"Yeah, and it felt good too," Clay said with a smile.

They got back to the ranch before eleven o'clock and got a good night's sleep. When Jack got up the next morning the sun was just coming up. He walked into the kitchen and was surprised to see the light was already on.

On the stove, he saw the coffee had been made and was still hot. He poured himself a cup and walked to the front door. Looking out the screen door, he saw

Clay down at the barn working on the balance rails. He had graduated to the highest rail and Jack watched as he walked gracefully across it and back without falling. Smiling, Jack walked back into the kitchen and started fixing breakfast.

They left for Lamesa at noon, taking their time on the drive. Jack wanted to stop in Hobbs and verify the shipment time for his hay. He also wanted to stop in Seminole and look at some more baling equipment. They would start baling hay next week, and he had made up his mind to buy a new hay baler.

It took them an hour to find the man in Hobbs and another hour of talking weather and hay conditions before they learned the hay would be shipped in another three weeks.

The stop in Seminole proved to be more productive. Jack found the hay baler he was looking for and purchased it on the spot, with guaranteed delivery on Monday. By the time they finished and drove the short distance to Lamesa it was already six o'clock. They drove straight to the arena, and after carrying the saddle and gear bag to the area behind the chutes, Clay hurried off to find the contestant board. His draw in the barebacks wasn't as good as he'd hoped. He drew a horse called Tic Tac that wasn't one of the better stock. He drew the same horse in the saddle broncs that he'd drawn in Seagraves—Crying Shame. When he told Jack, all he got was a wide grin.

"What are you smiling about?" he asked.

"That's a good horse," Jack replied. "You ought to be happy."

"I'm tickled to death," he answered back. "I've been wantin' a rematch with that cayuse since he threw me at Seagraves."

"Good," Jack replied, "but this time I want you to ride him."

"I plan to," Clay said with steely conviction.

Clay rode Tic Tac for all he was worth but only received a score of sixty-six. He'd hoped for a reride and approached the judges, but they wouldn't award him one.

Sometimes if a horse doesn't perform well, or a cowboy is fouled coming out of the chute or during the ride, the judges will award him a reride. The rules at most rodeos state that you can request one if you feel you deserve it, but it's up to the judge's discretion whether he allows one or not.

Clay was upset but he didn't let it get to him. Jack was impressed with the way the boy handled himself.

They watched the calf roping again from the grandstands and were behind the bucking chutes when the first horses were run in. Clay was number three in the order, and Crying Shame was waiting in the chute. Clay had his halter on and his saddle cinched down when the first rider left the gate.

Clay saw the rider slip to one side after the third jump of the horse. He knew he was going to get thrown and at that point should have pushed away from the horse and fallen free and clear. Whether it was inexperience or that the rider didn't realize the danger he was in, he slipped further down on the horse's side and with one more buck was thrown straight down, his foot turning sideways in the stirrup as he fell. As his head hit the ground he was jerked upward by the bucking horse, his foot hung up in the stirrup. He looked like a rag doll on the end of a stick as the horse bucked down the arena, his back feet grazing the cowboy's head each time they came in contact with the ground.

There was nothing the cowboy could do. He was at the mercy of the bucking horse. Most saddle bronc riders split the sides of their boots in an attempt to prevent such an accident, but sometimes even split boots won't come off if the cowboy's foot is wedged in tight.

One of the pickup men had shaken out a loop in his rope and moved in behind the horse. His loop settled neatly over the horse's head. He dallied around his horn and eased his horse to a stop, trying to prevent the saddle bronc from turning on top of the cowboy. He maneuvered his horse to the same side the cowboy was on so as to turn the horse away from his captive prisoner and hopefully prevent any further damage.

As the horse was brought to a standstill facing down the rope, several cowboys rushed forward. They eased down the rope, talking soothingly to the bronc until they had his head held. The fallen cowboy was unconscious as they released his foot from its trap. Dragging him away from the horse, they laid him on his back and moved away as the paramedics bent over him.

It took another ten minutes for the medical team to complete their examination. The cowboy regained consciousness before they brought in a stretcher and carried him out. Clay had been watching the whole episode and felt sympathy for the rider, but he shook it off and turned his concentration to the ride before him.

The arena was cleared and the second rider was ready. He nodded for the gate. His horse wasn't a strong bucker and he rode cleanly to the finish, scoring a sixty-five. Clay was ready when the arena director called for him, and he nodded for the gate.

Crying Shame came out of the chute ready to do battle with Clay again. He jumped high and came down stiff-legged, jarring every bone in Clay's body, but Clay was centered in the saddle and had a tight hold on the buck rein. The black went into a straight buck, kicking his back feet high into the air. Suddenly, while his back feet were in the air he pivoted on his front feet twisting his body to turn sharply right. This was the trick that had lost Clay in Seagraves, but this time he had been watching and saw Crying Shame's head move and was ready for it. He pulled hard on the buck rein and squeezed with his right thigh, and as the horse came around Clay was still in the saddle and spurring hard. The rest of the ride was picture perfect, with Clay in full command of the ride.

The whistle blew at the end of eight seconds and Clay was still spurring. He was elated with his ride and the judges gave him a seventy-two, which held first place through the rest of the bronc riders. It was harder to tell who was more pleased with the ride, Clay or Jack. Both were all smiles as they stood behind the chutes talking about what Clay had done.

It was a festive ride back to Roswell, with talk about the rides that had been made, and which horses had performed well, and which cowboys would make it to the top and which wouldn't. "You know I thought you were crazy when you told me walking those rails would improve my riding, but I can sure tell a difference since I've been doing it."

"I'm sure these new bronc riders probably have some newfangled way of doing it, but all I know is the old ways, so that's what we got to work with."

"You won't hear me complaining," Clay said and Jack raised his eyebrows in a look of disbelief. "Well not much anyway," he said, grinning.

Sunday was a leisurely day. They got up and went to church, ate lunch in town, and then drove back to the ranch, where they spent the afternoon playing cards and lazing around the house. Jack caught up on his back issues of *Farm and Ranch* Magazine, while Clay changed the stirrup leathers on his bronc saddle. Clay was sitting on the floor checking his handiwork when Jack spoke. "I got an association meeting tomorrow night. If you wanna go into town with me, you're welcome to."

Clay had been so caught up in the events of the past few days that he'd forgotten his father's threats. Jack's mention of the association meeting brought it all home. "Uh, yeah, I'd like that," he stammered.

"You gonna go by and see Shirley?" Jack asked with a hint of a smile.

"Uh, I guess," Clay said, his mind churning. He knew he had to get some more information to pass along to his old man or he'd catch him off guard like he did last week. Clay had no desire to meet face-to-face with his father again, though he knew he would probably have to in order to carry out his plan. Hopefully, that wouldn't be for a while.

"Well, my new hay baler is being delivered tomorrow and I want to get some hay cut so we can try it out and make sure it works."

"I'm starting to sweat, just thinking about it," Clay said.

"Just think of it as part of your training," Jack said, grinning broadly.

"This is one part of training I could live without," Clay groaned.

"Well, you won't have to do it all by yourself. I've hired three hands to come and help."

"Who are they?" Clay asked with interest.

"Lewis Green, Brad Hall, and Chuck Tanner," Jack said.

"I know all of those guys," Clay exclaimed in a surprised voice. "Lewis and Brad ride bulls and Chuck rides saddle broncs."

"Yep." Jack said, "They're going to help us get the hay in and we're going to help them with their riding, starting next week."

Clay smiled. "You're a whole lot smarter than you look."

"I'll take that as a compliment," Jack said with a solemn face.

They were up early as usual the next morning. Clay worked for an hour before breakfast on the balance rails. After a big meal of eggs, ham and pan-fried potatoes, they hooked the mower up to the tractor. Clay started cutting the hay pasture while Jack pulled the old hay baler out of the barn and greased its parts. "I want it to be ready in case something goes wrong with the new one."

"That's not being very optimistic," Clay teased.

"One thing you learn about baling hay is to be prepared. I realize it's a new baler, but when I bought this baler it took me two weeks to get the kinks worked out of it before I could start baling. I lost almost the entire field."

By the time the baler arrived, Jack had several rows of hay wind-rowed and ready to bale. The hot southwest sun had dried it quickly and enabled them to begin baling shortly after noon. The new hay baler worked admirably, and by four in the afternoon they had baled all the hay they'd cut and were ready to call it a day.

After a shower and a quick bite, Clay drove Jack to

Roswell. The meeting started at seven and Jack liked to get there by six-thirty.

"Do ya'll meet in the sanctuary?" Clay asked, a plan forming in his mind.

"Nope, we meet in the basement in Fellowship Hall. That way we can make some coffee and relax."

Clay was lost in thought the remainder of the trip. He dropped Jack off at the front of the church and waited until he went in before pulling out of the lot. He drove down the street and parked three blocks away from the church and sat waiting. He kept the radio on for the noise but his mind wasn't on the music. Looking at his watch, he saw it was now ten after seven. He got out of the truck and after making sure the doors were locked, walked the three blocks back to the church. Not wanting to be seen, he ducked behind some bushes when he saw a car's headlights coming down the street. The car passed by without incident, and looking both ways to make sure no one else was around, Clay walked the remaining distance to the church.

Clay remembered the meeting was being held in Fellowship Hall, but he was eyeing a hallway that ran along beside it, separating it from the Sunday school rooms. In his mind's eye he recalled seeing the vent that had been in the wall between the hallway and Fellowship Hall. If he could position himself close to that vent without being detected, he could listen to the meeting and wouldn't have to question Jack about it later.

Opening the big doors that entered into the sanctuary, Clay eased inside, keeping his hand on the door until it silently closed behind him. The sanctuary was dimly lit and he could see the door in the corner that led to the stairs to the basement. He walked silently to the door and eased it open, and heard dim voices coming from below. Letting the door close softly, he tiptoed down the stairs, the voices growing louder the closer he got to the bottom. The stairs ended in a hallway, with Fellowship Hall on the right. The door to Fellowship Hall was about thirty feet down the hallway, and the vent was fifteen feet beyond that.

Clay eased along the opposite wall, walking slowly on the balls of his feet, the carpeted hallway muffling his steps. He could hear his heart thumping loudly as he passed the door. He could now hear the voices plainly on the other side of the wall as he neared the vent. Ben Aguilar was talking about the new men they had hired, and when they would begin their rounds.

As there was no need for it, the lights hadn't been turned on at this end. The only light in the hallway was a single overhead bulb at the far end. Clay moved past the vent, glad to be engulfed in darkness.

He lay down on the floor and listened to the conversation from within. He heard the voices and tried to identify which voice belonged to each of the five men in the meeting. Besides Ben Aguilar and Jack, Clyde Lewis and Clyde Jones were there along with Travis Cunningham. Clyde Lewis had just asked Ben what areas he was going to concentrate on patrolling.

"We've got the three men we hired earlier circling the southern part of the county, with two of my deputies concentrating on that part as well. The four men we just hired will be relegated to the northern part of the county along with two more of my deputies."

"What roads will they be patrolling?" Clyde Jones asked.

Clay listened intently, making mental notes of the

things he would tell his father. He was so focused on
what was going on inside he almost made a fatal error
in staying too long. The meeting was ending and the
men were getting up to leave before he realized it was
over. Jumping to his feet, he moved quickly down the
hallway and was almost up the stairs when the door
of the hall opened. He didn't look back, hurrying out
the door at the top of the stairs and fairly running
down the aisle and out the front door. By the time he
reached the bottom of the stairs outside he was in a
full sprint, and didn't stop until he got to the pickup.

He fumbled with the key, trying to unlock the door.
He couldn't believe his hand was trembling as he finally got the key in the door and unlocked it. Starting
the truck, he put it in gear and raced around the corner. He had to come back to the church from the opposite direction to avoid suspicion.

Jack was silent as the men walked outside. He had
been the first to leave the meeting, and had seen the
figure going up the stairway. He was shocked to see it
was Clay, hurrying from the basement and out of the
church. Why was he there? What could he possibly be
doing in the church basement? If he was there to pick
him up he wouldn't have been hurrying out, and now
he was nowhere to be seen. Standing there, with these
questions running through his mind, he saw Clay
turn off Main Street into the parking lot. Saying good
night to the other men, he walked to the pickup, not
sure how he was going to handle this situation.

Clay had his nerves under control when Jack
climbed into the pickup. "Did ya'll have a good meeting?" he asked innocently.

Jack tried not to look at him as he answered. "It
went pretty well I think."

"Did they hire the new men?" Clay asked.

"Hired four more," Jack answered.

"Good. Maybe with all these patrols they'll catch the thieves soon."

"I hope so," Jack said. "I'm tired of all these meetings, but at least it's giving you a chance to see Shirley. How's she doing?"

"Fine." Clay didn't like lying to Jack, and his response was weakly spoken.

"You'll have to invite her out to the ranch sometime. I'm sure she'd like to see where you're living now."

"She works all week. It'd be hard for her to come during the week and we're usually gone on the weekend."

Jack nodded. "I'd like to meet her. Maybe she can get off sometime. Or," he said as if it was an afterthought, "she could come to a rodeo with us."

"Uh, yeah, she'd probably like that," Clay said but his voice didn't sound that positive.

Clay was in the field early the next morning, cutting hay while Jack began raking what they had cut the day before into large wind rows. It was a full day's work and they kept at it all day with Clay cutting and Jack wind-rowing. By the end of the day they had the field ready to bale.

"We'll start baling in the morning as soon as the dew dries," Jack said that night after supper.

Clay could only nod. He was exhausted from the day's work and had no energy left for conversation. He hadn't gotten a chance to call his father that day, but he hoped he could tomorrow. The sooner he got the evidence he needed, the sooner he'd be able to turn it over to Ben and hopefully put an end to his father's dirty dealings.

Jack was just as glad there was no conversation that night. He had plenty of time during the day to think about Clay's presence in the church the night before. He could think of no good reason for him to be there and no reason for him to sneak around about it. He wasn't sure he could carry on a conversation with him without asking why he'd been there, and he wasn't sure he wanted to know. He was thankful there would be other people around tomorrow. He needed some more time to think about it.

Chapter Eighteen

Lewis Green, Brad Hall, and Chuck Tanner showed up the next morning at seven o'clock. Jack had the baler ready to go. The hay trailer, a flat bed, was hooked up to the other tractor. By putting the tractor in low gear and heading it down the rows of bales, little correction was needed for it to stay on track while the boys loaded and stacked the hay.

Hauling hay is one of the hottest, most strenuous jobs there is. Once they had the wagon loaded they took it to the barn, unloaded it, and stacked the hay inside. There was little or no breeze in the barn, and soon all four boys were soaked with sweat after the first load.

"I ain't gonna be able to ride any bulls by the time we get through with this," Brad Hall said, wiping the dripping sweat from his brow.

"Think of it as training," Clay said with a grin.

"Training?" Lewis Green asked in disbelief. "I'd rather be training around April Bowen's swimming pool. She sure does look good in that new bikini she got."

"How would you know?" Chuck Tanner asked. "She ain't invited you to swim since she started going out with Ron Tallman. Seems he's the only one that ever gets invited over to her house anymore."

"That shows what you know. She invited me over two weeks ago. We swam all afternoon. She made me lunch and even gave me one of her dad's beers to drink."

"You're full of it, Lewis," Brad Hall said, laughing. "I happen to know April and her folks have been gone on vacation for the past two weeks, and Ron went with them."

Lewis looked at him in surprise, his face giving him away. "I know that, but I didn't think you did. You got to admit it sounded good though." All four of them laughed as they drove back to the hay field.

Jack was pleased with the amount of hay he got out of the meadow. The counter on the baler registered six hundred and thirty-two bales of hay. Counting the eight broken ones that he had to go back and rebale, he got six hundred and twenty-four bales on his first cutting. Hopefully, if the rains kept coming, he would get at least one more cutting this year.

He washed the baler off and was putting it in the barn when the boys brought in the last load of hay.

"Ya'll unload that and come up to the house. Mrs. Avery brought over some homemade ice cream for us. I'm going to go ahead and get started on it, and if you hurry, there might be some left." He chuckled as yells of protest followed him to the house.

"Hey, Clay," Brad Hall said, "what's it like living with old man Lomas?"

Clay thought about the question. How could he possibly tell them what it had been like these past few months. How could he explain to them that it was probably the best thing that had ever happened to him and he couldn't imagine living anywhere else or with anyone else. "It's all right," he said.

"I bet he's really hard to get along with," Lewis said, throwing up another bale of hay.

Clay grabbed the bale and threw it further up the

stack to Chuck. "Nah, he's not so bad, and he's really helped me with my riding. I've been placing at almost every show."

"Really?" Lewis asked. "I'll bet he makes you toe the line though, doesn't he?"

"Sort of," Clay said, "but he keeps me in shape and he's taught me a lot."

"Do you know what happened to his son?" Chuck asked. "My dad said he got killed and that Jack Lomas almost died too. He wouldn't tell me what happened but it must have been real bad."

"Yeah, my uncle once told me that Jaimie Lomas— that was Jack's son, had fallen in with the wrong bunch and had done something that had put him at odds with Jack, but he wouldn't tell me what it was, just that he and Jack were having problems when he was killed," Lewis said.

"You know, it's strange how nobody talks about what happened," Clay said. "It's like they all know but they won't say anything."

"My dad says it's out of respect for Jack. He says when Jaimie died everyone that knew what happened agreed not to talk about it," Chuck explained.

"That's weird," Clay said. "I've never heard of anyone keeping a secret that long. Much less a whole town."

"You're right. I guess that's why Jack Lomas always seemed so mysterious to me," Lewis said.

Clay said nothing more, but he couldn't help wondering what had happened between Jack and Jaimie. He remembered that night in Roswell when his father had said Jack wouldn't even side with his own son. He wondered if that had anything to do with the secret surrounding the Lomases. He was sure he didn't want to find out the answer from his father.

Once they were finished unloading, the boys washed the sweat off at the horse trough before going to the house. Mrs. Avery had brought by two buckets of homemade ice cream, and both buckets were licked clean by the time the boys had had their fill.

"That was some good ice cream." Chuck sighed.

"I'm glad you liked it," Jack said. "It cost me six dozen eggs and a slab of bacon."

All the boys looked at him in surprise. None of them thought Jack had arranged for them to have ice cream. The three newcomers looked at him in a different light, but Clay smiled to himself. How could anyone explain Jack Lomas?

"Who's ready to ride some rough stock?" Jack asked.

All four spoke at the same time, affirming that they were indeed ready.

"Well, I figured you'd be too tired from hauling hay, so I thought we'd wait until tomorrow to ride." The boys couldn't hide their disappointment. Jack fought to keep from smiling as he looked at the clock. It was two o'clock in the afternoon, almost time.

"Okay, let's go down to the arena and get things ready."

They were all smiles as they hurried from the house, grabbing their gear bags out of their pickups as they went. Jack followed behind, looking down the road expectantly.

The boys were running the bulls into the chutes when Jack saw the telltale sign of dust pluming along the caliche road. He knew it was the visitors he'd been expecting and eased away from the arena to greet them.

The Ford pickup with the cab-over-camper pulled up into the yard. Jack greeted the three occupants as they stepped out. "Hello, Ted," he said to the older of the three. "It's been a long time."

"Too long," Ted Gravely said, extending his hand. He was a short, stocky man with a powerful grip. "You probably know these two gents by reputation. Greg King, Harry Tombs, this is Jack Lomas."

"Howdy, Mr. Lomas," they said in unison, reaching to shake his hand. Both were world champion bull riders. Ted Gravely had helped teach both the intricate art of bull riding. When Jack had called him, he had promised he would get Greg and Harry to stop by and give Clay and his friends some pointers.

"I watched you ride at the national finals in 1968," Greg King said. "Jack, you won the national championship that year."

"You must have been in diapers in nineteen sixty-eight," Jack said smiling.

"Not far from it," Greg responded.

"It's great to meet both of you," Jack said, "and I got four boys that will be real pleased to meet you also. I want to thank you both for coming out and spending your time helping them."

"We're glad to do it," Greg said.

"Let's go down to the arena and I'll introduce you to the wild bunch."

Four boys stood with mouths opened wide as Jack introduced them to Greg and Harry. Each of the four boys knew the men by name and stood awestruck as the men they read about, watched on television, and wished one day to emulate, stood right there before them.

"Well, boys, are you going to stand there gawking or are you going to shake hands with these gentlemen?" Jack asked, grinning at their open idolization.

Greg and Harry had set up their schedules so they

could spend the next few days helping the boys. Jack
invited everyone to stay over, and for the first time in
years he fired up the old grill and cooked steaks for
everyone.

The boys spent the evening listening to Jack, Ted,
Greg, and Harry tell stories about their experiences
traveling the rodeo circuit. They asked question after
question of the four, and would have stayed up all
night listening to the tales had Jack not finally put an
end to it by saying, "All right, boys, that's enough
for tonight. If you're planning on doing some riding
tomorrow you better get to bed." After listening to
their objections that they weren't tired, he said,
"Well if you ain't tuckered out I reckon you can go
on out to the barn and restack the hay on the far
end."

"I was just thinking it was past my bedtime," Brad
said hurriedly.

"Yeah it's way past my bedtime," Lewis chimed in.

Jack made sure everyone was comfortably bedded
down for the night and finally crawled into bed. He
was surprised he didn't seem to be as tired as he usually was after a day in the hay field. "I must be getting
used to this kind of life," he said to himself as he
closed his eyes.

They didn't get started very early the next morning
due to the late night before. By the time they got the
bulls loaded into the chutes the sun was already
threatening to make it a hot day. While Clay, Brad,
and Lewis worked with Harry and Greg on the bulls,
Jack instructed Chuck on the finer points of saddle
bronc riding, working with him first on the ground,
then in the chute.

Greg and Harry started with verbal instructions to

make sure that the boys understood the basics of riding bulls.

It was almost noon before the first ride was made, with Greg and Harry yelling instructions and filling in as bullfighters.

By the time they started bucking out, Jack's front yard looked like a used car lot, as the families of the boys started showing up along with other spectators who had gotten word of the events taking place down at Jack's ranch. Of course having two world champion bull riders there didn't hurt in attracting the crowd.

Clay awoke that morning with a gnawing in his stomach. He knew he had to call his father that day and tell him about the meeting. He had just finished riding the Brahma and they were getting Lewis ready on the brintle bull when he saw his opportunity and quietly slipped away, working his way through the crowd, walking rapidly to the house. Going to his bedroom, he went down on his knees and retrieved the device he'd bought from under the bed. Pulling the miniature tape recorder from its hiding place, he unraveled a long wire with a suction cup on its end and walked to the kitchen phone. Taking the receiver from its cradle, he licked the suction cup and stuck it to the outside of the ear piece. After getting instructions from the sales person, he'd brought it home and tried it out to make sure it worked. He'd called Shirley one afternoon while Jack was outside and, as he played back their conversation later, was satisfied with the results. Though the voices coming from the recorder were scratchy with static, he could still plainly hear the conversation.

Praying his father would be home, he dialed the

number and clicked on the recorder. After the third ring his brother answered.

"Is the old man there?" Clay asked, showing no respect for his father.

"Hey, runt, we were beginning to think you weren't going to call."

"Just put him on," Clay said, impatience clear in his voice.

"Keep your pants on, squirt." Clay heard him calling Jason Tory, and a moment later his father's slithery voice came on the line.

"It's about time you called. I was beginning to think we were going to have to come and pay you a visit."

"This is the first opportunity I've had to call," Clay replied.

"You got anything more to tell me?" the older Tory asked.

"I got the locations where the patrols will be," Clay answered, "but I want to know what you're going to do." He was hoping to get the evidence he needed on tape, but Jason Tory wasn't going to make it easy.

"What did you find out?" Jason asked, anger and impatience now creeping into in his voice.

Clay outlined all that he'd heard at the meeting. He gave the details of where the patrols would be located and how the sheriff's department would be monitoring all the calls and dispatching each of the units.

"Which roads will these patrols be on?" Jason asked.

"No one will know that but Ben Aguilar. All I can tell you is the general area."

"That makes sense," Jason said. "I wish we knew the exact location where they'll be, but at least we know the general areas. You better not be lying to me, Junior, or you know what will happen."

Clay started to ask again what he meant to do with the information, but Jason Tory cut him off. "If you get any more information you call me. And you better hope what you've told me is right." He hung up the phone before Clay could say anything more.

He stood there for a moment holding the dead phone in his hand. He knew he'd failed to get the information he'd needed and his spirits fell as he hung up the phone. He'd just given away vital information to the man he felt certain was responsible for the cattle thefts and he had nothing to show for it. He couldn't go to Ben with this. Ben would probably arrest him and throw him in jail. He put the tape recorder back under his bed and left the house.

As the screen door closed behind him, Jack suddenly stepped out of his bedroom. He'd been in there getting a tube of antibiotic creme from his night stand to put on a cut Chuck had gotten. He hadn't heard Clay come in, but he had heard him talking on the phone. Not meaning to eavesdrop, he couldn't help but hear what Clay was saying. His heart had almost stopped as he heard Clay revealing information about the patrols and their locations, something each of the members had sworn not to disclose. Now he knew why Clay had hidden in the church, but he didn't want to believe it. Not Clay, not again.

He sat down on his bed feeling old and tired. What was he going to do? His first thought was to call Ben and tell him everything. Looking back later, he would regret not doing that very thing. If he had, everything would have come out in the open and they could have taken the appropriate action, but at the moment all he could think of was his feelings for Clay, and what had happened to another young man in a similar situation long ago. He couldn't go through that

again, he *wouldn't* go through it. Jack stood up, his resolve strengthened. He knew he'd have to do an acting job that would make a Hollywood star proud if he
was going to pull this off. He walked back down to
the arena with the salve in his hand.

The rest of the day went by without a hitch. They
stopped at noon to eat the picnic lunches the ladies
had brought. After lunch they rested and talked about
the morning rides. Greg and Harry were kept busy
talking to the new arrivals.

Clay and Chuck each rode the three saddle broncs.
Jack gave instructions to each in turn, complimenting
them on the things they did right and correcting the
things they did wrong. No one could see the turmoil
raging inside of him as he worked with each of the
boys.

By six o'clock, the festivities of the day had winded
down until only a few people were left. The horses
and bulls were in the pens. Greg and Harry were on
their way to a rodeo in Arizona and Ted had to get
back home. Chuck, Lewis, and Brad had also left,
thanking Jack for his help and promising to follow his
instructions.

As soon as everyone left, Clay went to do the
evening chores. Jack walked wearily to the house. He
had managed to get through the afternoon, but he
knew it would be harder for him to act as though
nothing was wrong with just Clay in the house. He re-
signed himself to the fact that he'd either have to do
it, or call Ben. "If I don't have an answer in a week, I'll
call Ben," he said to himself.

Clay did most of the talking during supper, with
Jack only interjecting small comments. The excitement
Clay felt was equal to Jack's misery.

"I can't believe you got Greg King and Harry Tombs here," Clay said.

"I had a little help," he responded.

"Well in case I forgot, I just want to say thanks. You really made Lewis and Chuck happy, and Brad was sure riding a lot better by this afternoon."

"I'm glad I could help," Jack said, his voice void of emotion.

Clay noticed and asked, "Something wrong?"

Jack knew he wasn't playing his part well, but he couldn't see how Clay could sit there talking as if nothing had happened, when he'd betrayed the trust he'd given him. "I'm just tired," he said. "It's been a long two days and I guess it's starting to grind on me. I'm going to bed to get some sleep. We got a rodeo tomorrow night."

"Yeah, I'm pretty tired too," Clay said. "I'll wash the dishes so you can go on to bed."

"Thanks," Jack said, walking wearily down the hallway to his bedroom.

Clay noticed Jack's shoulders were sagging as he walked away, but he just attributed it to his weariness.

Chapter Nineteen

Clay was entered in the Tucumcari rodeo Friday night and Amarillo Saturday night where the Hightowers were providing the stock. That meant they would be spending Friday night away from home. Jack had called the neighbors and asked them to take care of the chores Saturday. They left at noon Friday, Clay drove, his excitement from the previous two days still evident as they traveled Highway 20 to Fort Summer, the place where Billy the Kid was buried. He talked almost nonstop the entire trip. Though Jack was still upset over the phone call he had overheard, he was able to successfully hide the fact from Clay by putting it out of his mind and focusing on the rodeos they were going to. He found he could even carry on a conversation without his voice betraying his feelings.

Tucumcari, located on Interstate 40 west of the Texas/New Mexico border, is a town of about seven thousand residents with plenty of hotels and motels. Sitting halfway between Amarillo and Albuquerque, it's the resting place for many a weary traveler. Now it was decorated with large banners advertising the annual rodeo.

They arrived at the rodeo grounds at five-thirty. Finding the contestant board, Clay found he'd drawn Dirty Harry in the barebacks, a good horse by all accounts. He'd drawn Titan in the saddle broncs and Lonesome Dove in the bulls. He'd entered the bull riding only after Jack had given his reluctant approval.

Jack helped Clay set his bareback rigging in place and cinch it down. Third out, he rode to a score of seventy, which placed him second for the night. As was their custom, they watched the calf roping from the grandstands before returning back to the bucking chutes for the saddle bronc riding.

Clay placed his saddle on Titan while Jack slipped the bronc halter over his head. "You remember all the things I told you?" Jack asked.

"I think so," Clay said. "Keep my mind in the middle and watch his head."

"That's the important part," Jack replied.

Clay climbed on Titan's back and nodded for the gate. He rode to the whistle and scored a seventy-two to move into first place.

"That could hold," Jack said, grinning for the first time that day.

"It felt good," Clay said, returning the smile.

They went back to the grandstands to watch the steer wrestling, one of Jack's favorite events. Steer wrestling requires a team mounted on horses, one is the bulldogger or steer wrestler, the other is the hazer. His job is to keep the steer running in a straight line for the dogger.

The steer wrestler starts from behind a barrier just as the calf ropers do, allowing the steer a head start. Once out of the box, the steer wrestler rides up beside the steer, then drops off his horse on the steer's back. They use long-horned cattle, mostly Mexican breeds called Corintés. These cattle are a cross between Mexican cattle and Texas Longhorns, chosen for their wide horns and smaller size. This same type of steer is also used in the team roping.

Once the steer wrestler drops down on the steer, he grabs the animal's left horn in his left hand and the right horn in the crook of his right elbow. As his horse passes the steer, the steer wrestler's feet are out in front. Once they hit the ground, he pulls the steer around in a sliding stop and twists the steer to the ground. One of the old-time bulldoggers once joked the best way to learn how to bulldog was to get on the running board of a pickup while someone drives down a rural road at thirty miles an hour. When you come to a mailbox, jump off and grab it.

Three point eight seconds was what it took to win the steer wrestling that night.

Clay wanted to watch the barrel racing, and Jack laughed at him. "I don't see why you'd want to watch a bunch of girls run around the barrels."

"I always like to watch good horses work," Clay said with a sheepish grin.

"Uh huh," Jack said, not believing him for a minute.

They watched half the barrel racing before returning to the chutes. The bulls were run in and Clay's bull was in the sixth chute. He set his bull rope and waited for the event to start.

The bull riding started with the first rider getting thrown. The second rider had no better luck, and the third only made the first two jumps before hitting the dirt. The fourth made a qualified ride and scored a sixty-eight while the fifth rider scored a sixty-three.

Clay went over in his mind the things he'd learned from Greg and Harry, then nodded for his turn.

Lonesome Dove was a large Brangus, half Angus and half Brahma bull, with plenty of power and agility. Clay not only made the whistle, but scored a seventy-five. The crowd loved it, applauding and shouting for him the entire ride. They were on their feet as the whistle blew.

After the bull riding was over, Clay was leading in the bulls and the saddle broncs, and sitting second in the barebacks. "Not a bad night's riding," Jack said, impressed with Clay's improvement.

As they were leaving the chute area and heading to their pickup, several girls were standing by the gate. "Hi, Clay," they greeted him, and he responded with a wave. "Are you going to be here for the dance tonight?" one of them asked.

Clay shook his head. "Sorry, but we're headed for Amarillo tonight."

The look of disappointment was plain on the girls' faces as he waved good-bye and followed Jack to the pickup.

"Looks like you're getting a following of buckle polishers," Jack said, looking back at the girls still standing there.

"Huh?" Clay asked, looking back also.

"Buckle polishers is what we used to call 'em in my day. They're the girls that come to the rodeos to pick up cowboys to take 'em to the dance. They usually go for the top winners, hoping to get wined and dined in fine style. They all gather the next day to talk about the night before. Nothing wrong with it, if you're willing to spend all your winnings on 'em."

"Why the term buckle polishers?" Clay asked.

"Because when you do finally get to the dance they hug you so close while you're dancing, so all their girlfriends will be jealous, that your buckle gets polished in the process."

"Oh," Clay responded. "Sounds like it might be

fun, but just remind me of one thing if I ever latch on to one of 'em."

"What's that?" Jack asked, amused by Clay's response.

"To give you all my money to hold for me."

Jack threw back his head and laughed. "You're smarter than I gave you credit for."

"I'll take that as a compliment," Clay responded.

They drove into Amarillo around midnight and found the motel where Will and Dottie were staying. Once in the room, they both fell asleep instantly and were still asleep at nine o'clock when Will beat on their door. Clay, being closest, opened the door, blinking at the bright sunlight coming in the door. "Good morning," Will said in a loud voice that made Clay wince. Leaving the door opened, he crawled back in bed and pulled the covers over his head.

"Get up, you lazy bums!" Will shouted.

Jack was sitting up in bed by now, trying to wipe the sleep from his eyes. "Why are you in such a good mood?" he asked as Will came into the room and closed the door.

"It's a beautiful day out there and we had a great crowd last night, and tonight should be even better," he said. Part of the stock contractors' pay is a percentage of the gate fees, so the more spectators there are, the more he gets paid.

"I'm glad you're having such a good day, but that ain't no reason for you to come in here waking up hardworking people that didn't get to sleep until early this morning," Jack said.

"Hardworking, my aunt Fanny," Will said, laughing. "You two been lazing around, taking life easy while I been busting my hump to get a rodeo put on here."

"Uh huh," Jack said. "It's your boys and your wife that do all the work while you come around giving us working people a hard time."

Will laughed. "You two get up and I'll buy you breakfast."

Jack looked over at Clay. "Hurry up and get dressed. You're witnessing history in the making if Will Hightower is offering to buy."

Will snorted. "I used to get stuck with the check all the time when we were on the circuit. Of course, I was the only one winning and therefore the only one with any money, so I had to foot the bill."

"You're coming down with a bad case of old-timer's disease. It's done addled your brain, Hightower. The few times you did win and collected any money, there were so many people around with their hands out collecting what you owed them that there was none left and I'd have to carry you again."

"Ha! Look who's talking about old-timer's disease. Why, you old wore out, sorry excuse for a bronc rider, you mooched off me so much I was able to count you as a dependent on my income tax."

Clay pulled the cover from off his head. "I'd love to lie here and listen to you two old geezers go on about who carried who, but I'm going to get in the shower and see if I can wash off some of the bull you two are throwing around in here."

"Geezers," Will said indignantly.

"Bull," Jack chimed in, just as indignant. "Why, I'll have you know every word that was spoken was the pure Gospel as best we remember it."

Clay laughed. "That's the problem, your memories are about as long as your hair, or what's left of it."

With that he walked into the bathroom and closed the door.

"I don't know what's gotten into these youngsters today," Will said, "insulting us like that."

"I know what you mean," Jack agreed. "Seems they just ain't got no respect for their elders."

Both men laughed. "I'll go and get Dottie," Will said when the chuckles subsided. "You get dressed and we'll meet you in the restaurant."

"We'll be there in a little bit," Jack said, still smiling at his friend.

After breakfast the four of them drove to a ranch outside Amarillo. Will had heard about a couple of bucking horses for sale and wanted to take a look at them.

"I'm thinking of taking my show to the pro circuit," Will told them on the way.

"That's a big step to take," Jack said. "Won't that mean all new bucking stock?"

"For the most part. I've got a few horses and three or four bulls that are already pro material. And I've already got an offer for the other horses and bulls."

"When are you planning on making this move?" Jack asked.

"Oh, I figure to wait until after the National Finals, that way I can start at the beginning of the season. I have to be approved by the Pro Rodeo Cowboy's Association before I can officially put on a pro rodeo."

"Can you be ready by then?" Clay asked.

"I'm pretty sure I can. I've already located most of the stock I'll need and I reckon I can get the rest between now and the first of the year."

"I think it's a good idea," Jack said. "What do you and the boys think about it, Dottie?" he asked her.

"It was the boys' idea," she said, "and I like the idea of going pro myself."

"I don't like it," Clay said.

"Why not?" Will asked.

"Because I like to ride your stock. You put on one of the best shows around. If you go pro, I won't be able to ride at your shows."

Will looked thoughtful for a moment. "I don't know how Jack feels about it, and I don't want to butt into something that doesn't concern me, but in my opinion you're about to go pro yourself. By the time I get started you should be ready to get your permit." The PRCA requires that its new members first get a permit. Once they have earned a thousand dollars, they then have the option of becoming a full card-holding member.

"He might be ready by then," Jack said. "We'll have to wait and see." His tone of voice betrayed his hidden feelings and both Will and Clay looked at him in surprise, but he said nothing more as he turned to look out the window.

Early that afternoon, while Clay was in the motel room resting, Jack approached Will. "Let's you and I go have a cup of coffee. I got something I need to talk to you about."

Seeing the look on his friend's face, Will said, "Sure thing, let me tell Dottie."

The two old friends sat across the table from each other. Will waited patiently while Jack sat stirring his coffee, his mind turning over the facts he'd discovered, while he decided how to tell his friend.

"Will," he began, "you know Clay pretty well. What do you think about him?"

Will's face showed his surprise at the question. "I

think he's a fine young man that has a tremendous amount of potential. Why do you ask?"

Taking a deep breath, Jack continued. "Because I overheard a conversation he had on the phone the other day and I think there's a possibility he's involved in something that could land him in jail."

Will looked aghast. "I don't believe it."

"I haven't wanted to either, but I'm afraid that's what's happening and I don't know what to do."

"What is it?" Will asked, his concern genuine.

Jack hesitated. "You've heard about the cattle stealin' that's been goin on in Chavez County?"

"Oh no, you're not telling me Clay's mixed up in that?"

"I'm afraid he might be." He went on to tell Will about Clay's being in the church the night of the association meeting and the phone conversation he'd overheard.

"From what you've told me it sounds like he might be involved, but all you heard was one side of the conversation. Have you said anything to Clay about it?"

"Not yet," Jack said. "I've been wrestling with this thing ever since I heard him on the phone. I just don't know what to do. That's why I'm telling you. I was hoping maybe between us we could come up with some answers. I don't want to make the same mistake again."

Will looked at his friend. "Jack, I know you think you made a mistake with Jaimie, but there's not a soul who knows what happened that doesn't know you bent over backwards to do what was right."

"I don't know that," Jack said. Will could hear the sadness and regret in his voice. "And it don't change the fact that he's gone from me forever."

Will placed his hand on top of Jack's. It was all he could do to help his grieving friend.

"Jack, let's not condemn Clay until we know all the facts. Let's see what happens over the next couple of weeks. If it turns out he is involved then I recommend going to the sheriff and telling him. Let him be the one that gets the evidence."

"And meanwhile, friends of mine could lose more cattle because of what he's doing. How will I face them if it turns out Clay was behind it and I knew about it and didn't say anything."

"I don't have an answer for that, but I do know what it will do to you and Clay if you're wrong. It could ruin both of you."

Jack didn't answer but sat there staring at his now cold cup of coffee. He knew Will was correct. If he was wrong it would drive Clay away. "I don't know what to do, but I do agree with you. I need to get some more facts before I make a decision. If I find out he's guilty, I'll take it to the sheriff and let him handle it."

"That's the best way, but I want you to know I still feel like Clay's a good kid. If he's mixed up in this it's not because he's trying to get something. What I mean is he's not doing it for the money. Have you ever heard him talk about wanting money for anything?"

"Come to think of it he's never mentioned the need for any. All he seems to care about is rodeoing," Jack said.

"Uh huh, 'cause that's all he does care about," Will said. "That's why it's hard for me to believe he'd get mixed up in anything like you're talking about. He's doing what he always wanted to do and he's enjoying it. When I see the two of you together I'm almost envious. You're both doing what you enjoy. I don't see Clay risking all that to steal cattle."

"Yeah, not to mention going back to jail," Jack said.

"Huh?" Will asked, looking at Jack in surprise.

Jack looked up quickly, realizing the mistake he'd made, then with a sigh he continued. "That's the way Clay and I got hooked up. He was in jail for stealing a pickup. I know now it was a trumped-up charge, but he was going to Juvenile Hall and the sheriff talked me into taking him for a year. He's been afraid of going back to jail since. That's why I reckon I find it so hard to believe he'd get involved in this mess."

"It doesn't make sense," Will agreed. "I wish you the best of luck. If there's anything Dottie or I can do, just let us know."

"Just pray everything will work out for the best," he said, "one way or the other."

Jack and Clay pulled into the rodeo grounds at six o'clock and went through the ritual of carrying Clay's gear to the area behind the chutes. They found the contestant board and the listings. "I drew Copenhagen in the barebacks," Clay said, running his finger down the page. "And it looks like I drew Lucky Seven in the saddle broncs, and Bronson in the bulls."

"You won on Copenhagen in Ruidoso, and Lucky Seven's a good horse, I saw him buck out in Pecos. What do you know about Bronson?" Jack asked.

"He's that gray bull over there," Clay said, pointing to a large bull that looked like a cross between a Charlois and an Angus.

"He's a big one," Jack said, taking in the size of the bull.

"He sure is," Clay emphasized with pride, as if the bull belonged to him.

"As long as you don't try to dance with him," Jack said, "I still can't think of a good reason why anyone would want to crawl on the back of one of those brutes."

"I can't answer that question. All I know is that whether I'm on a bronc or a bull, the feeling I get when I have a good ride is like nothing else I've ever known. It's kinda like knowing you," Clay added.

"Like knowing me?" Jack asked, surprised by the statement.

"In a way it is," Clay said seriously. "When I first met you I didn't like you, but after I got to know you and found out you were more bark than bite, I couldn't imagine not being around you and the ranch and going to rodeos. I can't tell you why. It's just a feeling, like riding bulls."

Jack felt a lump come to his throat. He knew what Clay was talking about. He couldn't explain it either, but he couldn't imagine his life being any different than it was now and he couldn't imagine not having Clay around.

"I reckon I know what you mean," Jack said. His voice came out husky and he turned quickly away.

"Why don't we go get something to drink?" Clay said hurriedly, to cover the awkwardness of the moment.

"Sounds like a good idea," Jack said, falling in beside him. He put his hand on Clay's shoulder as they walked side by side. Clay smiled at the gesture.

A score of seventy-two from the night before was winning the bareback riding. Clay rode Copenhagen to a score of seventy-one to place second.

First place in the saddle bronc riding was a seventy-four, with second place a sixty-nine and third a sixty-two. Clay rode Lucky Seven to a score of seventy-one, which held to give him another second.

"You've done some good riding tonight," Will said to Clay later, as they stood inside the arena watching the barrel racing. "Jack's training is really helping isn't it?"

"It sure is," Clay affirmed. "You know, at first I thought some of his ideas were crazy, but after seeing what they did for my riding, I have to say he knows what he's doing."

Will chuckled. "When it comes to riding broncs, Jack Lomas knows more than most people forgot, but when it comes to people he's got a lot to learn. Jack's always lived by his own code. A code that says there's a right way to live and a wrong way to live and you have to live the right way. To him it's all black and white, and there's no gray areas. And he's right for the most part, but with people there's going to be gray areas, areas that you can't put into one category or the other because of circumstances, and that's where Jack has problems."

Clay looked at him thoughtfully. "I get the feeling you're trying to tell me something, but I'm not sure I follow you."

"I reckon what I'm tryin' to say—and not doing too good a job of it—is that there's not a man alive better than Jack Lomas, but he's human and he's made mistakes and he'll make more. But always remember, he makes his mistakes for the right reasons, so if in the future you think he's made a mistake, look at it from his point of view."

Clay laughed. "Don't ever go into politics, Mr. Hightower. It takes you too long to say Jack Lomas is human like the rest of us but he's not likely to admit it."

Will Hightower looked stunned then laughed. "Maybe you should go into politics. That summed it up exactly. That's Jack Lomas."

"I appreciate what you said, Mr. Hightower, and I want you to know I appreciate all you and Mrs. Hightower have done for Jack and me."

"Don't mention it," Will said. "We've been glad to help, and, Clay, if you ever need us for anything you just holler. I mean—anything, anytime."

Clay looked at him and for a moment he almost told him about his father, then thought better of it. He knew Will would tell Jack and that could lead to nothing but trouble.

"Thanks, Mr. Hightower, I really appreciate it."

Chapter Twenty

Clay's ride on Bronson showed he was in command the entire time. Bronson came out of the chute and turned into a right spin. Clay dug his spur into the bull's side and spurred with his left foot. He was ready when Bronson came out of the spin, dropped his left shoulder, and attempted to pull Clay down into the well, the place between a bull's neck and his shoulder in the direction he's turning. A bull has a better chance of hooking a cowboy if he can pull him into this area, especially in a spin. Clay leaned back and pulled up on his rope, preventing himself from being pulled down. The remainder of the ride was all Clay's as Bronson bucked first left then right, kicking his hindquarters high in the air with each buck.

The eight-second whistle blew and Clay waited for Bronson to move to the left before throwing his leg over his neck and stepping off. Bronson stopped bucking and turned to glare at Clay, then shifted his attention to the clown in the barrel and the bullfighter behind it, while the other bullfighter moved quickly between Clay and the bull. Bronson, the two bullfighters, and the barrel clown entertained the crowd. The bullfighter turned the barrel on its side, then rolled the barrel at the big bull.

The ladies in the crowd screamed as the bull

charged, then butted the barrel, sending the clown inside rolling. Once they saw the bull was going to play, both bullfighters got involved in the act, keeping the barrel between them and Bronson. While one bullfighter kept the bull's attention, the other ran around behind and swatted him on the tail. The crowd held their breath as the bull turned and charged, but the agile bullfighter moved quickly behind the barrel.

It was time for the other bullfighter to show off his stuff. While his partner kept the bull's attention, he backed away about forty feet and when he was sure Bronson's focus was on his partner, he sprinted toward the barrel as fast as he could. Stepping up on the barrel he jumped high in the air, placing one foot on Bronson's back as he came down. He landed agilely on the ground, and was up on the chute gates before the bull could turn around.

Bronson was herded from the arena to the applause of the crowds as the bullfighters took their bows. Clay scored an even seventy on his ride, which put him in second place. There were eight riders left, and he knew he would be lucky if it held.

He held second until the next-to-last ride. The bull was a tough Brangus and Cole James rode him to a score of seventy-five to take first place. Clay managed to place third and was well satisfied with his night's work, which netted him a little over five hundred dollars.

Clay and Jack waited after the rodeo was over to collect his check from Dottie. "You did real good tonight, Clay," she said, handing him his check.

"I had some good stock," Clay said, complimenting her right back.

"Ya'll be careful driving home," she said sweetly as she gave each of them a hug.

"We will," Clay said. "Jack's snoring keeps me awake."

Dottie laughed. "I'll bet it does. I've listened to him and Will snore more than once. I swear those two could lift the roof off a house when they get going."

"We'll see you in a couple of weeks," Jack said. "Say good-bye to Will for us."

"I will," Dottie said, turning to the other contestants who were waiting for their winnings.

It was a long drive back to Roswell. Clay was still high on winning. The thought kept him awake for the first two hours while Jack slept. But by the time they got to Clovis he had to stop. As he pulled into an all-night convenience store, Jack woke up. "What's up?" he asked, yawning and wiping the sleep from his eyes.

"Nothing, I've just got to take a break."

"You want me to drive?"

"Nah, I'll be all right as soon as I get a cup of coffee."

He walked inside and poured himself a cup of thick coffee from the pot and made small talk with the cashier as he paid. He started out the door but stopped in his tracks as the headlines of the Sunday paper caught his eye. CATTLE THIEVES STRIKE AGAIN IN CHAVEZ COUNTY it read. His heart raced as he stared at the paper, knowing he was probably responsible for someone else's cattle being stolen.

He was wide awake as he got back in the pickup.

"You all right?" Jack asked.

"Sure. Why wouldn't I be?" Clay asked, his voice reflecting the anger he felt at his father.

Jack looked shocked. "Because you looked tired. I was just wondering if you were getting too sleepy to drive."

"Oh," Clay said, realizing Jack knew nothing about the cattle thefts, "I'm fine now. I just needed a little coffee."

"If you get too tired, pull over and I'll drive," Jack said.

"I'll be fine," Clay said putting the truck in gear.

They got home at one-thirty in the morning and both of them went straight to bed. Jack got up at nine but let Clay sleep in until ten-thirty, when he walked into the kitchen barefooted and shirtless. "How come we didn't go to church today?"

"I didn't figure it would hurt to miss one Lord's Day. I knew you were tired after driving half the night."

"I was beat but I could have made it to church."

Jack waved his hand as if to say it didn't matter. "Why don't we drive over to Jones's this afternoon and see how they're getting along?"

"Sure," Clay answered, "we going for any particular reason?"

"Yeah, I've got a hankerin' for some of Mary's desserts."

"How do you know she'll have any dessert?" Clay asked.

Jack arched his eyebrow. "The day Mary Jones doesn't have dessert will be the day we'll be going to her funeral."

After lunch they drove to the Joneses' house. Jack had called Clyde earlier to make sure they were going to be home. As Jack had predicted, Mary had an apple cobbler with ice cream waiting for them. Jack had a small piece while Clay ate a large bowl.

"If you stayed around here, Clay, you'd soon weigh

more than those bulls you ride," Clyde Jones said, looking at the heaping bowl in front of the boy.

"That's for sure," Clay agreed. "This sure is good, Mrs. Jones," he said and was pleased to see the delight on her face.

"It's good to have someone here who appreciates my cooking," she said.

"Why, Mary," Clyde said, "you know I appreciate your cooking. It's just that if I ate all you tried to feed me, I wouldn't be able to get through the barn door."

"Ha! The day you get fat, Clyde Jones, will be the day I quit cooking," she said.

Jack grinned. "If I ate like this every day I'd weigh three hundred pounds," he said, pushing the empty bowl away.

Clyde looked at the empty bowl and said, "If you're finished I want you to come down to the barn and look at a cow I got. She's got something in her foot and I can't figure out what it is."

"Sure," Jack said, and looking at Clay and the dessert in front of him, he said, "Go ahead and finish your pie, we won't be long." Clay nodded and put another spoonful in his mouth.

Walking out the door, Clyde waited until they were away from the house before he spoke. "So what's so important that you had to drive out here on a Sunday to talk to me."

"It's about Clay," Jack said, and went on to tell him about the phone conversation and Clay's sneaking around in the church that night.

"Hmmm, sounds like something's going on. You think Clay's gone bad?" Clyde asked.

"I don't want to think he is," Jack replied, "but he's involved. Did you read the paper this morning?"

"Yeah, there was another theft Friday night."

"Uh huh," Jack said, "and it was in the exact spot where there were no patrols. And I overheard Clay telling someone on the phone where our patrols would be."

"So what are you going to do?" Clyde asked.

"That's why I'm here. You still friends with Horace Little?"

"I wouldn't say I was ever friends with him," Clyde said indignantly, "but I still see him every now and then." Horace Little was a man who had his finger in every underhanded deal in Chavez County and the surrounding areas.

"It's a pretty good bet he'd know who was behind these thefts," Jack said.

"I'm sure he knows," Clyde said with a nod, "but whether I can get him to tell me is another matter."

"I've know you to be real persuasive," Jack said.

"That was in my younger days," Clyde said, getting Jack's meaning, "but for you and Clay, I'll find out. I'll stop by and get Howard to go with me. He enjoys talking to people." Howard Dilton stood six foot six inches and weighed two hundred and seventy pounds, all solid muscle. Clyde had taken him in several years ago when he'd been down on his luck and helped him get back on his feet. He now had his own cattle hauling business, was married, and had two boys that were going to be as big as he was. His wife stood a little over five feet and didn't weigh a hundred pounds, but she made Howard toe the line. The two of them were the topic of many humorous conversations at the local coffee shops.

Jack chuckled. "I'd like to be a fly on the wall when you take Howard in to see Little. I'll bet you could even get Horace to tell you where he's stashed all the illegal money he's got."

"That's something I don't want to know," Clyde said with a frown. "I'll go see him the first of the week and give you a call if I find out anything."

"I appreciate it, Clyde. I wouldn't ask you to do this if there was another way."

Clyde waved his hand in dismissal. "I don't know why you didn't come to me sooner. One thing though, Jack: I'm going to tell you exactly what I find. What will you do if you find out Clay's involved?"

"I'm going to stand beside him," Jack said with resolve. "I didn't do that last time and that mistake has haunted me since."

Clyde looked at his friend and saw the sadness in his face. All he could do was hope that this time, things would be different.

Clay came out of the house and the two men turned at the sound of the door slamming behind him. "I reckon that cow will live," Jack said as they started for the house.

"There's one over there," Jack said, shaking out his loop. They had driven the pastures the day before, checking all the cattle they could see from the pickup. Several calves had the beginnings of pinkeye and there were some with runny noses. It was a hot summer day and both the men and the horses were sweating from the exertion.

Jack was pointing to a three-hundred-pound red Brahma cross calf. "His nose is running pretty good."

"Yep," Clay said, making his loop, "it's your turn." Each one took a turn going first. If one of them missed it was the other's turn to try and rope the animal. Jack had missed three loops already this morning while Clay had missed only one.

Jack walked his horse toward the calf, trying to get

as close as possible before the calf ran. The red calf stood with its head up, watching Jack. When he got within fifteen yards, the calf wheeled on his back feet and ran, tail in the air. Jack was riding his favorite horse, a black named Magic. Magic stood fifteen three hands tall; a hand is a measurement of six inches, about the width of a man's hand. The black horse weighed almost twelve hundred pounds, but had the speed of a smaller-sized horse.

When the calf bolted, Magic, sensing his rider's will, leapt forward, covering the distance separating them in three strides, and Jack's loop sailed out to settle neatly over the calf's head.

Clay was close behind as Jack turned the calf back. He rolled in behind and threw his heel loop, neatly catching both of the calf's back feet. He was riding a sorrel horse named Logan that he'd been training for the past four months. Logan stopped on his haunches as Clay pulled his slack, stretching the calf between the two horses. Jack dismounted while Magic held the rope taut.

Taking a syringe and bottle of antibiotics from his saddle pouch, he quickly gave the calf an injection. Remounting, he rode Magic forward until there was slack in the rope, while Clay kept his heel rope tight. Dismounting again, he eased up the calf's head and removed his rope from his neck while Clay kept the young bovine held down. Once Jack was back on his horse, Clay rode forward, allowing the calf to kick free of the heel rope. Unhurt but frightened, the calf ran bawling to his mother, who had stood by watching with motherly concern.

It was two tired cowboys who rode back to the house late that evening. Clay started the chores while Jack went up to prepare supper. "I sure need to hire a cook and housekeeper," he said to himself as he opened the door. The phone rang as he walked into the kitchen, "Hello," he said, grabbing the receiver off the wall.

"Hello, Jack," came Clyde Jones's voice.

"Clyde, how ya doin'?"

"I had a visit today with Horace Little," he said.

Jack perked up. "How did it go?" he asked, almost dreading the news that was coming. "Did he know who was behind the thefts?"

"Oh yeah, he knows. I didn't even have to threaten him with Howard. Once I asked him about it he told me everything I wanted to know. Seems he doesn't care too much for the folks pulling these cattle thefts."

"Who is it?" Jack asked, dread sounding in his voice.

"It's Clay's father and brothers," Clyde said. "At least they're the ones doin' the rustling. There's someone else who's doin' the buyin'."

"Who's that?" Jack asked.

"It seems to be some big-shot outfit out of Texas. Apparently they come into an area and get in with the local riffraff, and get them to do the stealing, then they have some Podunk hauling company carry them out of state. When they came into these parts they went to Horace first but he turned them down flat, said he didn't want nothin' to do with an outfit that wanted to work that way. So they went to the Torys."

"Did he know anything about Clay?" Jack asked.

"Nothing much, but he did voice an opinion that I thought was worthy of mention."

"What's that?" Jack asked, interested in anything that could clear this mess up.

"He said he wouldn't put it past Jason Tory to hold something over the boy to get him to cooperate."

"Like what?"

"He didn't say. Just gave it as a possibility," Clyde said, "but it makes a lot of sense and if you think about it, it's the only thing that fits. Why else would Clay jeopardize everything he has going?"

"It does seem like a good possibility," Jack said, thinking about it.

"Yeah and it brings up a whole new list of problems," Clyde said.

"It sure does," Jack agreed. "Like what does he have on Clay, or what has he threatened him with?"

"Exactly," Clyde said. "I'd walk carefully with this if I were you."

"You mean don't start stirring things up."

"You got it, partner."

Jack gave a weary sigh. "Thanks, Clyde, I really do appreciate your help."

"I won't say I was glad to do it, but I'm glad I could help."

Clay came in the door just as Jack hung up the phone. "Who you talkin' to?"

"Clyde Jones. He was telling me about an old acquaintance of ours," Jack said.

"What's for supper? I'm starved," Clay said, accepting Jack's explanation.

"Beef stew," Jack said, opening the refrigerator and pulling out the bowl he'd put in there that morning.

"Yum," Clay said in mock appreciation.

"You're welcome to cook us something different," Jack said.

"I'm too tired or I would," Clay said, washing his hands at the kitchen sink. "Your beef stew is good, but a fella can only take so much of a good thing."

"You're right," Jack said looking at the bowl in his hands. "I think I'll hire us a cook and housekeeper."

Clay stopped scrubbing with the handbrush. "Are you serious?"

Jack laughed. "Is my cooking that bad?"

"No," Clay hurried to say, "it's just that with all the work we have to do it would be nice to come home to a hot meal already prepared."

"It would be nice," Jack agreed. "I'll put out some feelers tomorrow while I'm in town and see if there's anyone available. There may not be any decent cooks that want to come out and cook for two mangy men."

"One mangy man and a good-lookin' young man," Clay corrected.

"Apparently you haven't gotten a good whiff of yourself lately," Jack said. "You smell like those calves we doctored today."

Clay sniffed the air. "Is that me? I thought that was you. I was ready to dig a hole and bury you for dead."

"As tired as I am I right now, I feel like I did die," Jack said, stirring the stew.

"I know the feeling," Clay admitted. "I could sleep for a week right now."

"Well, plan on sleeping in tomorrow. I got to go into town and while I'm there all you got to do is take some mineral blocks over to the south and north pastures."

"Really?" Clay groaned. "That's all I got to do?"

"That's all." Jack smiled.

Though Clay was worn out, once he went to bed sleep eluded him. His thoughts were on the cattle thefts of the last week and his part in making them possible. He didn't kid himself that Jack didn't know about them, but he wondered why he hadn't said anything.

Both his body and mind tossed and turned. He had to find some way to stop his father and put an end to these thefts. Jack was going into town tomorrow, and perhaps he could get through putting out blocks soon enough to go into town and pay a visit to his father. He could take the tape recorder and hopefully get his father to admit to his part in the thefts, then take the tape to Ben and get him to do something about it. It wasn't a plan that he particularly liked but it was one that could work. He held no illusions about what his father would do if he found out his son was setting a trap for him.

By the next morning Clay had set his resolve to carry out his plan. Jack cooked him breakfast and helped him load the mineral blocks into the Dodge. "I'll probably be gone most of the day," Jack said, slamming the tailgate shut. "You should be finished with this by lunchtime: That'll give you some time to work on your weights and the balance rails."

"Uh, I was wonderin' if it'd be all right with you if I went into town for a little while this afternoon?"

"Sure," Jack said. "If there's something you need, I'll be glad to pick it up."

"No I want to go by and see Brad. He's ordered a new rope and I want to check it out." It was true that Brad had ordered a new bull rope, but Clay had no intention of going by. He hated lying to Jack but weighing the alternatives, he knew it was the only way.

"Okay," Jack said, "but don't stay out all night. We've got to get things ready for branding next week."

Clay smiled. "I won't be late. I should be home in time for supper."

Jack watched Clay drive out of the yard before turning to the Ford pickup. He had several things to do in town today and he wanted to stop by and see some of his neighbors. They were going to start branding next week and as was the custom, neighbors helped each other, sharing the work on each ranch. He was also going to put an ad in the paper for a housekeeper and cook. It was funny, he thought as he drove the caliche road to town, before Clay came he'd never considered having a woman in his home again, but now for some reason it seemed like the thing to do.

Clay drove the rough pasture roads faster than was safe. The Dodge bounced over the ruts and holes, sometimes causing Clay's hat to be pushed down over his ears from hitting the ceiling so hard.

He unloaded the last mineral block at the north windmill and jumped back in the pickup, stirring up a dust cloud as the tires spun out. Pulling into the yard a little before eleven o'clock, he hurried in the house to change clothes. Jack had fixed him two sandwiches and he gulped them down with a glass of milk while he changed his shirt and jeans. He was back in the Dodge and heading into town at ten minutes after eleven, the tape recorder and microphone lying on the seat beside him.

Stopping at a fast-food restaurant in town, he bought a soft drink and went into the rest room, placing the tape recorder in his pocket. Choosing an empty stall in the rest room, he positioned the small recorder in his pocket, where he could easily turn it on. Connecting the external microphone, he ran the wire under his shirttail and brought it out at his belt, checking to make sure it wasn't visible but that it would still be able to pick up conversation. Satisfied with the results, he left the restaurant and drove to his father's house. He was both relieved and worried to see his father's pickup parked in the litter-strewn yard.

Clay sat in the pickup looking at the house where he'd spent most of his years. What little paint remained on the house was faded and peeling, and many of the boards were rotting and in need of replacement. The roof was missing shingles and leaked during rainstorms. Clay could remember his mother placing all her pots and pans around the house to catch the water coming in, all the while cussing his father for being too lazy to fix the roof, and him cussing her right back for being too lazy to cook and clean. It was a constant fight that went on day after day. Clay's mother had only one passion and that was the daytime soap operas that came on TV. She watched them day after day and could tell you what was happening with every person in every soap, all the while chain-smoking cigarettes. There were ashtrays sitting on every piece of furniture in the house, each one running over with cigarette butts and ashes, while empty TV dinner trays and empty beer cans littered the living room and kitchen. TV dinners were the main staple in the little two-bedroom house. Clay's memories of the cluttered house made him shudder. He could remember having to clear a path through the trash and dirty clothes just to get to the bathtub.

Summoning his courage, he stepped out of the pickup and walked up to the door. He almost knocked, then thinking better of it, reached in his pocket and clicked on the tape recorder before turning the knob on the door and stepping inside.

The stench that assaulted his nose made him balk momentarily, but he closed the door behind him and walked into the living room.

The sight before him was a familiar one. His mother sat on the sofa, surrounded by empty TV trays and old magazines, a cigarette hanging out the corner of her mouth. She was intent on her soap opera and only looked up as Clay walked in, offering no greeting, no motherly concern for her youngest son, just her interest in the soap opera on television. Jason Tory was lying down in the old broken-down recliner, his eyes closed, and snoring. He hadn't shaved in several days and his face was covered with the stubble of a beard. Clay would have bet his last dollar he was hungover. His oldest brother, Warren, was on the floor sleeping, probably hungover as well, Clay thought. There was a radio playing in the back room and Clay figured his brother Randy was asleep back there.

He walked over to his father and shook his arm. "I wouldn't wake him up if'n I was you," his mother said. "He tied on a big one yesterday and he'll be meaner than a snake."

"I've got to talk to him," Clay said, shaking him harder.

The older Tory moaned and shifted in the chair and opened his bloodshot eyes. It took him a moment to get his eyes focused and another moment to recognize Clay.

"What do you want?" he asked angrily.

"I came to give you some more information. You said you wanted to know if I heard anything."

Clay knew nothing new but he'd made up some things on his way over to help lead his father into the trap he had planned.

Jason Tory let the footstool on the recliner come down with a bang, moaning as his head came forward. "What you got that's so important that it couldn't wait?"

"They're moving the patrols down in the county. They figure that's where the next cattle will be stolen," Clay said.

Jason's eyes came wide open. "Whereabouts are they going to be workin'," he asked.

"From just south of Roswell on down," he said.

"That's good, that's real good," Jason Tory said. "Where did you hear this bit of information?"

"I overheard Jack and Ben talking on the phone," Clay said, shifting nervously on his feet.

"You don't say," Jason Tory said, looking at him suspiciously, "and when was this?"

"Day before yesterday," Clay answered with confidence.

"Day before yesterday, huh? How come it took you until today to let me know about it?"

"It was the first time I could get away," Clay said, starting to feel nervous.

"Why didn't you call me?"

"Because Jack's been with me the whole time and I couldn't call," Clay said. "I figured you'd be happy to get this information. Now you can hit one of the ranches in the northern part of the county."

Jason's eyes shot upward as he looked at his son. Reaching out his foot, he kicked Warren. "Get up, you lazy whelp," he said. Warren groaned and opened his eyes. Jason kicked him again. "Get up, your brother's here."

Warren peered through bleary eyes at his father, then at Clay. "Hey, runt. What'ya doin' here?"

"He's got some interestin' news for us. Seems he overheard Ben and Jack talkin' day before yesterday about movin' the patrols down to the lower part of the county."

Warren scratched his head. "That's good news, I reckon."

"Sure is," Jason Tory said, standing up. "Especially since Ben Aguilar has been up in Santa Fe since Saturday and I doubt very seriously if he called Jack Lomas long distance to tell him he was moving the patrols down south."

Clay swallowed hard. "I thought it was Ben he was talking to, maybe it was one of the deputies," he said.

"I doubt it," Jason said, advancing on his son. Warren had gotten off the floor and was beside his father. Clay was backing toward the door.

"Look, you're the one that wanted the information, I just brought it to you." He glanced over his shoulder toward the door. At that moment, Jason Tory sprang forward and grabbed him. Feeling his father grasp on his arm, Clay felt panic rise inside. He tried to wrench his arm free and run, but Warren, seeing his father grab Clay, rushed to grab his other arm. Clay's panic was now at full pitch. Pushing hard, he managed to throw Jason off balance and he stumbled backward. Jason bellowed as he started to fall and Clay swung a haymaker at his brother's head. In his panic he swung wild and instead of hitting his brother in the face as he'd intended, the blow hit him in the back of the head, bringing instant pain to his hand but having little effect on his brother.

Warren Tory shook his head while still tightly clutching Clay's arm. As his head cleared, he jerked hard on Clay's arm, propelling Clay toward him. At the same time he drove his knee into Clay's midsection, forcing the air from his lungs.

Clay had forgotten how much Warren liked to fight. It was he who had taught Clay much of what he knew about brawling, and he'd been taught the hard way, taking beating after beating from his older brother until he'd learned to give as good as he got. But now Warren had him at a disadvantage and was taking pleasure in making sure he didn't lose it.

As Clay doubled over in pain, Warren doubled his fists together and brought them down on Clay's neck. He went instantly to the floor, pain flashing through his head.

Clay started to rise, his thoughts still on escape. But as he came to his hands and knees, Warren stepped forward and kicked him in the stomach, driving the air from him again. He brought his knees up to his midsection and gagged.

Warren was stepping in to kick him again when Jason yelled, "That's enough! I want him able to talk."

Clay heard the words in his pain-filled mind, but all he could do was moan.

Clay's mother hadn't moved from her spot on the sofa and as Warren bent down and pulled Clay to his feet, she went back to watching television. The commotion had brought Randy from the back of the house. "What's going on?" he asked, seeing Clay being held roughly by his brother.

"Come on in here and help Warren hold him," Jason said. "I want to see what your little brother has up his sleeve."

Chapter Twenty-one

Clay was held sagging between his brothers. His stomach and head throbbed and he felt nauseous. "Hold him up while I see what he's got on him," Jason Tory said as the brothers lifted him none too gently.

Jason found the tape recorder immediately and jerked the wire that held the microphone. The wire broke loose and Jason cackled. "So, runt, you thought you could get me to admit to something, did ya? You almost had me there until you slipped up with Ben. Now what did you have in mind with this here contraption?"

Clay looked at him through hate-filled eyes, but said nothing. Jason Tory chuckled, then without warning, he backhanded Clay across the face. Clay felt blood fill his mouth as his lip split, his head rocked to the side.

"What did you plan on doing with this?" Jason asked again, his tone low and menacing.

"I was planning on giving it to Ben Aguilar," Clay said, his voice dripping with venom.

Jason Tory looked from the tape recorder to his son. "You remember what I told you I would do if you tried to double-cross me?" Clay just stared at him without answering. "I told you what would happen to Jack Lomas if you tried anything," Jason continued.

Clay tried to lunge at him but his arms were restrained by his brothers. "If you do one thing to Jack, I'll kill you," Clay spat.

Jason threw back his head and laughed. "You sure are a hellcat," he said and looked over at his wife. "It makes me wonder if you're really mine."

Clay's mother looked at him in surprise then rolled her eyes as if she couldn't believe his statement, and went back to watching her program.

Jason laughed again. "I reckon you are. I just don't know where you get your highfalutin ideas from. Why couldn't you have been like your brothers here. They like our lifestyle, being in the lap of luxury the way we are, but no, you wanted something else. So what am I going to do with you now? Tie him up, boys, until I figure out what we're going to do."

They tied Clay's hands behind his back and bound his feet together, then sat him on the sofa on the end away from his mother. When she looked at him, Clay almost thought her eyes held sympathy but then she went back to watching TV and never looked at him again.

The three Torys went into the kitchen and gathered around the table, each with a beer in his hand. Clay could hear them talking as they tried to figure out what to do next.

"You reckon he's told anyone else what's going on?" Warren Tory asked.

"Nope. If he had they would have already been here to arrest us. I figure he was telling the truth about trying to get evidence to take to the sheriff."

"What are we going to do with him?" Randy Tory asked. "If he doesn't show back up at the ranch, won't Jack Lomas get suspicious?"

There was silence as Jason thought about the question. "Boys, things don't look too good. If someone's seen that Dodge parked out in our yard, they'll know he was here. If he was to come up missing they'd tell the sheriff. That wouldn't look good for us. We got to come up with a plan that won't lead back to us."

"If he don't show up at the ranch, Jack's going to go to the sheriff and they'll come straight here," Warren said.

"Hmmm, I think you just hit on it, Warren," Jason said with an evil smile.

Warren sat there looking proud of himself, though he had no idea what his father meant.

"We'll wait until it's good and dark, then we'll take Junior and the truck out to the Lomas ranch. Warren, you'll follow later in our truck—not much later, but late enough not to arouse any suspicion. We'll meet up at the turnoff. Junior here is going to help us get Jack Lomas. The trailer's due tonight to haul those cattle we got out of here. We'll load Jack and Clay on the trailer and send them along with the cattle. The people at the other end can take care of them when they get there. They'll just disappear. If anyone saw the pickup here, we'll just say he came by to get some of his clothes and we haven't seen him since. We'll play the worried, grieving family that wants to find their missing boy." Jason chuckled. "Why, we might even offer a reward for any information about our dear Clay."

Warren Tory frowned. "I don't think we should spend our money that way. Why waste money on a runt like that?"

Jason Tory reached across and slapped his oldest son upside his head. Warren reeled from the blow. "Why'd you slap me?" he asked, shocked by his father's sudden violence.

"Because you're too stupid to live, boy," Jason said. "We ain't gonna be payin' nobody, 'cause we're the only ones that'll know where they are, you idiot."

Warren sat there rubbing his head, and suddenly the light went on. "Oh yeah," he said, grinning like he'd finally gotten the punch line of a joke.

"It'll make people believe we really want to know what happened to our poor Clay if we're willing to pay a reward. Then we certainly couldn't have had anything to do with his disappearance," Jason said, explaining it to his two sons.

Clay could hear the conversation and felt his spirits fall as he realized they really meant to carry out their plan.

When darkness came, Warren and Randy came into the living room and unceremoniously pulled Clay to his feet. His hands were numb from being tied behind his back, and his legs, aching from lack of circulation, refused to move. They untied his feet and dragged him into the kitchen, where Jason Tory stood finishing off the last of his beer. "You know, you're really lucky Jack didn't find out about you telling us where the patrols were located. He probably would have turned you in to the sheriff, like he did his own son."

Clay looked up sharply. "What do you mean?" he asked.

Jason laughed at the look on his son's face. "You didn't know, did you?"

"Know what?" Clay asked, anger filling his voice.

"Old man Lomas caught his precious son Jaimie involved in stealin' cattle and he turned him right in to the sheriff. Just imagine, if he did that to his own son, what would he do to you? Why, he'd probably deliver you to the jail in person."

"You're lying." Clay spat at him, trying to break away from his brother's grip.

Jason Tory laughed. "Am I? I'll bet you've heard stories about Jack's son and wondered what happened to him. Everyone around here has kept it quiet. No one wanted to cause the great Jack Lomas any more pain than he'd already had to go through. I mean, after all, the poor man turned his only son into the law and got him killed. Why should he have any more pain than that?"

Clay stared at his father, knowing he was telling the truth, but hating him for telling it like he did. "How did his son die?" Clay asked tentatively.

"I don't know all the particulars of that. It was kept under wraps pretty well. It was some kind of car wreck or something," Jason said with a snide smile. "So you see, Junior, we're probably saving you from Jack Lomas and his sick sense of justice."

Clay stared at the floor. If his father was right, and he felt in his heart that he was, how would Jack react when he found out he was involved in all of this. Jack would never believe Clay was trying to protect him. He'd think he was helping them so he could get a share of the money.

"Come on, Randy, let's get him in the truck. I'll go out first to make sure nobody's watching. When I get in, you bring Junior out. Warren, you wait about fifteen minutes then follow in the pickup."

Jack walked to the screen door and looked up the road for the tenth time in the last two hours. The sun had already set and it was getting dark outside. Supper time had come and gone with no sign of Clay. He was beginning to get worried. He thought about calling the sheriff's office to see if there had been any accidents, but he knew if Clay had been in a wreck, they would have already called. He went back into the kitchen and poured himself another cup of coffee. Sighing fretfully, he sat at the table and tried to read one of his farm magazines, but found he couldn't concentrate on the articles. He'd already read the one on parasites in cattle three times and still didn't know what it said. He was thumbing through the pages, looking at the advertisements, when he heard the drone of a car engine. He remained seated and breathed a sigh of relief as he heard the engine slow and turn into the drive.

Clay was squeezed between his father and Randy, his hands still tied behind his back. They had stopped up the road and left the other pickup, and all four were in the front seat of the vehicle, packed like sardines.

Pulling into the yard, Jason took a handkerchief and stuffed it into Clay's mouth. "We don't want you yelling out a warning before we get into the house."

Stepping out of the pickup, Jason Tory hesitated before closing the door. Warren and Randy got out on the other side, closing the door behind them. Jason rolled his eyes and let the door close quietly. "Two doors slamming might make him wonder who was here," he said in a whisper to Warren, who instantly looked guilty and ashamed. "Remember," he said, still whispering, "I go in first. You bring him in right behind me." He pulled a pistol out of his belt and started up the sidewalk to the screen door.

Stepping up to the door, he opened it up and stepped inside, letting the door slam behind him.

"Is that you, Clay?" came Jack's voice from the kitchen.

"Uh huh," Jason said in voice loud enough for Jack

to hear. He turned and nodded to his sons, then walked directly to the kitchen, the gun held out in front of him.

Jack was looking at the door expecting Clay to come through it. When he saw Jason Tory step through the doorway with the pistol in his hand, he started to rise, surprise and anger registering on his face.

"Not so fast, Jack," Jason said, pointing the pistol menacingly at Jack's midsection. "Don't do anything we'll both regret."

Warren and Randy pushed Clay into the kitchen. Jack's shock at seeing the bruises and cuts on his face made him move toward him, but Jason Tory brought the gun up again. "Stay back," Jack stopped and slowly moved back to his place at the table.

Jason reached up and removed the gag from Clay's mouth. "Move over there beside Jack," he said, motioning with the barrel of the gun.

"You all right?" Jack asked, concern in his voice.

"I'm all right. I'm sorry about this," he said, feeling sick about letting Jack down.

"What do you want, Jason?" Jack asked angrily.

"Oh, we don't want anything from you, Jack, except a little of your time."

"They're going to send us out with a load of stolen cattle," Clay said.

"That's ridiculous," Jack said. "Ben already knows you're behind these cattle thefts. You want to add kidnapping to the charges you're already facing?"

All of the Torys looked at him in surprise, including Clay. "How'd you know?" Jason asked.

"I told you Ben already knows," he replied, hoping Jason would believe the lie. "He hasn't done anything because he wants to find out who else is involved. He knows it's somebody in Texas. He just hasn't found out who it is yet." He was hoping the information Clyde had given him was true enough to make Jason think the gig was up.

"Ben's been in Santa Fe all week. If he knew anything he'd be beatin' down our door to get us."

"He doesn't want just you. He also wants the guy you're shipping cattle to. He went to Santa Fe to get the district attorney's help."

Jason carefully thought about what he'd heard. Keeping his gaze locked on Jack, he mulled it over in his mind, finally coming to a conclusion. "Tie him up, boys. We're going ahead with our plan anyway."

"But what if he's tellin' the truth?" Warren asked, worried now.

"If he is it won't make no difference. Jack and your little brother will be in Texas. Harmon will take care of things on that end and we'll be long gone before Ben Aguilar can get enough evidence to do anything."

"You mean we're leaving here?" Randy asked in surprise and disappointment.

"We have to," Jason said. "If Jack here knows about us, you can bet others know as well. How they found out is beyond me, but we ain't got time to find out right now. You boys get old Jack here tied up and then go get our pickup."

Warren and Randy tied Jack's hands behind his back and sat him in a kitchen chair. Clay was made to sit in the chair across the table from him. They both heard the engine of the Dodge start up and leave the yard. Jason was roaming the house, looking around for something.

Clay sat with his eyes downcast. He couldn't bear to look at Jack. He felt the rancher's eyes on him but

he wouldn't look up to meet his gaze. Shame burned
through him.

"Looks like we're in quite a fix, doesn't it?" Jack
said.

Clay looked up at him, and instead of seeing the
anger he'd expected, he saw a small smile on Jack's
face. He stared at him for a few moments then said, "I
reckon we are. I'm sorry I got us into this mess."

"You didn't get us into this mess. Your father got us
into this."

"Yeah, but if I hadn't gone there tonight and tried to
get him to confess to the cattle rustling, we wouldn't
be in this pickle."

"Maybe, but then again it might have been worse,"
Jack replied.

"I don't see how it could be much worse," Clay
said.

"Oh, it could always be worse. The thing is, we got
to use our heads and if we get a chance we got to be
ready."

"You knew my family was involved in those cattle
thefts, but did you know I was telling him where the
patrols were?"

Jack didn't answer immediately, and when he did
his voice was soft. "I knew. I saw you the night you
were in the church and I overheard you on the phone
the day everybody was here. I was in the bedroom
getting a tube of antibiotic cream when you made the
call."

Clay's shocked expression didn't begin to express
what he felt. "Why didn't you say something?"

Jack let out a weary sigh. "I made a mistake once
and I didn't want to make another one."

"Jaimie?" Clay asked.

Jack nodded. "He was a lot like you except he didn't

want to stay and work on the ranch. He wanted things the easy way."

Jason walked back into the kitchen with Jack's 30-30 rifle tucked under his arm. "I don't reckon you'll mind if I keep this. I might want to do some deer hunting in my new home."

"They don't let you hunt deer in prison," Jack said.

Jason Tory laughed harshly. "That's good, Jack, but I ain't goin' to prison. I've been waitin' a long time to make it big and I've finally done it. I'm shipping this last load—with two extra head." He chuckled. "By the time Ben puts all the pieces together I'll be long gone with a new name and living respectable."

Jack chuckled derisively. "Jason, you ain't smart enough to live respectable. You'll be in prison before you see your next birthday, but at least you'll have your two boys in there with you. Yes sir, you can have your own little family business in there making license plates. I think I'll order me a personalized one just so I'll know it was you that made it."

"You won't be around to order anything, Jack. You're going to be in Texas, or should I say *under* Texas."

"Tell me something, Jason, how can you treat your own son this way?" Jack asked, nodding toward Clay.

"He ain't my son no more. He moved out, said he didn't want nothing to do with us. What would you do if your son said he didn't want anything to do with you? Oh, but that's right, your son said that and you turned him into the sheriff, isn't that right, Jack? Of course, it wasn't your fault he died as a result of it, is it, Jack?"

"You're a sick man, Jason. Just because Clay didn't want to go along with your thievin' ways isn't any reason to do this to him."

"But he was going to get evidence against us and turn us in to the sheriff. He even had a tape recorder hidden in his pocket. I couldn't just let him get away with that."

Jack started to reply, but stopped as they all heard the sound of the truck engine starting up the drive. "Hold on to that thought, Jack. I'll be right back," Jason said, turning and walking to the front door.

"So you were going to tape your father and brother's confession and take it to Ben?" Jack asked.

"It sounded good at the time," Clay said with a shrug.

"It would have been real good if it had worked," Jack responded, "but why didn't you just tell me and we could have done something about it."

Clay hesitated. "This is going to sound kind of strange considering the circumstances right now, but they threatened to hurt you if I told them."

Jack laughed outright. "You're right, it does sound kind of strange."

Chapter Twenty-two

Jack and Clay were placed in the back of the Torys' pickup. Their feet were bound to prevent them from attempting escape. Their backs were to the cab of the pickup, and each time the truck hit a bump, the bed frame jarred their spines.

"Now I know how a pool ball feels," Clay said, clenching his teeth and trying to move away from the pickup bed.

"I got a feeling this is going to be the good part of the ride," Jack said. "Riding in a trailer with a load of cattle all the way to Texas isn't my idea of a fun time."

"Is there any chance Ben's coming to the rescue."

"I wouldn't count on it. All that stuff I told your dad was a bunch of lies. I have no idea why Ben's in Santa Fe. I learned all about Jason's shady dealing from Clyde Jones. He once crossed paths with a known criminal and almost killed him, and since then he's had a sort of . . . um, an open relationship with him. This criminal told Clyde all about your dad and what he was doing."

"And you knew I was involved?"

"I figured you were. I just didn't know how or why," Jack said.

"Why didn't you turn me in to Ben when you found out?" Clay asked, trying to see Jack's face in the darkness.

"Like I said, I already made one mistake. I didn't want to make another."

"What happened?" Clay asked, sensing Jack wanted to talk.

"Jaimie was everything to me. My immortality so to speak. I wanted him to like the things I liked—the ranch, rodeo, horses—but he wanted everything easy. I guess I spoiled him, gave in to him too much. When I finally quit giving him everything he wanted, he started stealing. He was stealing cattle from all my neighbors, even stole some of mine to keep me from getting suspicious, but I found out. He always had too much money, bought too many things. I figured out what he was up to and told him to turn himself in. I told him I would stand beside him, get him an attorney, but he just scoffed at me. He told me he didn't want anything I had, he'd found a way to get what he wanted, so I went to the sheriff and told him everything. He was coming to arrest Jaimie that night. They met on the road. Jaimie had a horse loaded in the cattle trailer, on his way to steal more cattle. The sheriff turned around and started after him, and Jaimie panicked and tried to outrun him. He lost control and rolled the pickup and trailer. He was killed instantly. I've never forgiven myself since."

Clay sat in stunned silence. What an awful ordeal for a man to have to go through. He remembered Will Hightower's words in Ruidoso, *What Jack had gone through would have killed most men.* Those words came back to him as he considered what he'd heard. "I'm sorry, Jack. If I'd known I wouldn't have gone along with my father's demands."

Jack looked steadily at Clay. "You did what you thought you had to and you did it for unselfish reasons. There's no comparison between what you did and what Jaimie did. He stole cattle for selfish reasons. You went along with your father because he threatened me. I can't tell you how proud I am for what you tried to do."

Clay blinked and tried to swallow. "But look at the jam I got us into."

"Well, I didn't say you went about it in the right way," Jack said with a soft chuckle. "You should have come and told me when he first approached you."

"I was afraid he'd do what he threatened."

"If I'd known we could have been prepared. Ben could have had him watched," Jack said. "But that's all hindsight and you know what they say about hindsight?"

"What's that?" Clay asked.

"It has twenty-twenty vision," Jack said.

"Well you got any ideas about how we're going to get out of this mess?" Clay asked.

"We just have to wait for an opportunity. But meanwhile why don't you turn your back around here and let me see if I can work on those ropes."

Clay moved around until his back was against Jack's. Clay tried to avoid being seen by the three in the front seat, but they seemed intent on the road ahead of them.

"Where do you think we're headed?" Clay asked.

"We've been heading south for the last five to ten miles. The best I can figure we're close to Larry Shupes's place."

Jack worked at the knots binding Clay's hands. The coarse rope they used was hard on his fingers. His fingernails broke and bled and his arms ached from the effort, but he didn't stop.

"We're slowing down," Clay noted.

"We're going to Larry's west pasture. He's got some

holding pens about four miles down this road. We got maybe fifteen minutes before we get there. The knots are starting to come loose," Jack made himself concentrate on the ropes. He could feel the knots coming loose and tried to work faster.

Clay felt the ropes binding his hands slacken. He squeezed them together to loosen them more and heard Jack's grunt of triumph at the same time the pressure on his wrists was released.

"Quick. Untie your feet," Jack said as the ropes slipped away.

"Let me untie your hands first," Clay said, reaching for Jack's hands, but Jack twisted away.

"Listen to me. We don't have enough time. We'll be there in a minute. Untie your feet and get ready."

Clay hesitated only a moment before reaching down and untying the ropes on his feet while Jack watched the three in front.

Once the ropes were off of his feet Clay turned to Jack. "Let me untie you."

"No, we're there," he said, nodding to the front of the truck. Clay glanced through the windows of the pickup and saw the headlights illuminate a set of holding pens. There were at least thirty head of cattle in the pen. There was a one-ton pickup with a thirty-two-foot gooseneck stock trailer backed up to the loading chute.

"When we slow down you jump out the back and run, run as fast as you can. Change directions as you run. They're going to come after you, but you're smarter than they are so use your head. Charles Brown's house is about three miles due north—you can't miss it if you can find the oil top road that runs north and south. Get to his house and call for help. Tell the sheriff's office that they'll probably take the cattle north to Clovis then into Texas. That way they can stay on county roads."

"I can't leave you here. There's no telling what my father and brothers will do," Clay said.

"You're the best chance I've got of staying alive. Jason's not going to kill me if you can testify against him. He'll try to use me to get you to come back, but don't you listen to him. Now, get ready, we're almost there."

Clay tensed, ready to bolt as soon as the truck slowed.

"Clay," Jack spoke in soft voice.

Clay turned to look at him. "Sir?"

"Cowboy up and ride hard," Jack said with a nod.

"Yes sir," he answered in a confident voice.

Clay sensed the vehicle slowing and moved himself around to the back of the cab. Watching for the glow of the brake lights, he pushed his body up slightly with his hands and realized how sore his muscles were. He had been tied for hours now, and the beating he'd taken from his older brother had taken its toll.

The brake lights came on and the pickup slowed to turn. Clay knew it was time. "I'll have help on the way," he said, looking at Jack. Jack nodded and Clay pushed himself up and made it to the tailgate of the pickup in one stride. Grabbing the top of the tailgate, he hurtled over and down to the ground. His legs screamed in protest as he hit the hard dirt of the road and his knees buckled beneath him, but the adrenaline was coursing through him, his mind yelling for him to run. He was on his feet in an instant, running across the road they'd just come down. Dodging scrub brush and cactus, he ran into the darkness, changing directions as Jack had instructed.

The truck skidded to a stop, throwing Jack against the hard metal. He grimaced as his back collided with the hard edge of the pickup bed.

Jason Tory was out of the truck and running before it came to a complete stop. "Come back here, you little whelp!" he yelled, aiming the gun in the direction he had seen Clay run. Jack saw the move and feared the elder Tory was actually going to shoot, but as quickly as he aimed the gun he lowered it and jumped back into the pickup. Jack could hear him shouting orders to Warren and was thrown over as he slammed the pickup in reverse and mashed the gas pedal to the floor, turning the wheel sharply to the right.

When Warren jerked the pickup's automatic transmission into forward and stomped the gas pedal to the floor, the engine flooded, causing it to die. Jason cussed his son, calling him several names that caused Warren to become even more distressed, which resulted in his flooding the engine even more.

Jason yanked open his door and jumped out, running around the pickup and jerking the driver's side door open. He grabbed Warren by the shirt and dragged him from the seat. "Get out of there, you fool." Taking the driver's position, he frantically turned the ignition until the engine turned and finally caught, coughing and sputtering until it had expelled all the excess gas from the carburetor. Black smoke boiled from the exhaust and rolled into the bed where Jack sat, coughing and choking until Jason put the truck in gear and spun away.

Clay ran as he'd never run before. He thanked his lucky stars he was wearing his low-heeled roper boots. Darkness surrounded him with no moon to light the night. His eyes soon became accustomed to the inky dark and he could make out objects in his path, but not before he'd run into several mesquite bushes and yucca plants. His arms were scratched and his shirt torn, but he felt none of it as he ran. He could hear the sound of the truck engine moving in the direction he'd first run, but he'd changed direction and was running south. He knew his father would think he'd head back toward the road leading to town, but he'd actually gone in the opposite direction, then switched and headed west.

Topping a small rise, Clay looked in the direction of the holding pens. He could see the headlights of the pickup moving left then right in a searching pattern across the pasture. He could see the headlights bouncing and knew the truck was moving fast across the rough terrain. He knew Jack would still be in the back of the truck, and with his hands tied he would be battered unmercifully in the metal bed of the truck. But Clay knew if he didn't get away and get help they could expect a lot worse. Turning, he started into a slow trot. He'd have to conserve his energy if he expected to last.

"We'll never find him out here," Warren Tory whined.

Jason Tory knew his son was right, but he wasn't about to say anything. He also knew they had to get the cattle loaded and on the road while it was still dark. Their accomplice driver would already be nervous and if they spent any more time out here, he was likely to pull out, leaving them with a pen full of stolen cattle.

Turning the pickup in a wide arc, Jason headed back toward the holding pens, moving slower while continuing to watch for Clay.

Jack tried to sit up. He'd been thrown on his side

when the pickup turned around and had been tossed around like a sack of potatoes in the metal bed. He felt a lump rising on his head where he'd smashed against one of the wheel wells. His arms and back were battered and his tailbone had been slammed so many times it felt like it was broken. He'd finally been able to wedge the toes of his boots under the top of the bed where the metal had been turned under. By hooking his toes under this lip and pushing his back against the opposite side, he'd managed to keep from being slammed around so much, though he still took a beating.

When Jason pulled back up to the holding pens, the driver was in his truck and the engine was running. Jason pulled his pickup in front and blocked him from moving. Getting out of the truck, he walked up to the driver, who was sitting with his window down. "Let's get these cattle loaded," Jason said.

"Hey look, fella, I didn't bargain for any of this," the driver said to Jason's retreating back.

"Come on," Jason commanded, "we don't have that many hours of darkness left."

They ran the cattle up the chute and into the trailer with little trouble.

"Get going," Jason hissed, sliding the latch closed on the gate.

"Move your truck," the driver said, "and I'm outa here."

"Warren, move the truck, and try not to flood the engine while you're at it," Jason said sternly.

Jack watched the truck and trailer pull away. He wondered what was going to happen now. The three Torys had been standing by the loading chute talking, but now they were walking toward the truck.

Jason Tory looked in the back. "That was a stupid move on your part, letting that boy loose."

"Oh, I don't know," Jack said. "From where I sit I think it was pretty smart. He's free and can testify against you."

"He may be free but we won't be around for him to testify against. But you won't be alive to learn that."

"That's the problem with you, Jason, you're so stupid you think everyone else is too. They'll catch you and when they do they'll lock you up for so long you'll be an old man when you come out, if you even live that long."

"You better watch your mouth, Jack. Right now I feel the urge to do damage to something and you're real convenient, so don't provoke me. Let's go, boys," he spat, nodding toward the cab.

Jack leaned back against the bed of the truck and tried to get comfortable. His arms and hands were numb and his back, legs, and head ached badly. He thought about trying to watch where they were going, but figured it would be of little use.

The cool night air was a blessing as Clay ran. Though the evening was cool, sweat poured off his body and soaked his clothes. His feet hurt and his lungs felt as if they would burst, but still he ran. He'd found the oil top road Jack had told him about and by his estimation he had another mile to go. Slowing to a walk, he breathed in large gulps of air. He was alternating running and walking, running for ten minutes, walking for five. After his allotted five minutes he broke into a run again, and topping a rise, he saw the lights of a barn and house half a mile away. *That must be the Brown place*, he thought and picked up the pace.

* * *

Jack had finally dozed off as the pickup moved on blacktop. He was awakened when it turned off onto a rough gravel road. Looking up over the tailgate, he studied the surroundings. This place looked familiar, but he couldn't place it from his limited view.

The pickup continued on for another mile before turning again. This time it went only a short distance before stopping. Warren opened the passenger door and got out, and a moment later the truck moved forward again and stopped.

Must be a gate, Jack thought to himself. Warren returned to the pickup and got in, and they started up again. A few moments later the pickup came to a stop and the engine shut off.

The doors to the truck opened and Jason Tory spoke. "Warren, you get our stuff out of the barn. Randy, you get Jack out of the truck."

Jack struggled to sit up as Randy lowered the tailgate. He reached in and grabbed Jack by the boots and started dragging him toward the back, not caring that he was dragging him across the ridges of the truck and causing excruciating pain to shoot through Jack's spine.

When Jack's feet hit the ground, his knees wouldn't hold his weight and he collapsed to the ground. "Get up, old man," Randy Tory said, nudging him none too gently with the toe of his boot. Jack struggled to his knees and finally to his feet, with no help from Randy. He stood wobbling for a moment before he was pushed toward the front of the pickup.

Jason Tory was busy hauling sacks out of a shed while Warren started loading things from the barn. Jack saw him bring out a television set, a VCR, two camcorders, and other electronic equipment and load them in the back of the truck. Randy's job was to watch Jack, who was finally starting to get some feeling back in his legs. He watched the Torys go about their loading and wondered where all the items had come from, figuring most of them were stolen. Jason came out of the shed carrying a small metal box. He was holding it close to him as if it contained something valuable. Jack suspected it was part of the money he'd gotten from the sale of the stolen cattle.

Warren was still carrying electronics from the barn and noticed Randy standing idly by. "Why don't you tie him to that tree over there and give me a hand?" he said with anger.

" 'Cause Dad told me to keep an eye on him," Randy protested. Warren shook his head and put the stereo he was carrying in the back of the truck.

The eastern sky was beginning to show signs of daylight and as the darkness lifted, Jack looked around and studied his surroundings. He knew immediately where they were. He'd been close to this place on several occasions. Matt Hick's place was only a little ways from here and he'd been a visitor there many times. As a matter of fact, he'd passed by this very barn on his way to see Matt. He didn't know if it would matter or not, but it made him feel better knowing where he was, as if by knowing, he had an edge.

Chapter Twenty-three

The barn where they were sat in a small valley, bordered on either side by rolling hills. Looking down the road that ran through the valley, Jack could see three cars coming up fast. They were still four or five miles away but Jack knew they were sheriff's cars. His pulse quickened and he wanted to shout for joy, but his face remained expressionless, and he looked away from the cars so as not to draw Randy's attention to their inevitable appearance.

Jason was now helping Warren carry the items from the barn, and Jack was amazed at the number of things they loaded in the pickup. The Torys must have been stealing or fencing stolen items for quite a spell, he thought.

"There's one more TV and a stereo left in there," Warren said as he came out with another VCR. "I don't know where we're going to put them. The truck's almost fully loaded."

"Leave them," Jason said. "We've got enough."

"Hey, Jason, that's some nice stuff you got there," Jack said. "You going to open up your own store in prison? You ought to be able to trade a lot of that stuff for cigarettes and chocolate bars in there."

"Keep laughing, Jack, but if you'll notice, you're the one that's tied up and we're the ones with the truckload of goods."

Jack glanced down the road. The sheriff's cars had stopped over a mile away, as if waiting for something. He wanted to keep the Torys occupied.

"What do you plan on doing with me?" Jack asked.

"I'm glad you asked, Jack. I've been thinking about putting you down in that old well over there and leaving you," he said, pointing to a hole surrounded by stones. "I figure it'll take three or four days for you to die. Of course, I might make an anonymous call from somewhere up the road and tell them where to find you, or I might not." He laughed at his own sick humor.

Jack looked him straight in the eye. "You're about the lowest form of human life I've ever met," he said.

"Now, Jack, if you're trying to get on my good side, it's not working," Jason said.

Jack glanced down the road and saw the cars were now moving toward them. There were now four cars, and they were moving slowly so as not to make a dust cloud. They were less than half a mile away and would be there in less than a minute. "Where do you think you're going to be able to go that the law won't catch up to you?" he asked, looking back at Jason.

"Oh, now, Jack, you don't think I'm crazy enough to tell you that, do you?"

Jack chuckled. "Well, like I've been sayin' all along, Jason, you ain't too bright. I thought it might be worth a try." He was pleased to see anger come to Jason's eyes.

"Don't push it, Jack. I've taken about all I'm going to take from you."

Jack smiled inwardly. If he could make Tory mad, he might not hear the cars until it was too late. "Why, Jason, I wouldn't want to upset you for all the world.

My mother always told me not to make fun of the learning disabled. It's not your fault you're stupid."

Jason's face flushed crimson in anger. He stepped forward, balling his fist, and hit Jack full in the face. Jack's head snapped back and he tasted blood. Though he was weakened from the night's ordeal, he didn't go down. Shaking his head to clear it, he stood up straight and smiled at Jason. "I've been hit harder than that by women," he said.

Jason's face contorted in rage, and lowering his head, he charged at Jack, head-butting him in the stomach and knocking both of them to the ground. Jack hit the ground hard. His hands were still tied behind him and he had no way to cushion his fall. The air was knocked from him and he labored hard to breathe. Jason sat astride him and drew back his fist to strike again when Warren yelled, "Dad, the law's coming."

Jason whirled around and saw the cars coming up the road. They were almost to the gate leading into the barn. Jack was trying to suck precious air into his lungs when he heard Jason let loose a torrent of curses.

Jason saw the lead car crash through the metal gate and speed toward them. Warren and Randy were looking at him, waiting for direction. He glanced around and knew they couldn't make a run for it. Pulling the pistol from his belt, he reached down and grabbed Jack by the collar of his shirt and started pulling him up. "Get on your feet," he hissed, yanking harder.

Jason stepped behind Jack as the sheriff cars pulled to a stop fifty yards away. Six deputies stepped out of the cars, each one holding a rifle in his hands. Using the car doors as shields, they waited.

Jack saw Ben Aguilar step out the fourth car and he smiled when he saw the passenger he had with him. Clay opened the car door and stepped out. When he saw his father holding Jack he started forward, but Ben reached out and stopped him, then turned to look at Jason. "Give it up, Tory," he said in a calm voice. "There's no way out and there's no use making things worse than they already are."

Jason held the pistol to the side of Jack's head. "If you come any closer, Ben, I'm going to have to put a bullet in old Jack's head here!"

Warren and Randy stood off to one side, staring at their father. Both had thought he would give up, but now he was standing behind Jack with a pistol at his head. Neither had thought it would ever go this far, and they kept glancing at each other nervously.

"I want you and your boys to get back in your cars and drive out of here!" Jason said, shouting at Ben.

Ben looked around at the six deputies, each one now aiming his rifle at Jason Tory. "Sorry, Jason, but we can't do that. This ends here. Now throw down your gun and let Jack go."

Jason laughed maniacally. "I reckon you don't care too much for Jack here, Ben. Are you willing to see his brains blown out? If you and your deputies don't start moving out I'm going to squeeze this trigger."

"If you do, Jason," Ben said, "my deputies will open fire on you and your boys. Is that what you want? Are you willing to sacrifice your sons?" Warren licked his lips nervously and Randy edged behind his older brother.

"Dad," Warren said, his voice cracking, "let's give it up. They've got us. We can't get away."

"Shut up, you sniveling brat. We're not caught yet.

As long as we've got Jack they're not going to do anything."

"Yeah, but they're not going to leave, Dad. They won't let us go," Warren whined.

"Shut up, Warren!" he shouted. "Let me think." He stood behind Jack, the gun held only inches from his head. "You boys start backing toward the barn. We'll hole up in there until I can decide what to do."

The two boys started creeping back toward the barn, casting nervous glances at their father, then at the deputies holding guns. Jason tightened his grip on Jack's collar and leaned close to his ear. "You and I are going to move to the barn. If you stumble, trip, or in any way make a wrong move, I'm going to blow your head off. Now come on!" He pulled Jack backward, glancing behind him.

Ben saw their intent as they started to move. "Hold it right there, Jason," he shouted, but Tory ignored him.

"Keep moving, Jack," he said.

Ben watched, feeling helpless as the Torys moved into the barn. He knew it would be a long ordeal now.

"What are we going to do now, Pa?" Warren asked, peering out the window to look at the group of lawmen gathered outside.

"I don't know yet, but at least I got some time to think," he said. He walked to the window and peered out. He could see men moving into position, surrounding the barn.

Ben Aguilar now had his bullhorn out. "Jason, you might as well give it up before someone gets killed. Throw down your guns and come out. No one will hurt you. I promise."

Jason didn't respond. He had placed Jack in a sitting position in one corner of the barn and told Randy to watch him. Jason was now pacing the floor, careful to stay away from all of the windows. Warren was staring anxiously at his father. His nervousness was making him sweat. His shirt was soaked.

Outside, Ben looked at the sky overhead. It was going to be a hot day and there was little if any shade around. The barn would soon become a pressure cooker. He knew Jason Tory was a keg of dynamite that could blow anytime. He continued warning his men not to shoot as long as Jack was held hostage, a reminder of just how explosive the situation was.

The state police had moved into position to totally surround the barn. There was no way anyone could escape without being seen.

Ben tried again to talk to the Torys, but there was no response. From his hostage training he knew that was not a good sign. It was going to be a long standoff.

By noon the temperature in the barn was well over one hundred degrees. All four occupants were soaked with sweat and Jack was near to passing out, being unable to move away from the sweltering heat radiated by the tin on the side of the barn.

Jason Tory had alternated between pacing and sitting. No one had spoken in the past two hours. Warren had tried to reason with his father and had received a backhanded slap. Since then, he had been sitting on one of the work benches sulking. Randy had found a five-gallon bucket to use as a seat and now sat ten feet from Jack, fanning himself with a piece of cardboard he'd found.

Jack's heat-addled brain tried to think of some way out of the situation but he could see no way to disarm Jason. As far as he could tell, there was no way out of the barn except through the doors on either end or the

window on either side. He knew if he had a chance
he'd go out one of the windows, but they hadn't let
him stand up, much less get close to one.

Clay fidgeted back and forth along the row of cars.
He had asked Ben over and over what they were
going to do, until Ben had finally warned him to stay
back and be quiet or he'd have him taken to town.

It was soon four o'clock in the afternoon and the
sun was starting its slow descent toward the west.
Clay watched the barn for any kind of movement.
There had been none since the men had entered early
this morning. He wondered how Jack was holding up.
He had looked done-in early this morning and Clay
knew that being bound in the heat of the barn all day
would take its toll on the older man.

Clay had taken over the responsibility of bringing
fresh water to the deputies and state police during the
day as they held their positions. He wondered how
those inside were faring without water. As he moved
around the perimeter of the barn he had an opportunity to study the structure. The barn itself was only
ten or eleven years old, being constructed mostly of
tin and pipe. It ran east and west, with large sliding
doors on either end and one small door, the one the
men had entered on the east end.

It was a combination hay barn and workshop, Clay
surmised, with the hay being stored in the upper loft.
There were two smaller doors overhead, and on the
west end there was a boom and pulley used to hoist
bales of hay into the loft. He knew there had to be a
door in the floor of the loft that led to the workshop.
If a man could get inside the loft, he might be able to
catch them by surprise.

There was only one deputy watching that side of
the barn, a young man named Billy Trent. Clay knew

Billy fairly well and had spent time talking with him during the day as he brought water. He had kept him filled in on what was happening and carried messages to him from Ben, since they were trying to keep radio silence, so as not to tip off the Torys to any of their positions.

Clay told Ben about the loft and his idea, but Ben didn't feel the risk was worth taking. "They'll come out when they get thirsty enough," he said.

"But what about Jack?" Clay asked. "He didn't look too good when they took him in there. I don't think he'll make it long without water."

"I can't take the risk," Ben said and turned and walked away.

Clay held his tongue instead of arguing, and continued carrying water to the men, but the idea wouldn't leave his mind and he continued to run a plan through his mind, noting what it would take to make it work. By the time darkness started to fall, he had everything worked out. All it would take was a rope, a pair of gloves in his back pocket, and a whole lot of luck.

The bullhorn blared out once again. "Jason, give it up. Throw out your weapons and let Jack go. I promise you, you and your boys won't be harmed."

Jason looked up from where he sat. His eyes held the look of someone who had lost touch with reality. Jack shifted his position, trying to ease the pain in his back. His throat was parched and his body ached all over. He looked at Jason and knew the man was beyond reason. He had seen everything he'd planned for go up in smoke. Now he was in a predicament that was beyond his mental capacity to cope with. Jack knew it wouldn't take much more for the man to go completely over the edge.

Jason didn't respond to the bullhorn, but walked to the window and peered around the edge into the glaring lights from the patrol cars, then returned to his seat on the fifty-five-gallon drum and sat staring at the window.

Clay set his water bucket down before he reached Billy's position and followed the path around the small knoll where Billy sat waiting. Darkness completely blanketed them. There was no moon as of yet and Clay gave a silent prayer of thanks as he approached Billy's position. Clay had stayed away longer than he usually had. He had to make Billy believe that what he was about to tell him was the truth, and he wanted him anxious.

Rounding the knoll, Clay spotted Billy sitting with his back against a scrub oak. "What took you so long," he asked as Clay came up to him. "And where's the water? I've been out for half an hour now and I'm about to die. I can only imagine what those in the barn are feeling like."

"I didn't bring any water," Clay said and saw the disappointment in Billy's eyes. "Ben wants you to move around to the east side. They're going to move in and take them from that side.

"They're going to rush them?" Billy asked incredulously.

"No, they're going to move in and catch them by surprise," Clay said.

"Then I reckon we better get going," Billy said.

Clay had anticipated this and hurried to say, "You go on, I've got to go around and tell a couple of the others."

"All right," Billy said, hurrying off in the direction from which Clay had just come.

Clay didn't waste any time once he'd made sure

Billy was gone. Taking the rope from the place he'd hidden it nearby, he crept silently to the barn until he was below the boom. Fashioning a loop in one end, he swung the rope and threw it at the end of the boom. The rope hit the boom but the loop didn't go over and the rope fell back to the ground, hitting it with a thud.

Clay winced as the rope landed, knowing it might have alerted those inside. He waited, his back pressed against the wall of the barn. After a moment, making sure no one had heard, he coiled the rope again and made another loop. Taking a deep breath, trying to relax and picture himself roping cattle with Jack on the ranch, he swung the rope and threw. The loop settled over the end of the beam and tightened as Clay pulled the slack.

Taking the gloves from his back pocket, Clay grabbed the rope and began climbing, using his legs to wrap around the rope as he went. Once he'd made it to the beam, he pulled himself up and grabbed on to it, then inched along the beam until he was at its base, still outside the window. Looking along the edge of the window, he saw a frame had been built around it. It was only two inches wide but if he could grab hold of it he could swung himself in. Letting go with his right hand he reached over and grabbed the edge.

Now came the tricky part. Letting go of the beam with his left hand, he quickly grabbed the frame. Holding his feet up he swung inward, gripping hard with the tips of his fingers. He let his feet swing in and then back out until his swing slowed and he could gently let his feet down without making a sound.

Arched against the doorway, he pushed himself upright and stood in the darkness. Now that he was in, the problem was to find the door leading down to the first floor. Standing still, he let his eyes grow accustomed to the murkiness of the barn. He began making out bales of hay stacked on his left. He moved forward warily, making sure he made no noise as he moved.

Ben was standing by his car drinking another cup of coffee when Billy Trent walked up to him. "I'm here," Bill said. Ben looked up at him, surprise showing on his face. "What are you doing away from your post, Billy?" he asked, his voice a mixture of anger and bewilderment.

"Clay told me you were going in after them," he said, his voice trailing off as he saw the look on Ben's face.

"That little . . ." Ben said, throwing down the Styrofoam cup he held and splashing coffee on his patrol car. "Come on, that fool's gone into the barn. We've got to get up there."

Ben sent Billy to bring the other deputies and state police. When they were all gathered, he spoke quietly and calmly. "We got someone in the barn loft," he said, "and if he gets down below, we've got to be ready to move. I want two men on either side of the small door and one man by the two windows. We may have to create a diversion to help him," he said with a deep breath.

Clay eased forward, cautious step after cautious step. He'd already checked out the north side of the barn and found no door. He was easing along the south wall when he saw what he was looking for. There along the wall, he could see a spot clear of any loose hay. Looking hard, he could see the door's handle sticking up. Easing forward, he knelt and grabbed it.

Warren Tory sat alone in the darkness contemplating his future. As he saw it, he would soon be either dead or in prison. Between the two he was sure he preferred prison over death, but if things continued as they were he felt certain his father was going to take this all the way. Outnumbered and outgunned, there was no way they could come out of this alive. He felt like crying. He was still sitting on the tool bench when he felt something thin stick him in the shoulder.

Reaching up, he pulled it off and looked at it. It was a piece of hay, and the only place a piece of hay could have come from was up above. Looking up, he could see the outline of the hayloft. Following it around, he could just make out the dim formation of the door and the ladder that came down the wall behind him and to his left. As he watched the door, he was startled to first see it open slightly, then open wider. He opened his mouth to call out, but closed it just as quickly. It was time for this to end, one way or another.

Clay opened the door and eased it back, letting it down gently, leaving the stairway open. Sticking his head through the door, he peered into the barn below. He could make out the images below from the headlight shining through the windows. He saw his father sitting on a drum, his back to him. He spotted Jack in the corner and Randy sitting on a bucket nearby, his head bent over as if asleep. Looking around, he gave a start as his eyes fell on Warren, realizing he was being watched. Clay started to jump back, fear clutching at his spine. Expecting to hear Warren shout a warning, he was shocked to see his brother turn back around and stare at the opposite side of the barn.

The ladder Clay had to go down was located on the opposite side of the barn. It was partially illuminated by the headlights, which meant Clay would be in the light part of the way down. Taking a deep breath, he stepped on the first rung and eased himself down, moving as silently as possible. He crept down stealthily, one rung at a time, turning to watch his father and brothers.

Jack opened his eyes. He had been dozing, but something had awakened him. With agony, he pushed himself up to a sitting position and looked around. Randy sat on his bucket with his head in his hands, apparently asleep. Jason sat with his back to him, still staring at the wall. Looking around, he saw Warren on the workbench staring at the same wall. Then his eyes caught a movement and his heart stopped. He recognized instantly who was coming down the ladder, but wondered why. It should have been a deputy, not Clay. He looked back at Jason, but he remained in the same position. Then he looked at Warren and wondered why he didn't turn around. Surely he could hear or even sense Clay behind him.

Clay continued his downward descent. He held his breath, expecting at any moment to hear his father's yell. He still didn't understand why Warren hadn't called out, but he was thankful he didn't. He stopped as his foot came in contact with the concrete floor. Glancing around, his eyes sought out each of the four men in the room. Through the dim light he could just make out each of them. Jack was staring at him as he stepped away from the ladder. Clay caught his eye and nodded to him, then moved along the wall toward him.

The workbench Warren sat on was only two feet away from where the ladder came down. Spotting a large crescent wrench, Clay reached over and picked it up, then started moving slowly along the wall. He had no plan from this point. He only knew he had to do something to help Jack.

Jack watched him move along the wall. He held his breath, expecting at any moment for Warren to turn and see him. Feeling certain he would shout a warning, the boy just sat staring at the wall like his father did.

Clay moved around a table, now close enough to reach out and touch Jack. He looked at him and gave him a weak smile, then turned and started toward his father, keeping his steps light and slow. He was within four feet of Jason when he raised the wrench over his head.

Jack would never know if it was the movement itself or if Jason sensed someone behind him, but at that moment he turned his head and saw Clay behind him. Clay's heart lurched in his chest as Jason's head came around. Jason still held the gun in his hand and as he turned, he started bringing it up. Clay didn't hesitate as he saw the gun. Lunging forward, Clay swung the wrench at Jason's arm. It hit Jason's forearm and he let out a scream of pain, dropping the pistol. Clay raised the wrench again but before he could swing again Randy hit him from behind, driving the wind from him and knocking him into Jason, who staggered backward but kept his feet.

Clay was down on his hands and knees when Jason straightened up. Randy had stepped back after knocking him down and watched as his father picked up the pistol with his left hand, and swung around to take aim at Clay. Jason was awkwardly pulling the hammer back with his left hand as the door burst open. Looking up, he saw Ben Aguilar come charging through the door, two deputies right behind him.

Swinging the gun around, he tried to bring his

sights to bear on the three men when the first shot
rang out, catching him in the right shoulder and spinning him around. Staggering but regaining his balance, he now stood facing Jack Lomas. In that
moment he saw the man he thought was to blame for
spoiling everything he'd worked for. Bringing the gun
up, he thumbed back the hammer again. The ominous
click was the last sound he ever heard as three bullets
hit him in the back and slammed him forward, where
he fell in a heap on top of Jack.

Nobody moved for several moments. Then Clay
pushed himself off the floor and stood up. Looking at
his brothers, he saw they were both staring at where
their father lay.

Ben walked over and pulled Jason off Jack and
helped Jack sit up. He felt for Jason's pulse but he already knew he was gone. Clay stood in shock until
his eyes came to rest on Jack. In an instant he was on
his knees in front of him, his arms tight around the
rancher's neck, tears pouring from his eyes. Clay was
squeezing Jack so tightly he was coming close to
choking him, but Jack said nothing as he felt the
warm tears drip onto his shirt.

Ben took in the scene and stepping behind Jack, he
quickly untied his hands. As his hands were freed,
Jack wrapped his arms around Clay and hugged him
to his chest, the tension draining from him. Ben
walked away quietly, a broad smile on his face.

The deputies handcuffed Randy and Warren, and
loaded them into the car, then started taking inven-
tory of the items in the pickup. They went through
the barns and shed, checking everything for more
stolen items and evidence. Jason was covered with a
blanket, awaiting the coroner's arrival.

Jack and Clay stood to one side, watching until Ben

came up to them. "I ought to throw you in jail," he said, looking sternly at Clay. "That was a foolish stunt you pulled, young man. You could have gotten yourself and Jack killed in the process."

"I'm sorry," Clay said sincerely, "but I couldn't sit by and wait, knowing Jack was in there."

Ben turned to Jack. "I don't know if putting you two together was the right thing to do or not. He's starting to act more and more like you every day." Then smiling, he asked in softer tone, "How you holdin' out?"

"I've been better," Jack said, leaning against the big oak tree at the end of the barn. "How did you know where we were?" he asked.

Ben looked over at Clay. "His mother called and told us. She told us where the holding pens were too. We were headed there first when we got Clay's call. I sent one of the deputies to pick Clay up while the rest of us headed here. The state police picked up the cattle just this side of Clovis."

Clay looked at Ben, confusion written on his face. "My mother called you? You didn't tell me that."

"I wanted to wait until it was over before I told you," Ben said.

Clay shook his head. "I can't believe she called and told you. I didn't think she cared."

Ben looked at him with sympathy. "You never know about a mother. She said she couldn't let him hurt you. I reckon she always cared more than she let on, but she couldn't show it around Jason."

Clay nodded, then looked up at Jack, concern showing on his face. "Ben, we need to get Jack to the hospital and have him checked out. You think you could have one of your deputies drive him?"

"I don't need to go to no dadburn hospital," Jack

protested. "All I need is to get home to my bed and get some rest."

"You're going to the hospital and get checked out," Clay said adamantly.

Jack and Ben looked at him, both astonished by his stand. Jack turned to Ben and smiled, though it hurt through his cut lips. "I reckon I better go get checked out at the hospital."

Ben nodded. "I reckon you ought to. I'm just about finished here. I'll drive you myself."

Ben walked away to give instructions to one of his deputies. Clay glanced over to where his father lay. "You know, I don't feel any regret that he's gone. I don't think I've thought of him as my father for a long time."

"He wasn't a father," Jack said. "He was just a man who happened to be responsible for bringing three boys into this world. It takes more than that to be a father."

Clay nodded, looking thoughtful. "You're right and it takes more than just being sired by a man to be a son." He looked up at Jack to see if he got his meaning and was pleased to see Jack nod at him warmly.

As they moved toward the car, Clay took Jack's arm and put it around his shoulder. "Here, lean on me," he said.

Jack smiled at him. "I think I will," he said.

The hospital took X rays of Jack's back and tailbone and determined that nothing was broken. Clay made them call Dr. Johnson, who showed up to read the X rays and give Jack a thorough examination, finally pronouncing him capable of going home. "You're going to be sore for several days," he said, "and it'll be a spell before you can sit in a saddle, but you should heal with no problem. Just take it easy and don't strain your back."

Clay had stayed during the entire examination to make sure everything was all right. "Shoot, Doc, you don't have to worry about him taking it easy. Ever since he got me out there I've been doin' all the work. All he does is sit in his rocking chair and give me orders."

Jack looked at him wide-eyed. "Why you shriveled up little peanut! I haven't been able to get an honest day's work out of you since you showed up!"

Dr. Johnson laughed at the two of them. "You two are suited for each other. I don't think either of you has the sense to be by yourselves. Now both of you get out of here and I don't want to see either of you back for at least a month. I got *real* patients to take care of."

Jack and Clay grinned at the doctor. "I've given you a prescription for some pain pills," Dr. Johnson continued. "I recommend you take one and stay in bed for the next couple of days."

"That sounds like a good idea to me," Jack said, sliding off the examination table and buttoning his shirt, "if I can get this whelp here to be quiet long enough."

Clay grinned at him. "I reckon I'll be asleep as soon as you are."

Ben was still sitting in the waiting room when they came out. "You two ready to go home?" he asked.

Clay looked from him to Jack. "I'd like to go by and see my mother before we leave town," he said.

Ben looked at Jack and seeing him nod, said, "Sure, Clay, I'll drive you by."

As they pulled up into the yard of the run-down house, Clay sat looking out the window of the car.

This had been his house for most of his life, yet it had never felt like home. Now all he saw was the trash in the yard, the peeling paint, and the broken screen door. He opened the car door and stepped out, feeling like the weight of the world was on his shoulders. "Take all the time you need," Ben said. "We'll wait for you."

"Thanks," Clay responded, turning and walking up the dirt path that led to the kitchen door.

He didn't knock, but just opened the door and went in. He heard the television in the living room and knew she was there. He walked around the kitchen table and stopped in the doorway that separated the living room and kitchen. His memories of the night before flooded back to him. Had that just been last night? he asked himself.

Laura Tory sat on the sofa, her eyes staring at the program on the television set, but Clay could see she wasn't really watching. He cleared his throat, hoping she would turn toward him but she continued to stare at the set. "Mama," he said, but still she didn't look up. "Mama, they're not coming back."

Laura Tory finally took her gaze from the television and looked at her youngest son, but the faraway look in her eyes made Clay wonder if she really saw him.

"He was going to kill you," she said, "and he was going to take your brothers and leave. He didn't tell me but I overheard him talking. He was going to go and leave me alone after all the years I put up with him and his sorry ways. Is he in jail?" she asked.

Clay shifted his feet and looked down. It was a moment before he could get it out. "He's . . . he's dead, Mama. He tried to hold Jack Lomas hostage and they shot him. Warren and Randy are in jail."

"When will they be home?" she asked.

Clay took a deep breath. "They're charged with being accessories to grand theft, kidnapping, and receiving stolen property. I don't think they'll be home for several years."

"But they can't lock up my boys," she pleaded, as if saying it would make it so.

Clay looked at her with sympathy. "I got to go, Ma. Jack and the sheriff are waiting for me. I'm sorry things had to turn out this way, but I wanted to stop by and say thank you for calling the sheriff. If it's any comfort to you, you probably saved Jack's life."

Laura Tory just sat staring at him blankly, so he walked over and kissed her on the cheek. It was the only time he could remember kissing his mother. She touched the spot on her cheek where he kissed her, but she was back staring at the television. Clay turned and walked away. He looked back at the house once more before getting into the backseat of the car.

"You all right?" Jack asked, looking back at him.

"I think so," he said, "but I sure could use some sleep. This playing cops and robbers really takes it out of a fella."

Jack and Ben laughed as Ben backed the car out of the Torys' driveway. "I'll keep an eye on her for you," Ben said as he looked in the rearview mirror, seeing Clay looking at the house.

"Thanks," Clay said, leaning back in the seat and closing his eyes.

They were halfway to the ranch when Jack sat up straight and startled both Ben and Clay. "Oh my gosh!" he nearly shouted.

"What's the matter?" Ben asked, looking around.

"I hired your cousin Julie and her husband, Terry, to work for me and they were going to be there first thing this morning to start. What will they think when they get there and we're not there?"

Ben laughed. "Quit worrying. When they arrived at your place this morning and found all the lights on and nobody home they called the office and we told them where you were. Julie's already cleaning house and Terry's taken care of the chores. They'll be there waiting for you."

Clay looked surprised. "You hired *two* people to work?"

Jack turned and smiled at him. "Well, I figured if you were going to go pro, we'd have to start making a lot more rodeos, and we have to have someone to take care of the place while we're gone."

Clay grinned at him. "You really think I'm ready to go pro?" he asked.

"Not yet," Jack said, "but by the time you get all that hay I've ordered unloaded and stacked you should be."

Clay grimaced. "Another of your famous training programs, huh?"

"Nope." Jack laughed. "Just a good way to get my hay unloaded."

Ben laughed at the expression on Clay's face. "That's what I call a good deal," he said.

Chapter Twenty-four

Jack was still moving slowly a week later, so Clay and Terry were taking care of the ranch. Branding had been postponed for a couple of weeks to ensure Jack would be available.

Julie and Terry were in their early forties. Terry had lost his job when the ranch he worked on was sold. Julie had also been looking for work when Jack approached her and offered her the job of head cook and housekeeper. She had eagerly accepted and had asked if he knew of any job for Terry. Knowing Terry as he did, Jack offered him a job as well. The couple were staying in the extra bedroom in the main house until the trailer house Jack bought could be brought out and set up.

Julie, upon hearing of Jack's ordeal and seeing his condition, immediately assumed the position of personal nurse. She made sure he followed the doctor's instructions to the letter and worried over him like a mother hen. Clay and Terry loved Jack's predicament and rode him without mercy about following his nurse's orders until he threatened to have both of them working on windmills for the rest of the summer.

Ben stopped by to see how Jack was doing and to fill him in on what had happened since the night of Jason's death. "We found out who was behind the cattle thefts," he said, sitting at the kitchen table. "It was a group of men out of Pampa. Seems they've been operating for a couple of years without being caught. The Texas authorities arrested them last week and have charged them with ten counts of grand theft. They should be out of business for a long time."

It was the beginning of the second week when Jack brought up the fact that Clay had already missed several rodeos. "Are you going to enter any this weekend?" he asked as they all sat at the kitchen table eating the scrumptious breakfast Julie had cooked.

"I was waiting for you to get well before I entered," Clay responded.

"Hmmph," Jack spat out. "I ain't never been sick." Julie raised her eyebrows at him and he quickly revised his statement. "Well, I ain't," he said. "I've just been a little stove up, but I'm better now and I don't see any reason we shouldn't make a couple of rodeos."

Jack paid no attention to the scowl Julie directed at him and looked at Clay. Clay glanced first at Julie then at Terry, who was grinning. "You sure you don't need to wait a little longer before you start bouncing around in the pickup? You know the doctor told you to take it easy." Clay grinned at Julie.

"Maybe you ought to wait a little longer," Julie said with sincere concern in her voice. "The doctor told you to take it easy, and he knows best."

Jack's face clouded with frustration and anger. "I'm fine," he said adamantly. "I have taken it easy long enough now. I'm ready to go to a rodeo and by gosh, we're going. Clay get in there and get entered."

"Yes sir," he said, still grinning like a possum. It was all Terry could do to keep from bursting out laughing.

"Don't you have some work to do?" Jack asked, glaring at him.

"Can I finish my breakfast first?" Terry asked, somehow managing to keep a straight face.

"Only if you wipe that silly grin off your face and hurry up."

While Clay was on the phone, Jack pulled Julie aside and in a hushed tone told her, "Clay's birthday is this Saturday, but I want to have a party for him here next Monday. Do you think you can arrange for his friends to be here and maybe whip up a cake for him?"

Julie was all smiles as she assured him she would take care of everything.

Clay entered in the Big Spring, Texas, rodeo Friday night, and since Will and Dottie were putting on the show in Abilene, Texas, he entered there Saturday night.

By Friday, Jack was grouchy as an old bear. Nothing pleased him and nobody could do anything right. It was a relieved Julie and Terry who watched them pull out of the driveway. "I swear I think that man would have eaten all of us alive if he hadn't left when he did," Julie said, shaking her head.

"I can remember when he was happy just to stay here on this ranch and be left alone. Things sure do change," Terry said with a smile.

Clay was sitting second in the barebacks, winning the saddle broncs and placing third in the bulls when they left Big Spring. They pulled into the hotel in Abilene at eleven-thirty that night. Ben and Dottie had just gotten there and were kept awake until early morning listening to Jack and Clay tell about the incidents that had taken place. "It's a wonder you two are still alive," Dottie said, shaking her head in amazement.

"I reckon the Good Lord was lookin' out for us," Jack replied.

"I always heard he looked out for fools and little children," Will said.

"If that's the case he must be sittin' on your shoulder," Jack retorted. He caught Will's eye and motioned with his head. Will smiled and excused himself, leaving the room. In a moment he returned carrying a large box covered with wrapping paper and a large bow on top. He walked over and set in on the bed next to Clay. "Happy birthday, Clay."

Clay looked first at the box then at Will, Jack, and Dottie. "Go ahead and open it," Will said.

Clay tore the wrapping paper, then ripped open the box. His eyes opened wide when he saw what was inside. "I can't believe it!" he said, pulling out the contents. A new bronc saddle and halter lay on the bed.

"The saddle is from Jack. The halter is from Dottie and me," Will said.

"I can't believe it," Clay repeated, a lump now in his throat. "I don't know what to say."

"Just say you like it," Dottie said. "That'll be enough."

Clay shook his head. "No, that won't be enough. I've never been given anything like this in my life. You've all given me more than I ever thought I'd have and now this."

Jack placed his hand on his shoulder. "Son, you've given us all something too. You've given me more happiness than I ever thought I'd have again. This is just a small token of my appreciation."

Clay smiled as tears formed in his eyes. He turned to face the man who in six months had become more of a father to him than his own father had ever been. Jack opened his arms and Clay gladly embraced him.

Dottie smiled through her tears and as soon as Clay stepped back she hugged him to her. "You've turned into quite a young man," she said, stepping back. "We're all proud of you."

"Yes we are," Will said, hugging him in turn.

Dottie finally had to break the party up at four in the morning. "Come on, Pa, we got livestock to care for in the morning."

"No we don't," Will said. "I figure the boys could handle it without me, so I told them to take care of it."

Dottie looked at him in shock. "I don't believe it! You mean you finally decided you didn't have to be there to run the whole thing, and that your boys might be able to do just fine without you?"

"Well, not everything, but I reckon they can start earning their money every now and then so I can sleep in. I reckon I've earned it."

"I didn't think I'd ever see the day," Dottie exclaimed. "Come on, let's get to bed so I can enjoy not getting up early."

Will, Clay, and Jack laughed as Dottie hurried from the room.

"In case I didn't tell you," Clay said as the three stood in the room, "thank you for the halter."

"You told us," Will said, slapping him on the shoulder.

When the Hightowers had left, Clay turned to Jack. "Thanks for the saddle. I still can't believe it."

"You're welcome," Jack said. "You know it will have to be broken in before you can ride in it."

"Yeah I know," he said, running his hand over the rough leather, "but I plan on breaking it in real quick."

*   *   *

Everyone slept late the next day and then just lounged around the hotel pool or sat in the room talking.

"I've just about got everything ready to start producing pro shows," Will said as they sat in the room.

"You still plan on making January your start time?" Jack asked him.

"That's the plan," Will replied. "I've got most of the stock lined up and I've got a definite buyer for the stock I've got now, so I should be ready."

Jack rubbed his chin. "I reckon Clay ought to be ready by then too. As a matter of fact, I figure it wouldn't hurt to go ahead and get his permit and maybe make a few shows just to get the feel of what he'll be up against."

"That's not a bad idea," Will said.

Dottie Hightower sat listening to the two of them, then glanced at Clay, who was sitting on the bed, not saying anything. Coming to her feet she placed both hands on her hips and faced the two men. "You two beat anything I've ever seen. Here you are planning Clay's future like it was your own. You haven't even asked him how he feels. Are you going to plan who he marries and how many children he has?" she asked, letting out a sigh of frustration.

Jack and Will looked at each other, then at Clay and finally back at Dottie. In unison they said, "Yes!" and broke into laughter. Dottie gave them a venomous look and turned to Clay. "I feel sorry for you. These two will plan your entire life if they think they can get away with it."

Clay grinned at her. "I don't think there's anything to worry about. Since I've been around these two, I've come to find out they're mostly hot air. They do a lot of talking but when it comes to any action they just kind of fizzle."

Dottie threw back her head and laughed. "I guess he's smarter than I gave him credit for. He's already got you two figured to a T."

Will looked at Jack then said, "You know, you try to help someone out by giving them the benefit of your vast experience and knowledge and they throw it back in your face. I think maybe we ought to find us someone who'd be more grateful and turn this young whelp loose."

"I tend to agree with you," Jack said, looking sadly at Clay and Dottie.

"You two are so full of bull, it drips off you," Dottie said. "First of all there ain't no one that's going to listen to you two, and second you ain't got no vast experience and knowledge worth listening to. All you got is a bunch of stories that are one-fourth fact and three-fourths fiction."

Jack and Will both feigned hurt looks. "I reckon we ain't appreciated, Jack," Will said. "Why don't we go over to the café and get us a cup of coffee?"

"That sounds like a real good idea," Jack said, grabbing his hat and winking at Clay and Dottie. Clay and Dottie waited until they closed the door on their way out, then they broke into laughter. "I guess we better go with them," Clay said, picking up his hat. "We can't let those two loose on unsuspecting folks."

"You're right about that," Dottie said, opening the door.

The rodeo began at seven o'clock. Jack and Clay were behind the chutes waiting for the grand entry and pre-rodeo announcements to be completed.

Will drew Copenhagen in the barebacks, Big Foot in

the saddle broncs, and Double T in the bulls. "You've drawn good tonight," Jack said. "If you ride all three you could win the whole shooting match."

"What do you mean if? I plan on riding every one of 'em."

Jack laughed. "If you weren't we'd be on our way home right now."

Clay was the fourth rider out in the barebacks. Copenhagen was holding true to form, bucking hard using his sunfish move several times before lining out and bucking straight. The judges awarded Clay an amazing eighty-two, which held first place through the remaining riders.

Big Foot was a large bay horse that had the moves of a horse a whole lot smaller. Clay hadn't ridden the horse this year, but had drawn him in the past. "He bucks hard and moves quick," he said to Jack. "You've seen him buck before, you know how he moves. What do you recommend?"

"Watch his head. Keep your rein tight and ride the hair off him," Jack said.

"That's pretty well the way I had it summed up," Clay said with a smile.

Big Foot came out of the chute on his back feet and pushed off hard, going high in the air while twisting his body. Clay kept his feet over the points of his shoulders when his front feet hit the ground, raking him as he lunged again. After three jumps Big Foot hit the ground and pulled a reverse, moving backward as fast as he could while vaulting into the air. It was a hard move to stay in time with but Clay continued spurring, and when Big Foot lunged forward, he was right with him, spurring on every jump. When the whistle blew, Clay dismounted in a flying leap and landed on his feet instead of waiting for the pickup men. Jack watched the move with wary displeasure.

The ride was good enough to put Clay in third place.

When Clay walked back to the chutes, Jack was waiting for him at the unsaddling chute. "You put on a real good ride," he said.

"Thanks," Clay said. "It sure felt good."

"And that dismount was a real grandstand," Jack said, watching him closely.

Clay looked around from the fence, sensing Jack's displeasure. "I reckon I did do a little showing off."

"Uh huh, and what if you'd busted your knee or twisted your ankle?"

"I guess I didn't think about that," Clay said with remorse.

"No, you didn't. I know when you make a good ride it makes you feel invincible, but you've got to use your head and not take silly chances."

"Yes, sir," Clay said. "I won't do it again."

"Good. Now let's get your saddle and get ready for the bull riding."

Double T was one of Will's best bulls. He was planning on keeping him as part of his pro stock. He was part Hereford and part Brahma, a large bull that had come off a ranch in west Texas.

Will and Jack helped Clay pull his rope. Will checked the flank rope to make sure it was set right, then climbed down into the arena, saying, "Make a ride, cowboy."

Clay pounded his gloved hand into a tighter fist and moved up on his bull rope and nodded for the gate.

Double T turned and came out of the gate, and as his front feet hit the ground, his hindquarters shot into the air until he was almost vertical. Clay leaned back until his back was resting on Double T's spine. When the bull's hindquarters started down, Clay came forward, making sure he didn't let himself go too far and overcompensate.

Double T started into a right-hand spin. Clay dug in with his right spur and waited to get in time with the bull before using his left foot to spur the tough hide.

Enraged, Double T came out of his spin, jumping high in the air and twisting his body, coming back to earth in a bone-jarring slam, then turning left. Clay had seen the move coming and dug in with his left spur. He didn't have time to spur with his right because Double T only made one circle before changing directions and lunging toward the chutes, which were only a few feet away.

Clay pulled hard on the bull rope and kept his feet pushed forward. All his mind and energy was concentrated on one thing—staying on Double T's back. When the whistle blew, Double T was only three feet from the chute. Clay swung his left foot forward and over the bull's neck, knocking his hand from the rope. He landed on his feet only a few yards from the chutes. Covering the distance in two lengths, he jumped up on the gate, his feet landing on the third board as Double T's hindquarters came around. The bull's large buttocks hit Clay's right foot, smashing it against the boards. Clay winced against the pain as he felt his ankle twist in his boot.

Double T was moved out of the arena and Clay climbed down off the chute, gingerly putting his weight on his foot. Though the pain was intense, he knew it was luckily only sprained and not broken.

The crowd was on its feet cheering and applauding, realizing they had just witnessed a winning ride.

The judges wrote their individual scores on their chalk boards and held them up for the announcer to see.

"Ladies and gentlemen," he said, the excitement electrifying his voice, "we have a new leader in the bull riding! Clay Tory has just ridden to a score of ninety-two points!"

Clay was beaming despite his pain as the crowd applauded and cheered. He'd finished the rodeo with two firsts and a third, increasing his bank account by at least six hundred dollars plus what he'd already won in Big Spring. He had a new saddle and halter and a bright future—what more could he ask for?

As Clay limped toward the arena gate, Jack came along beside him. "Let me help you," he said, taking Clay's arm and putting it around his shoulder. "You can lean on *me*."

Clay smiled at him. "Looks like I get to sit back and take it easy for a while."

"Don't count on it. We got more rodeos to make. I figure if you keep winning like this, I can retire and you can support me."

They both laughed as they walked through the gate and out of the arena.

Epilogue

As the cold weather passed away and the days grew longer, the spring grass began breaking through the soil, stretching toward the sun and bringing new life to the range. Clay was loading hay in the back of the Dodge and Jack was carrying wire and posts out of the barn when they heard a car coming up the road. "Looks like Ben," Jack said, throwing the wire and posts in the back of the truck and pulling off his gloves.

"Wonder what he's doing out here?" Clay asked, wiping the sweat from his brow.

"I don't know, let's go find out."

In November of the previous year Clay had gotten his PRCA permit and joined the ranks of the professionals. It had taken him only three rodeos to fulfill his requirement for pro status and since then he and Jack had traveled the circuit, leaving Terry and Julie to look after the ranch. As summer approached, the rodeos increased in number. They planned each month around the *Pro Rodeo News,* the publication that listed the upcoming rodeos, contestant standings, and placings for past rodeos.

Will and Dottie Hightower became pro rodeo stock contractors in January. Jack and Clay tried to schedule as many of their rodeos as possible. Clay continued to practice in the arena at the ranch. It wasn't unusual for crowds to gather on any given day during the week to either watch or participate. Jack had invited all the young boys who wanted to participate in rodeo to come out and use the arena. He furnished the stock and gave instructions. He loaned money to those who couldn't afford entry fees. He even bought roping and dogging horses for several of the boys who couldn't afford their own.

Shirley Roberts started coming to the ranch on a regular basis. At first she was timid and shy around Jack, but she soon got used to his gruff nature and even began to taunt him the same as Clay.

After Warren and Randy's trial, they were sentenced to ten years in state prison. Clay began to see his mother on a regular basis. She had taken a job at one of the stores in Roswell, and was leading the semblance of a normal life. The last time he'd gone to see her, he was surprised to see the house clean and tidy. "I guess I got so used to the mess that it didn't bother me, but with your father and brothers gone I just couldn't stand living like that anymore." Clay helped her paint the outside and clean up the yard, and called her several times a week to see if she needed anything. He'd heard through the rumor mill that she was dating an insurance salesman, and he couldn't help teasing her about it when he called.

Ben pulled his patrol car to a stop in the yard and stepped out as Jack and Clay walked up. "Hey, Ben," Jack called out. "What brings you out this way?"

"Oh, I was just in the neighborhood and thought I'd drop in and see how things were going."

"I got some coffee we can heat up," Jack said. "Come on inside and we'll have a cup."

"Best invitation I've had today," Ben said, following the rancher into the house. Clay brought up the rear, sensing this was more than a casual visit.

Jack lit the burner on the stove and set the old coffeepot over the flame as Clay got three cups from the cupboard and set them on the counter.

When the coffee was poured and all three were seated, Jack looked at Ben. "Now what really brings you out this way? And don't tell me you were just in the neighborhood."

Ben laughed and reached into his shirt pocket, pulling out several folded papers. He laid them on the table in front of him and looked at Jack and Clay. "You're a free man," he said, looking at Clay. "You've served your time and now you're free to do what you please, as long as it's legal." He grinned.

Clay looked at the papers lying on the table. He'd forgotten about being a ward of the county and it dawned on him that he'd been with Jack because he had to be. Now that he was free, would that change things?

Jack looked at Ben and then at the papers. "Does this mean he doesn't have to do what I tell him anymore?"

"Did he ever do what you told him?" Ben asked with a laugh.

"You make a good point," Jack said. "I reckon I've put up with his hardheaded abusive ways for so long I just got to thinking he was doing what he was suppose to."

Clay's eyes widened. "What do you mean my hardheaded, abusive ways? Seems to me *you're* the hardheaded abusive one, making me do all the work around here while you sit back and take things easy."

Ben smiled at the easy banter between the two.

"Well if you two will sign these papers, Clay here will be all through with the Chavez County Court system for the time being."

Clay didn't miss Ben's innuendo. "I'll be through with it for forever," he said.

"Now don't go making any rash statements." Ben smiled. "I figure if you stay around Jack very long, I may have to arrest you for killing him. Of course there's not a jury in the county that would convict you. They'd call it justifiable homicide."

"Hmmph," Jack snorted. "They'd call it justifiable homicide if I were to do away with the sorry excuse they got for a sheriff."

Jack and Clay signed the papers Ben had brought out, then Ben pulled two checks from his pocket. "These belong to you two."

Both Jack and Clay looked puzzled as they each stared at the checks in their hands. "What are these?" Jack asked.

"That's the money the county owed you. Fifteen dollars a day for you Jack, and five dollars a day for Clay. You two never picked it up. Of course we know Clay had his savings account from his winnings."

They looked at him in surprise, both with guilty looks on their faces. "Yeah we knew, but we also knew Clay got a bum rap and as long as he kept his nose clean we weren't going to say anything. By the way, now that you've served your time, and since it occurred while you were still a minor, you have a clean record."

"That's good to know," Clay said. "That should help me in my homicide trial."

Ben chortled as Jack gave him a scathing look.

After Ben left, Jack stood in the yard looking down the road. Clay had started for the hay barn but stopped when he noticed Jack wasn't coming. "What's the matter?" he asked, turning around.

Jack didn't answer for a moment. Then looking toward him, he spoke. "You're free to go now if you want to."

Clay felt a lump come to his throat. "I know," he said softly, then looked at the house and around at the barns and arena. "But this is home. If you'll let me, I'd like to stay."

Jack felt tears come to his eyes. They'd never talked about what would happen when Clay's time was served, and for a moment when Ben had told him that Clay was free to go, he had wondered if maybe Clay wanted to leave. Now, he knew the bond that had formed between them was solid. They belonged together, for only they knew how much they needed each other and the excitement they shared in the crazy sport they called rodeo.

"This is your home for as long as you want to stay," he said.

"Then it looks like we'll be together for a long time," Clay said.

"I like the sound of that," Jack said, putting his arm around the younger man.

They both laughed as they walked into the arena.

Don't Miss the Next Exciting Entry
in the Rodeo Riders Series . . .
Rigged to Ride

Early in April, a meeting took place in a suite at the Sands Hotel in Las Vegas, Nevada. It was a meeting that would drastically impact professional rodeo and the National Finals for the remainder of the year. It involved two men of imperial wealth, Tom Larrs and Harmon "Hank" Tallridge. Tom had made it big in the building boom in California in the late seventies, then increased his holdings through wise investments and careful planning. His greatest passion in life was gambling, but only if the stakes were high and the odds were great.

Hank Tallridge had accrued his vast fortune in the electronics industry. After four failed marriages and numerous bad relationships, he had found solace in the casinos of the Vegas Strip. It was there he'd met Tom Larrs. Their shared passion for gambling forged an alliance that kept them both looking for new ways to test their luck and feed their appetites for excitement by betting large sums of money on Lady Luck, and waiting to see which way she would turn. They had long tired of the normal games available in the casinos, though each would occasionally enter a high-stake poker game. They bet on every baseball, basketball, football, hockey, volleyball, and soccer game played. They wagered on every event of the Olympics, and on every kind of race there was. In any given week, each of them had somewhere between a hundred and fifty to three hundred thousand dollars out in bets. Like two junkies, they needed more and more to satisfy the fire within. Now, as they sat in the plush room at the Sands, looking at the two separate sheets of paper spread on the table before them, they both knew that what they were about to embark on would be one of the largest gambles of all times. One sheet of paper listed the top thirty national contenders in each of the rodeo events. On the other sheet of paper was a list of fifteen of the wealthiest people in the United States, all known for their passion for gambling.

"Did you contact all of the people on your list?" Hank asked.

"Yep, how about you?"

"Everyone of them, and they're all in."

"All of mine, too," Tom said. "Each one will wire five hundred thousand to the bank account in the Caribbean by close of business tomorrow."

The idea for this gambling extravaganza had come to Hank while he sat watching the Professional Rodeo Cowboys Association National Finals the year before. As he thought about what it took for each of the cowboys to qualify for the finals, and how many times the leaders changed during the year, he realized what a long shot it was for anyone to finish in the number one spot. An injury, bad draws, financial problems, family problems— anything could impact the odds of making it to the finals. The chances would change constantly, and as far as Hank could see, no one could determine what those odds were. What a gamble!

Tom and Hank worked out the details over a period of two months. They first compiled the list of men and women that would be invited to their game, then they made a list of the top thirty contenders in each of the six events; bareback riders, saddle bronc riders, bull riders, calf ropers, steer wrestlers, and team ropers, both headers and heelers. They decided not to include women's barrel racing, mainly because of Hank's bad luck with women. He thought having women on the list would jinx him. Though Tom thought the event would add another degree of excitement to the game, he agreed to the women's omission. A gathering of all fifteen participants was then planned for the following week in the very same room the two men sat in now. Tom having reserved the room for a month at a time. The meeting was timed to coincide with the release of the latest standings. All the contestants' names would be placed in various bowls. Those in first through third place would be placed in one bowl, fourth through eighth in another, and so on. There would be fifteen participants because that was the number of top contestants that worked more than one event. Each of the fifteen would be allowed to draw names from each of the bowls in turn, until all names had been drawn. The names each person drew would comprise his team for the season. Each team would be ranked by the amount of prize money they won. The contest would last through the finals, with the winner of the pot being the holder of the team that won the most money. The winnings amounted to a staggering seven and a half million dollars.

Little did Tom and Hank know what they were creating, nor did they know how it would affect the rodeo world. "Just think—we have eight months to watch the game and see how Lady Luck plays her hand," Hank said, the excitement gleaming in his eyes.

"And we won't know until the end which way she'll go. It's all solely in her hands," Tom replied. Little did he know how untrue those words would be.

Clay reined in the dapple gray he was riding and waited for the Jack Lomas to ride up beside him.

"How many did you count?" Jack asked.

"One hundred and seventy-four," Clay answered.

"I counted one fifty-five. That makes three hundred and twenty-nine head. There's only one missing, and we probably just overlooked her," Jack said, removing his hat and wiping the sweat from his forehead.

They had been riding since daylight, checking the cattle in the north section of the Lazy L Ranch, the spread that Jack Lomas owned near Roswell, New Mexico. It was the place that Clay had called home for the past two and a half years, ever since his brief run-in with the law.

"The calves are looking good, but if we don't get some rain soon, the cows are going to start dropping weight," Clay said, surveying the cows standing around the tank by the windmill.

"Yep, and the grass ain't gonna hold out much longer. It's been two months since we had any rain to speak of," Jack said, frowning through the dust stirred up by the cattle milling around.

Looking at the sky, Clay sighed. "And it don't look like we're gonna get any today."

"I reckon not," Jack replied. "Let's head back to the house. I'm hungry, and I saw Julie rolling out pie crusts this morning. I'll bet she's making some more of her apple pies."

"I wish you hadn't told me that," Clay said groaning.

"Why not?"

"Because it's still an hour to the house, and I'm starving. If it weren't for the fact that it's bad to run horses to the barn, I'd race you back for the first piece of pie."

"I'd take you up on the challenge, but as it is I reckon we'll have to hit a fast trot and get there as quick as we can," Jack replied.

The ground-eating trot was also a bone jarring one if you happened to be riding a rough horse, and Clay was definitely riding one today. The dapple gray was a stout quarter horse that Clay had trained himself. He loved the performance the horse gave when it came to roping and cutting cattle. In fact, he loved everything about him. Everything, that is, except his trot.

Jack smiled from behind as he watched Clay's backside bounce in the hard seat of the saddle. Moving his own horse up beside him, he asked him, "You ready for your rematch this weekend?" Jack was talking about the saddle bronc horse Clay had drawn at the upcoming Salina, Kansas, rodeo. It was a horse called Outlaw, a top bucking horse that had been to the National Finals three years in a row. Clay had drawn him two months before in Tombstone, Arizona. Outlaw had won the battle, throwing Clay six seconds into his eight-second ride.

"I'm ready. I should have ridden him last time," Clay said in a voice that reflected the anger he still felt at his performance.

"You should have," Jack said, "but you didn't. Now you have to put your mind to it and ride him this time. Don't let that move he's got throw you off again."

Clay chuckled. "It sure is a sneaky one. He throws his head to the right then ducks left. The only horse I've ever seen do that."

"He's good, alright. That's why he's made it to the finals three years in a row."

"How do you ride a horse that moves his head one

way then turns the other? You've always taught me to watch their heads in order to follow the direction that they're going to turn."

"That's true on most horses, but I reckon there's always an exception to the rule. You'll have to tighten your seat and keep your rein a little firmer and not anticipate which way he'll go."

"Oh, that ought to be easy," Clay said, smiling.

"That's the only thing I can tell you. You might talk to Billy Ettinger. He won the Ft. Worth rodeo on Outlaw," Jack said.

"Yeah, I know." Clay sighed. Billy Ettinger was in first place in the standings, while Clay was sitting third just behind Ron Bowers. Both men were great guys, but the competition between the three was fierce as they vied for that coveted first-place title. "If I see him in Salina, I'll ask him what he did to cover him."

"He'll sure tell you," Jack said.

"I know, that's what hurts," Clay said rolling his eyes. "And if I make a qualified ride on him, he'll never let me forget it was him that made it possible."

Jack broke into laughter. "If you make a qualified bronc ride on Outlaw, you'll probably win the saddle bronc riding and that'll probably move you into second place in the standings. You can throw that back at him. That should take most of the sting out of it. You got to learn to look at the bright side of things."

"Believe me I try that all the time when I'm working with you. The only problem is, I can't find any bright sides," Clay said, laughing.

Without batting an eye, Jack responded. "Well I guess you won't be wanting any of that apple pie then, since that sure isn't a bright side to this day."

"Well maybe there are one or two bright sides," Clay said, grinning, "but they're few and far between."

The two carried on their easy banter as they covered the distance to the ranch house, where Julie had a late lunch waiting for them.

As they unsaddled their horses, Jack thought back to the time when he had first met Clay. The boy had gotten into trouble with the local sheriff on a trumped up charge of grand theft auto. Ben Aguilar, the Chavez County sheriff, had seen potential in Clay, and rather than let the judge send him to juvenile hall, he had asked Jack to take him in for a year. Reluctantly, Jack had agreed. It had been a stormy start since both possessed a streak of stubbornness. Neither had been willing to give an inch in the beginning, but each had a love for rodeo, and through that they had found common ground to forge a friendship. It was a friendship that had survived some of the most trying times imaginable.

Clay had served his one year of county time on the ranch, and had stayed on with Jack, helping with the ranch and traveling to rodeos. It was a situation that suited them both.

Clay was now participating on the professional rodeo circuit. His first year as a professional had been a learning experience for both of them. Clay had finished in eighteenth place in the saddle bronc riding, twenty-second in the bareback riding, and seventeenth in the bull riding, just two places out of the finals. Though it had been disappointing, he had vowed to work harder and make it in all three events this year.

As Jack and Clay finished unsaddling their horses and turning them into the large corral by the barn, Terry Stevens came driving up in the ranch's old Dodge pickup. Terry was Julie's husband. Jack had hired them both to take care of the ranch while he and Clay traveled from rodeo to rodeo. Terry was just coming in from working on a windmill, and stopped at the barn when he saw Jack and Clay.

"How's the calf crop doin'?" he asked, stepping out of the pickup.

"They're lookin' good right now, but if we don't get some rain soon we're goin' to have to start feedin' 'em," Jack said, looking again at the sky as if he could somehow will rain clouds to appear.

"It is dry," Terry agreed. "But there's still plenty of grass in the north pasture, and the east pasture looks pretty good, too."

Jack nodded, his mind mulling over the options they would have to face if it didn't rain soon. "Clay and I'll be gone for about two weeks. We're going to rodeos in Oklahoma, Missouri, Kansas, and Colorado. We'll take a look at things when we get back and see what we need to do."

"We should get at least one cutting off the hay field," Clay added.

"It won't be much of a cutting," Jack said. "I doubt we'll get four hundred bales."

Clay pointed to the large dirt tank that served as a watering place for the barn stock and the cattle during gathering time. "I was thinking the other day that if we could find some way to use the water from that tank to irrigate the hay pasture, we might be able to get enough hay to hold us over until it rains."

Jack looked at the tank, then at the hay pasture. The tank was almost three acres wide and about twenty-five feet deep. "If we use the water out of there, we won't have anything to water the stock with," he said, though his mind, seeing Clay's logic, was already trying to conceive of ways to get the water into the field.

"If we don't get some hay, we won't have any stock to worry about," Clay responded. "We could use the gasoline pump to flood the hay field. It'll take a little work directing the flow to get an even cover, but it should work."

"A little water on that field right now would make a lot of difference in the amount of hay we get," Terry said.

"It sure would," Jack agreed.

"I'll get everything working while you two are gone. I'll water it in the evenings so the water won't evaporate. With two weeks of water, we'll have hay ready to cut by the time you get back."

Jack nodded. "Sounds like a plan. Now let's get up to the house and get something to eat. My stomach is rubbing my backbone."

Julie and Terry were young, in their early thirties, but Julie took care of Jack and Clay as if they were her children. Cooking and cleaning for them was only part of her responsibilities, as she saw it. She also made sure they ate right, doctored them when they were hurt, and if one of them so much as sneezed, she was there instantly with cough syrup and a thermometer. Jack once made the comment that he wished she and Terry would have some kids of their own so she would quit mothering him all the time. But the truth was he loved the attention she paid him, and her constant worrying was comforting. So when she scolded all of them for coming home late and fussed about the lunch she'd prepared having turned cold, Jack just chuckled and patted her on the arm. "Now, Julie, you know when we're out working cattle we can't quit until the job is finished. Besides you're such a good cook it tastes good even when it's cold."

Julie slapped his hand away in mock anger. "You're so full of bull, Jack Lomas. Now go wash up while I finish heating up ya'lls lunch." Though she acted upset, it was easy to see Jack's compliment pleased her immensely. Clay and Terry exchanged winks as Jack left the kitchen grinning.

Jack and Clay left early the next day. The Ford four-door pickup they drove had a cab-over camper that served as their motel on wheels, complete with shower, bed, and a small refrigerator that could run on either propane or electricity. There was a rooftop air conditioner that was powered by the small generator they had installed on the bumper of the truck. Julie had packed their clothes in the camper's small closet, and had stocked the refrigerator with snacks and as many prepared meals as she could fit into the confined space. She constantly admonished them about their eating habits on the road, and made them promise they would eat wholesome meals.

Jack let Clay do most of the driving while he navigated, having only gotten them lost on a few occasions, much to Clay's teasing delight.

The first rodeo Clay was entered in that week was in Oklahoma City that very night. "I can remember when the national finals were always held in Oklahoma City," Jack said as they crossed the Texas–Oklahoma border. "I know the finals have grown and done better since they moved them to Las Vegas, but there was something about having them in a cowtown like Oklahoma City that can't be replaced."

"They may miss something," Clay said with a grin, "but money isn't one of them. The pay-offs have quadrupled since they moved to Las Vegas, and you have to admit it's a heck of a lot more exciting there than in Oklahoma City."

"Maybe," Jack responded sullenly, "but there's still something missing that can't be found in Vegas."

"I don't care if they're held in Podunk, Rhode Island— as long as I make 'em," Clay said.

Jack smiled at him. "I reckon I felt the same way."

"What was the greatest thing about making it to the finals?" Clay asked, glancing over at Jack.

Jack thought for a moment before answering. "There were a lot of great things about making the finals. Of course, the first thing is the fact that you beat out a lot of good people to get there. Then there's the knowledge that you're going to get a shot at the best stock there is. But if I had to pick the best thing about going to the finals, I guess it would have to be the excitement I saw in Marie's eyes when we got to Oklahoma City. I guess that's probably one of the reasons why I love this city so much."

Clay felt a lump rise in his throat at the mention of Jack's deceased wife. "You made it to the finals four times, didn't you?" he asked.

"Four times in seven years, and every time was just as exciting as the one before. Marie was just as excited to be going, too. The year I won the saddle bronc riding she was on cloud nine. You would have thought she was the one doing the riding, the way she carried on," Jack chuckled as the memories flooded back to him. "And I guess in a way she did make every ride. Sometimes it's harder to sit in the stands and watch than it is to actually ride. I've learned that myself since I've been watching you."

"I just hope I have someone, someday, to share my victories the way you had Marie," Clay said.

"You got me," Jack said, looking at him and grinning.

"That's true," Clay said, "but I don't think it's quite the same. I'd like to have someone give me a big kiss when I make a good ride, and I sure don't want it to be you."

"You don't know how happy that makes me," Jack said.

The rodeo grounds were a buzz of activity as they drove through the contestant gate. The rodeo wouldn't start for another hour, but both Jack and Clay liked to arrive early early in order to talk to the other cowboys. It was one of the few times they got to socialize and catch up on the news of what was going on elsewhere on the circuit.

Since Clay had turned pro, he was able to call in and find out what stock he'd drawn, so he knew ahead of time which bull and horses he'd be riding. And like the other cowboys, he knew most of the stock either by experience or by reputation. He had drawn X7—Red Rocket—in the bull riding; number twenty-eight, Double Trouble, in the barebacks; and number three fifteen, a horse called Doctor Death, in the saddle broncs. Double Trouble was the only animal Clay had reservations about. The sorrel horse did not have the reputation of being one of the top bucking horses in the Ray Carrie bucking string.

Ray Carrie was one of the top stock contractors on the pro circuit. His stock was consistently voted into the finals. The top fifteen cowboys in each event that made it to the finals voted on the stock they wanted to ride. This insured the year's best stock was at the competition.

The Oklahoma City rodeo kicked off with the grand entry, followed by the invocation and the National Anthem. Then the bareback riding event began.

Clay was slated to be the fifth rider, so he settled in to watch the first four. Cory Hickman, the third rider, scored a seventy-four to take the lead. Jack helped Clay set his rigging and gave him words of encouragement as he eased down into the chute and worked his hand into the handle, rotating his hand to heat the resin on his glove and the leather handle, making it sticky. Easing onto Double Trouble's back, he set his feet on the chute over the points of the horse's shoulders. Reaching up, Clay pulled his hat down tightly on his head and nodded to the gate man.

Double Trouble pivoted on his hind feet and lunged into the arena. Clay's spurs remained over the points of the horse's shoulders as its front feet hit the ground, satisfying the mark-out rule.

Double Trouble spun right and leapt into the air, coming down stiff-legged and hard. The jolt shook Clay's body, but he kept his hold and maintained his balance, all the while raking his spurs along the horse's shoulders as it leapt forward.

Double Trouble bucked straight down the fence of the arena. Head down and kicking high, he gave Clay a good ride all the way to the eight-second whistle.

The pick-up men moved in as Clay worked his hand from the rigging handle. The man on his right grabbing him around the waist, Clay slid easily to the ground.

The judges gave Clay a score of sixty-nine. It was not good enough to place and Clay knew it, but he had learned that that was how a rodeo event went. Sometimes you draw well, and sometimes you don't. He smiled as he walked back to the chutes to get his bareback rigging, knowing he did the best he could. There was a time when he would have been upset, but Jack had convinced him it was futile to worry over a ride that had already taken place. It was much better to focus on the rides yet to come.

Jack was waiting for Clay behind the chutes. "You put on a good ride," he said as Clay climbed up on the platform with his bronc saddle.

"Would have been better if I'd had a better horse," he said, then held up his hand as Jack started to say something. "I know, I know, that's rodeo—you pay your entry fees and you take your draw, but it doesn't hurt to want the best horse."

Jack chuckled. "No, it doesn't hurt, as long as you

know it's not always going to happen and accept it when it doesn't."

Clay laughed. "I've learned that lesson already.

"I guess you have," Jack said. "Let's get something to drink."

"Good idea. I think I swallowed half the dust in this arena."

They watched the calf roping and steer wrestling while they waited for the saddle bronc riding event to begin. As they were walking back to the chutes, they passed an area where several young ladies were sitting on their horses. Clay glanced at them and smiled, and was turning his attention back to the chutes when a female voice called out to him. "Hi Clay."

He turned and looked in the direction of the voice and instantly recognized Tamara Allen as the one who had spoken. "Hi Tamara," he said, with a wave of his hand.

"Good luck on your ride," she said, smiling brightly at him.

"Thanks," he said grinning back, then hurried to catch up with Jack, who had continued toward the chutes. As he caught up with him, Jack gave him a bewildered look. "What?" Clay asked, surprised by the look.

"You got at least twenty minutes before you have to start getting ready for your ride. Why didn't you talk to Tamara? She's definitely interested in you."

"Uh, she's just being nice," he stammered.

"She's bein' nice alright, and she especially likes being nice to you. I've seen how she looks at you and I've seen how you watch her. The chemistry is there—all you have to do is add the ingredients."

Clay grinned in embarrassment. "And what are the ingredients?"

Jack cocked an eyebrow at him, then said, "Conversation is the first one. Start there and everything else will fall into place."